# V THE ORIGINAL MINISERIES

## BOOKS BY KENNETH JOHNSON

*V* (with A. C. Crispin)*
*V: The Second Generation**
*An Affair of State* (with David Welch)

*Denotes a Tor Book

# V

## THE ORIGINAL MINISERIES

### KENNETH JOHNSON
### and A. C. CRISPIN

**TOR®**

A TOM DOHERTY ASSOCIATES BOOK
NEW YORK

This is a work of fiction. All of the characters, organizations, and events portrayed in this novel are either products of the authors' imaginations or are used fictitiously.

V: THE ORIGINAL MINISERIES

Copyright © 2008 Warner Bros. Entertainment Inc.
WB SHIELD: ™ & © Warner Bros. Entertainment Inc.
(s08)

Edited by James Frenkel

A Tor Book
Published by Tom Doherty Associates, LLC
175 Fifth Avenue
New York, NY 10010

www.tor-forge.com

Tor® is a registered trademark of Tom Doherty Associates, LLC.

Library of Congress Cataloguing-in-Publication Data

Johnson, Kenneth, 1942–
V: the original miniseries / Kenneth Johnson and A. C. Crispin.—1st ed.
    p.  cm.
"A Tom Doherty Associates book."
    ISBN-13: 978-0-7653-2199-2 (hardcover)
    ISBN-10: 0-7653-2199-8 (hardcover)
    ISBN-13: 978-0-7653-2158-9 (paperback)
    ISBN-10: 0-7653-2158-0 (paperback)
  1. Human-alien encounters—Fiction. 2. Imaginary wars and battles—Fiction.
I. Title.
PS3610.O3595 V16 2008
813'.6d—dc22

                                                      2008034327

First Edition: November 2008

Printed in the United States of America

0  9  8  7  6  5  4  3  2  1

*This book is dedicated to the Whileaway Writers Co-op,*
*that irrepressible, egalitarian Gang of Six I'm fortunate*
*enough to have as friends—movers, shakers, and artists all.*

**ANNE**
**DEBBIE**
**O'MALLEY**
**SHANA**
**TERESA**

*—A. C. C.*


**TO THE HEROISM OF**
**THE RESISTANCE FIGHTERS**
*—past, present, and future—*
*this work is respectfully dedicated.*

*—K. J.*

# ACKNOWLEDGMENTS

I'd like to extend a special acknowledgment to my editor, Harriet P. McDougal, Vice President of Tor Books, for her encouragement, advice, and paw-holding during the writing of this book.

Warmest thanks are also due Pixie Lamppu, who really *cared,* and helped whenever possible.

—A. C. C.


To my friend and literary companion, editor Jim Frenkel, I extend my sincere appreciation—not just for his shepherding of this novel, but for the personal dedication he brought to *V: The Second Generation*.

—K. J.

# V

## THE ORIGINAL MINISERIES

# 1

THE GUERRILLA ENCAMPMENT WAS SET UP IN THE REMAINS OF AN old village. The mud and cinderblock huts, the remains of a bombed-out church—even a pottery shop, wares still baking in the summer heat—all seemed to huddle, forlorn, dying, bullet-torn things.

Tony Wah Chong Leonetti wiped at the sweat on his forehead as he parked the ancient jeep beneath a sagging thatched overhang. "Looks the same . . . Why do they always look the same?" he mumbled.

"Why do what always look the same?" Mike Donovan shifted his camera to his shoulder and panned it quickly around the camp, his alert green eyes searching for the best angles, the most telling shots.

"Guerrilla hideouts. No matter what country—Laos, Cambodia, Vietnam—they all manage to look the same. Guess people on the run are basically alike, never mind their nationality." He rummaged in the backseat, dragged out a bag containing his sound equipment. Mumbling softly to himself, he tested the mike, listened to the playback in his earphones, finally nodding in satisfaction. Donovan, meanwhile, had climbed out of the jeep to meet a dark-haired woman who was approaching, her AK-47 not quite pointing at them.

Her voice was hard, her eyes reddened with dust and exhaustion. "You are Donovan?" she asked in broken English. "Juan told us you would be coming."

Donovan nodded.

"Carlos is not here right now. You must wait."

Donovan looked doubtfully at the dusty camp. "How long?"

"I do not know. Wait." Purposefully she turned on her heel and left.

Donovan looked back at Tony. "Hope he's on his way. I'm starved, and the prospects for chow don't look very promising, do they?"

Tony sighed. "I suppose we could always grab one of those chickens over there."

Donovan grinned, looking suddenly much younger. "Wouldn't be the first time, would it?"

"No—" Leonetti turned. "Did I hear an engine?"

"You sure did." Donovan began checking the settings on his camera.

A truck, heavily laden with armed guerrillas, trundled bumpily into camp. Groans from the wounded mixed with shouts of greeting broke the hot silence as other fighters emerged from the broken buildings and ran toward the vehicle. Donovan and Leonetti followed, stepping aside as men and women carrying stretchers passed them.

"Looks like they weren't so lucky, wherever they've been," Tony observed, listening to the babble of rapid Spanish and the moans of the injured. Some of the forms handed down from the truck didn't stir.

Donovan trained his camera on a bloody face, feeling, not for the first time, like a ghoul—living off the suffering and death of others—then thought, as he always did, that suffering and death served no useful purpose at all if nobody knew of them. His job was to see that people knew what was happening.

One man was shouting orders above the din. Tony glanced over. "Carlos?"

Mike Donovan nodded. "Must be." Raising his voice, he called, "Excuse me, are you Carlos? Juan said you would talk to us about the attack last night. How bad was it? How about your losses?"

The man swung down from the truck. He looked to be in his mid-thirties, and he might have been handsome if not for the sweat and blood streaking his face. He brushed irritably at a wound by his left eye, causing fresh red to well and drip. At Donovan's hail, he turned, glared at them. "Of *course* we suffered losses, man. You don't go up against a force like theirs without expecting losses!" Angrily he turned, striding past the truck. The sleepy camp was now a welter of activity, as men and women struggled to load gear into trucks and jeeps.

Leonetti moved his microphone in a circle, picking up the sounds of the camp—the running feet, the squawk of frightened chickens, the heavy thumps as the fighters loaded the trucks. He glanced over at Donovan. "Looks like they're moving out, Mike. Think we should take the hint?"

Donovan, intent on a shot, nodded abstractedly, then focused on the leader. He was shouting:

"*¡Saquen primero los camiones de municiones!*"

Tony shook his head. "What'd he say?"

Donovan started after Carlos. "'Get the ammunition trucks out first.'"

"Oh, shit," Tony mumbled. "They must be expecting trouble."

Donovan was already out of earshot. Catching up to the guerrilla commander, he shouted, "How many losses?"

The man's mouth twisted into an ugly line. "Seven men and women killed. A dozen wounded." Looking back at his fighters, he shouted, "Jesus—*imuebe el jeep! ¡Lo iestá tapando todo!*"

Donovan looked over at the offending vehicle to make sure Carlos wasn't referring to the old wreck he and Tony had finagled, was reassured that it was another. He took a close shot of the man's face as he directed the evacuation. "You're wounded too."

As if realizing for the first time that he was on camera, that what he said would be relayed to millions of television viewers, Carlos looked directly into the lens, his words biting: "These wounds are *nothing* compared to the wounds they've inflicted on my country." One of the medics approached, tried to dab at his eye, but Carlos brushed him aside to continue. "But we're gonna fight them. Till we win, man. You got that? Fight till El Salvador is *free!* Nothin's going to stop us! *You got that?*"

"Yeah," Donovan said, "I got that."

A sudden shriek tore the air behind them. Donovan and the guerrilla leader whirled to see an army helicopter roaring toward them, nearly skimming the tops of the trees surrounding the camp. Machine guns spattered bullets like deadly raindrops as the gunship began a strafing run straight down the dusty middle of the camp. Several people went down with the first blasts, and their screams battled the thunderous roar of the chopper, the staccato bursts of the guns.

Without realizing how he'd gotten there, Donovan found himself belly-down behind a broken wall, camera still perched on his shoulder. He began following the path of the attack chopper, panning the camera carefully as the helicopter turned and came back for another run. He was dimly aware of a blur beside him—a blur that resolved itself into Tony, sweating and covered with dust, but still gamely clutching his sound gear.

He could barely hear his partner's voice over the chaos. "This don't look so good, Mike."

Donovan couldn't believe the shot he was getting of the gunship, guns blazing, as it roared back through the village. His voice grated from the dust he'd swallowed, but his tone was jubilant. "You kidding, man? It's great!"

Across the camp a truck exploded as the gas tank was hit— and at almost the same moment the woman who had first spoken to them doubled up with a shriek. Several people ran to help her; others began firing back at the enemy. Bullets kicked up dirt only feet away, and Tony Leonetti grabbed Donovan's arm. "Come on—the hell with the great shots!"

They ran, weaving and dodging, hampered by their gear. Yet it was so much a part of them that neither newsman thought of abandoning the equipment. They dodged behind another wall, closer to a building, huddled against a new assault from the chopper.

Tony flinched as a bullet whanged past him. "Donovan— you're gonna get me killed this time, I swear to God!"

Donovan turned and grinned, his teeth flashing in his dirty face. "Hell, Tony, you're going to get another Emmy!"

"I'm gonna get a bullet in my earphone!" Leonetti shouted back, grimly keeping his sound equipment operating. "Tell my wife my last thoughts were of—"

"Look!" Donovan's shout cut through Tony's words. "Look at him!"

Carlos had run to a downed comrade just as the helicopter turned, bearing down on him. Bullets began peppering the ground before them. The guerrilla leader stood, his .45 automatic pistol in both hands, coolly sighting along the barrel at the approaching chopper. As it came within range, swooping even lower for the kill, he squeezed off several rounds, aiming for the pilot, clearly visible behind the glass bubble of the cockpit.

Just as it seemed that the next burst of machine-gun fire would destroy the leader, the gunship pilot sagged limply in his seat. The helicopter wavered, dipped, then slipped over the treetops, losing altitude with every second. The ground shook with the force of the explosion, and Donovan could feel a puff of warm air against his face, even at this distance. "Unbelievable! I don't believe it! Did you see that?"

Tony nodded vigorously, grabbing his arm. "What's *really* unbelievable is that we're still alive, chum! Come *on!*"

Donovan was still shooting as his companion dragged him into their beat-up vehicle, which was still, amazingly, intact. Leonetti gunned the motor, hearing the beating thunder of another helicopter closing on the camp, now blazing with gunfire and flames from exploded vehicles. Letting out the clutch with a jerk, he sent the jeep fishtailing through the camp, heading back toward the road they'd traveled earlier that morning. He glanced over at the cameraman, then grinned half in admiration, half in exasperation. Donovan was training his camera back the way they'd come, leaning backward to catch a shot of the helicopter as it followed them.

"I wish we had a Tyler mount!" he shouted as the camera bounced on his shoulder.

Tony Leonetti sighed. "I wish we had a tank." But Donovan, still shooting, didn't hear him. The jeep careened along the road, crossed a creek, raising a spray of water. Suddenly the vehicle lurched sickeningly as a rocket exploded near them, sluicing water over the jeep and its occupants.

Donovan's voice reached Tony dimly, though the soundman knew his friend must be shouting at the top of his lungs. "Hang in there, Tony! This isn't any worse than Cambodia!"

The Asian man laughed, shaking his head. "At least if you bought it there, I could'a passed for one of them! Where the hell did that chopper go?"

The question was answered as they topped a small rise in the road. The chopper was hanging a few feet above the ground, waiting for them.

Tony turned the wheel quickly, but not before the copter fired a burst. The jeep swerved again as Leonetti gasped, grabbing at his arm. Donovan quickly reached for the wheel, steadying the careening vehicle as the chopper lifted off overhead. Glancing quickly at his partner's arm, the cameraman saw a new blotch of scarlet staining Tony's hibiscus-flowered shirt. "You okay?" he shouted, as his partner took over the driving again.

"You kidding?" The wind whipped Tony's black hair back from his sweatband. "I'm loving every minute of this!"

Suddenly another rocket went off directly in their path. The jeep, already overbalanced, slipped sideways, overturning in the ditch beside the road. Overhead they could hear the thunder of the chopper as it homed in on them.

Donovan was thrown atop his partner, out of the overturned jeep, but the soft dirt of the roadside kept them from being more than shaken up. All of the cameraman's instincts reacted to the beat-beat of the helicopter blades. They had to reach the shelter of the trees!

Donovan scrambled up, camera still clutched firmly. Turning, he pulled the soundman to his feet, noting with part of his mind that the gas line had ruptured and that flames were licking along the splattered fuel.

He was alarmed by Tony's pallor beneath his tan. "Can you run?"

Tony turned to see the fire. "I have a choice?"

"I'm going to draw their fire. You haul ass over to those trees. They'll give you a little protection." He cast a quick glance upward at the helicopter, which had turned and was heading back for them. He threw himself forward. "Go, Tony!"

"No, Mike! We go together—"

Donovan was already running. "Get your can in gear! Go!" Behind him he could hear Tony heading for the trees.

Donovan zigged across the mud flat, hearing the bullets beginning to spang almost on his heels. Even as he increased his speed, he realized that there was nothing ahead of him except another bend of the creek—broad, shallow, but nearly impossible to run in. Rusting in the middle of it was the hulk of a once-orange pickup, Swiss-cheesed with hundreds of bullet holes.

*Hide in the shelter of that?* he wondered, thinking that the truck would provide little cover from the bullets. But there was no place else to run.

He turned, cradling the camera, only to see the chopper settle down to within a few feet of the water as delicately as a broody hen arranging herself on her nest. *Shit*, he thought, *this is it.* In sheer defiance—with a wild thought that perhaps the chopper didn't realize he was a newsman—Donovan raised the camera and began shooting directly at the faces of the two men in the helicopter. His eye narrowed on the viewfinder of the camera as the chopper moved even closer and Donovan peered sharply at the man sitting next to the pilot.

*It can't be! Ham Tyler—what the hell is he doing here?* The former CIA agent was now part of a highly secret branch of covert U.S. security operations. He had dogged Donovan's heels before—in Laos. Donovan had heard rumors that the right-wing "patriot" (*his* term, not Donovan's) was responsible for some of the more notorious mop-ups of guerrilla forces here in El Salvador, but hadn't been able to verify them.

But even as Mike Donovan recognized the man in the copilot's seat, the helicopter abruptly lifted, turned, and went zipping away. *Huh? Now why the hell—*

Donovan turned to see if by some miracle a tank had rolled up behind him (*in total silence?! Don't be foolish, Mike . . .* ) and nearly dropped his precious camera. Even as he heard the low, pulsing hum, his startled eyes took in the huge shape drifting toward him over the distant mountains, dwarfing even their vastness.

Donovan felt his jaw sag; his mind screamed that he must've bought it—he couldn't still be *alive* and seeing this. Automatically his finger tightened on the shooting button, and he heard the camera record the incredible vision.

An oblate spheroid, just as he'd heard it described in those UFO stories, but it was so *big*! His fuddled mind tried to absorb the enormity of the ship, but as it loomed closer and closer, his sense of proportion simply gave out. A mile in diameter? More. Two miles? More— *Big*—

Finally it stopped, hanging in midair like an impossible dream. Donovan heard Tony shouting behind him, and turned to wave reassuringly at the soundman. As he slogged through the water toward his friend, one thought ran through Donovan's head like a broken record: *How many people in history have been saved from having their asses shot off by a flying saucer?*

THE WHITE MOUSE SAT UP ON HIS HIND LEGS, WHISKERS TWITCHing, as he heard the cage door rattle. Food time? But his stomach told him no, it was not food time. Instead he felt a hand grasp him gently, lift him carefully, then turn him over. He recognized the scent, the voice that spoke, and did not struggle.

"Come on, Algernon. Show Doctor Metz your tummy."

"Remarkable!" Doctor Rudolph Metz leaned over to scrutinize the mouse's furry belly, then picked up a magnifying glass to inspect it more closely. "The lesion's nearly healed!"

The blonde young woman in the lab coat smiled, pleased by Metz's reaction. "Yes. In a few more days it should be completely normal." She stroked the mouse's head with one finger, then gently put him back in the cage.

Doctor Metz raised bushy salt-and-pepper brows, regarding her as intently as he had the mouse. "You know how long my research staff has been searching for that formula, Juliet?"

Juliet Parrish smiled, but shook her head. "It wasn't all my doing. Ruth helped a lot."

Ruth Barnes looked up from a microscope across the lab. "I heard that, and don't you believe it, Rudolph. She did it all."

"Well, I was very lucky." The fourth-year medical student carefully examined the latch on the mouse cage, not meeting the older man's eyes.

Metz nodded. "Luck happens in science, but usually only when accompanied by hard work and inspiration. The truth here, Juliet, is that you are very, very gifted. Research comes naturally to you."

Coming from Doctor Metz, this was an extraordinary compliment, and Juliet couldn't stop the flush of pleasure that warmed her face. Glancing over at Ruth, she saw the older woman give her a "thumbs up" sign of approval.

Metz watched the mouse as he frisked around his cage. "And furthermore, I warn you that Ruth and I are going to try and steal you from the med school. If you could devote your full time to biochemistry, you might—"

The laboratory door slammed back against the wall with a bang, making them all jump. Silhouetted in the doorway was a breathless young black man. "Have you heard about them?"

"Heard about what, Ben?" Doctor Metz was puzzled.

Doctor Benjamin Taylor flipped on the television set that sat high on a shelf in the lab. The small portable's face filled with Dan Rather's well-known countenance—at this moment, a very grave countenance:

"... but wherever the reports have come from—Paris,

Rome, Geneva, Buenos Aires, Tokyo—descriptions of the craft have all been identical. And—" He broke off, plainly listening to a voice in his earphone. "I'm told that our affiliate station KXT in San Francisco now has this visual."

The screen filled with the image of a huge vessel looming in across San Francisco harbor, filling the screen, so vast that the Golden Gate Bridge below it looked like a Tinkertoy. The three in the laboratory could hear the awe in Rather's voice-over:

"Yes, there it is—Good Lord, the size of it! Ladies and gentlemen, this picture is coming to you *live* from San Francisco."

Almost at the same moment, the four scientists heard a low, pulsing hum, barely within the range of human ears. The mice, however, shrilled and began to race frantically around their cages.

Juliet glanced over at Ben. "Do you think—"

As if in answer to her question, Dan Rather spoke from the television screen: "I'm also getting confirmation that *another* of the giant ships is moving in over Los Angeles!"

"Oh, God," Ruth said. The four scientists stared at each other.

ANTHROPOLOGIST ROBERT MAXWELL LEANED CLOSER TO HIS prize, brushing carefully at a vacant eye socket with far greater gentleness than he used when bathing his three-year-old daughter. Even so, Arch Quinton put up a cautioning hand. "Gently, gently, Robert. She's a verra' special lady . . ." His Scots burr was most pronounced when he was excited, and Maxwell grinned to himself, thinking that he'd never seen the older man more ecstatic over a discovery—though Quinton would die rather than break out of that "dour Scot" cover he affected.

"So your examination of the hip socket verified that she

was female?" he asked. At Quinton's nod, he continued, dabbing carefully at the blackened, jagged teeth, "Upper Pleistocene, for sure, Arch. Much older than any we've uncovered at this site, wouldn't you agree?"

Quinton nodded. "The artifacts seem t' bear you out, lad. Also, look at her forehead, here—" His hand, which had been raised to brush gently at the wispy fragments of hair, paused, then turned into a point. "Robert, look at that!"

Even before Robert Maxwell could turn, he heard the sound—a vibrating pulse throbbing in his body as well as his ears. He turned to see a giant craft, silver-blue, sliding toward them as smoothly as if it ran on an invisible track. His hand tightened convulsively on the brush, and he pressed his body closer to the cliff, as though he would interpose himself between his find and the spaceship.

ELIAS TAYLOR SQUATTED ON THE FIRE ESCAPE, GLANCING QUICKLY around to make sure he was unobserved. Not much chance that anyone would be home, since it was the middle of the day, but Elias had never been caught yet, and didn't intend to break his record. Satisfied, he quickly taped the small pane over, his movements neat and economical. Then, a quick tap with a rock and—presto! The young man's teeth looked doubly white against his dark countenance as he grinned. Easy. Elias liked jobs that were easy.

Once inside the apartment, he trotted through the tiny rooms, looking for items that would be easy to carry, simple to fence. A Walkman caught his eye, and he flipped it on, listening intently to make sure that the tone was good.

A sock stuffed under the mattress of an unmade bed yielded nearly a hundred in cash. Elias grinned again as he counted it, shaking his head. *They always hide the bread in the same places. Most folks have no imagination . . .*

The only other thing that interested Taylor was a portable

television. He turned it on, grimacing as he saw it was only black-and-white. *Cheap suckers, I swear,* he thought, ready to turn it off and make his exit. Black-and-whites were so cheap that it wasn't worth his energy to steal them anymore. His fingers hovered over the "off" switch, arrested by the image on the screen, what looked like (but couldn't be!) a *live* shot of a big UFO! Hastily he turned the sound up.

". . . along the Champs-Élysées. We repeat, this picture is coming live from Paris, where yet another giant UFO is moving overhead."

Elias sat, eyes widening, as the picture changed to a squadron of jet fighters scrambling into the air. The voice continued:

"The Pentagon reports that fighters from the Tactical Air Command bases around the United States have approached these monstrous UFOs, but all jets reported interference with their onboard guidance and electrical systems, forcing them to break off their attempts."

The scene shifted to a mob rushing madly along a street, cars jammed in the middle, honking insanely—complete and utter chaos. Even the cops looked spaced-out, and no wonder, thought Elias, seeing another of the giant ships hanging (how the hell did they *do* that trick?) overhead. The scene reminded him tantalizingly of another, something he'd seen in the past, in a movie. As the camera panned to reveal the Washington Monument, Elias whistled softly to himself. "Shit," he mumbled, "it's old Klaatu and Gort come to Earth for real this time!"

The announcer was still talking: ". . . making it impossible to get within a mile of the craft. Missiles fired at the ships simply go astray, then detonate harmlessly well out of range. Police and troops are trying to maintain an orderly evacuation of the nation's capital . . ."

"Hell, too," mumbled Elias. "That sure don't look orderly

to me!" He fingered the Walkman, wondering how this new development would affect the prices Reggie would give him on this stuff . . .

". . . and all the other cities that are threatened by this unprecedented happening, but roads and highways everywhere are jammed with traffic. Accidents have paralyzed all or most of the major arteries. Other craft are known to be approaching or hovering over at least seven other major U.S. cities—Houston, New York, San Francisco, New Orleans—yes, and this is now confirmed, Los Angeles . . ."

"L.A.?!" Elias nearly dropped the Walkman, rousing to realize that he was in a stranger's living room, and that the rightful owner might reappear any moment. Hastily he slid one leg over the windowsill, afraid to look up.

He heard it before he saw it. Clutching the Walkman, Elias decided to take the rest of the day off.


MIKE DONOVAN PULLED A BLANKET OVER TONY'S GENTLY SNORING form, and moved forward to the Learjet's cockpit. Dropping into the copilot's seat, he glanced at the instruments. "Ahead of schedule," he commented.

Joe Harnell, the pilot, nodded. "How's your friend?"

"He's fine. The Scotch and codeine put him out. I can take her for a while, if you want to stretch your legs."

"Ever flown one before?" The pilot glanced quickly at Donovan.

"I've piloted almost everything except the shuttle, one time or another. Used to fly recon in Nam. Did you find out where we can set down?"

The pilot stood up, watching as Donovan took over the controls, then nodded approvingly before answering the newsman's question. "Yeah. So far Dulles is still open. We'd better take it. They're shutting down all over."

Donovan considered. "No, I got a hunch that New York is

going to be the place to be as far as news goes. How about JFK?"

"Closed."

Donovan shrugged, grinning. "Let's open it. They can't roll up the runways, can they?"

"Hell, too. The FAA would have our—"

Donovan snapped his fingers. "No, I've got a better idea! La Guardia's much better!"

Harnell stared at him. "You nuts? That'd mean flying this sucker right *under* the goddamn thing!"

"Yeah! Think of the shots I could get!"

"No way, Mike."

Donovan grinned at him. "Come on, think of the bucks the film will be worth! I'll share the credit with you . . ."

Harnell stared at him in disbelief. Donovan gave him a wink and went to get his camera.

THE NEXT MORNING THE BERNSTEIN FAMILY, STANLEY, LYNN, THEIR son Daniel, and Stanley's father, Abraham, watched in amazement as Mike Donovan's film showed the view of the underside of the great craft that hung over New York City. Like the one in Los Angeles, where the Bernsteins lived, it had remained stationary and silent throughout the long (and at least for Lynn Bernstein) sleepless night.

Daniel, who was eighteen, was fascinated by the spacecraft. All his life he'd been waiting for something exciting to happen to him, and here it finally had. Never mind that it had happened to the rest of the world too—something told him that this was what he'd been waiting for. He turned excitedly to his father, a thin-haired, sad-eyed man with a permanent stoop and the beginnings of a potbelly.

"They say it's a good five miles in diameter, Dad!"

His mother, Lynn, a nervous woman who might have been attractive if not for the deep lines between her eyes and her permanently thinned lips, wrung her hands in her lap, saying for the hundredth time to nobody in particular, "We ought to leave the city, don't you think?"

Stanley Bernstein glared at his son. "I told you before, Lynn, where would we go? The roads are jammed, they say. Besides, as the president pointed out, we ought to avoid panic. They haven't done anything to indicate they're hostile."

Old Abraham shifted uneasily on the couch. "I wonder if there is any place *left* to hide. Even the Germans during the war had no ships like these."

"Father," Stanley said reprovingly, "that doesn't help—"

Their attention shifted abruptly back to the television screen. A somewhat hoarse but still professional Dan Rather was saying: ". . . They have reported the same occurrence now in Rome . . . and Rio de Janeiro . . . Moscow . . . Yes, the reports are flooding in—that same tone is being repeated all over the world from the spacecraft hanging over our cities—"

The Bernsteins heard the pulsing signal simultaneously from the television pickup and also from outside their suburban Los Angeles home. A tone, swiftly echoing, then changing to a voice!

"Twenty-one . . . twenty . . . nineteen . . . eighteen . . ." The strangely resonant voice continued the countdown while the news commentator explained that all over the world people were hearing the same thing—each in the appropriate local tongue.

". . . five . . . four . . . three . . . two . . . one." After a second's pause, the voice continued, "Citizens of the planet Earth . . . we bring you greetings. We come in peace. May we respectfully request the secretary general of your United Nations please come to the top of the United Nations Building in New York at 0100 Greenwich Mean Time this evening. Thank you."

Stanley blinked. "What time is that?"

Dan Rather answered, obligingly, from the television. "The voice we have just heard requested the presence of the secretary general at the top of the United Nations Building in New York City at eight o'clock this evening."

Lynn clutched frantically at her husband's hand. "What will this mean, Stanley?"

Daniel turned to grin at her, ecstatic. "It means something is gonna happen, Mom . . . finally! Isn't it *great*?"

# 2

SUNSET WAS A DIM RED MEMORY ON THE NEW YORK WESTERN SKY as Mike Donovan panned his camera across the lights of Manhattan. Late summer wind whipped his already rumpled hair—the breeze was stiff this high up. The top of the United Nations Building. Donovan checked his watch again. Seven fifty and forty-five seconds. Not quite ten minutes to go.

The roof door slammed, admitting yet another crowd of journalists and technicians. Mike spotted a familiar black head and hurried over to greet Tony Leonetti, helping his friend carry his equipment over to the roped-off line. Donovan noted Leonetti's grimace as he moved his shoulder.

"You sure you're gonna make it, Tony?"

Tony grinned. "The news event of the *century*? Man, I ain't about to miss it!"

"Mike?" Both men turned as a woman's voice reached them.

Donovan's eyes held hers as she walked toward them, a tall, very well-groomed woman in her early thirties. Everything about her, from her expertly applied makeup and hairstyle to her level, measuring gaze, proclaimed her as one of the most prominent television reporters in the business. "Uh, hello, Kristine."

"Hello, Mike. Hi, Tony." She nodded pleasantly to Tony, who returned her greeting. "I heard you drew the TV pool. Me too."

Donovan smiled knowingly. "I thought I recognized your card in the pile downstairs. Figured you wouldn't miss this one."

She returned his smile a little sheepishly. "So where are we setting up?"

He pointed to the roped-off line beyond which stood a contingent of UN military police. With a nod, Tony excused himself to set up his equipment. Donovan hesitated, looking over at the bustle of camera crews, their faces ranging from strained worry to hectic gaiety. From far below he could hear the ever-present wail of sirens.

Kristine took his arm. "Mike? Let's get set up."

He started. "Yeah. I was just . . . thinking."

Her glance was knowing. "So was I. You could've at least said good-bye before you left that morning."

"I did. You were on the phone, hustling somebody for an assignment, and didn't hear me."

She paused, turned to him, her green eyes eloquent. "I'm sorry."

Donovan smiled, a little tensely. "So was I."

Their eyes held for several seconds, then she looked away. "What time is it?"

Donovan checked his watch. "Seven fifty-six."

Kristine hurried away to check her last-minute preparations. Donovan busied himself with his camera settings. The minutes crawled by.

At seven fifty-nine, a distinguished white-haired man emerged, flanked by armed escorts. Donovan recognized him as the secretary general and watched as he waved to the rooftop troops to lower their weapons. Donovan trained his camera on the gigantic floodlit shape of the alien craft hovering far above them, so enormous it dwarfed the tallest of the sky-scrapers. He could hear someone counting down under his breath.

One of the newsmen was speaking into a mike: "... and a hush has fallen ... not just here, I am sure, but around the world ..."

"Nine ... eight ... seven ... six ..."

*Five*, thought Donovan, *four, three, two, one*—

"... as eight o'clock strikes ... 0100 Greenwich Mean Time."

Donovan stared upward, the viewfinder of his camera pressed against his eye. His eye watered as he tried not to blink.

There! Something—hard to make out in that silver-blue vastness—a tiny dark opening! Donovan allowed himself that blink, then squinted back at the ship.

He zoomed in, centering directly on the opening, watched it fill with something—something that resolved into a stream-lined shape that detached swooping down toward them. Donovan could hear Kristine's cool, professional tones, and with one part of his mind admired her control—he knew she was as nervous as any of them, but her poise argued that she did this every day. "The smaller craft is moving at an angle downward, now—across Third Avenue and Thirty-Ninth—coming directly toward the UN Building."

Donovan pivoted to follow the craft as it slowed prior to landing. It gleamed white, with small dark triangles that could have been opaque windows at regular intervals. On what looked to be its nose was a red symbol of some kind, a combination of dots and lines, like nothing the cameraman had ever seen before, but holding a haunting familiarity never-theless. The craft descended with barely a whoosh of dis-placed air to mark its passage.

Kristine continued her commentary: "Now the craft is

drifting to a stop some ten feet in the air above our heads . . . Now it's landing . . . The air itself feels strange . . . vibrating slightly . . ."

A panel opened at the bottom side of the craft, just as the assembled crowd heard a voice—a strangely resonant, slightly echoing voice: "Herr General Sekreterare . . ." Donovan shifted the camera to pick up the secretary general as the man stepped to the front of the crowd, his face set in lines of calm determination, his back very straight.

The voice continued: *"Var intre rädd kom upp för trappan."* At the same moment a short ramp extruded onto the rooftop, resting there securely.

Kristine's voice reached Donovan, still poised, calm, but with a new tightness. "I think the voice spoke Swedish— that's the secretary general's native language . . ." She listened intently to a button in her ear. "Yes, I have the translation now . . . 'Mr. Secretary General . . . do not be afraid . . . Please climb the ramp.'"

Beneath his shock of white hair, the elderly man's face was set, his strides coming with a steady precision. He reached the ramp and began climbing, step by step, until he reached the top and disappeared. The armed guards raised their weapons. Donovan realized he'd been holding his breath only when his vision began to blur. He let it out slowly, his eye riveted to the camera's viewfinder, and waited.

There was a stirring at the top of the stairs, shadows moving within darkness. Then—a face! The secretary general emerged, moving with a quick vigor that was in huge contrast to the rigid strides he had taken to reach the craft.

Murmurs filled the rooftop, but Kristine's authoritative tones cut through them: "There he is! The secretary general is reappearing! He is apparently unharmed, waving cheerfully to the onlookers here on the roof of the UN Building . . . Just a minute. It looks as though he's going to address the crowd . . ."

The older man's educated, slightly accented tones reached Donovan clearly as he focused on the speaker's face. "My fellow citizens of Earth . . . these Visitors assure me that they come in peace and that they wish to honor all the covenants of our United Nations Charter. As you'll see, they are much like us . . . although their voices *are* unusual. They first asked me to speak on their behalf, but I felt everyone would be more comfortable if their Supreme Commander, who is aboard this vessel, spoke directly to you all. His voice will be heard around the world, in every language necessary."

The secretary general turned back to look up the stairs. Donovan focused past him on the dark opening in the belly of the shuttle. Movement—then he was seeing booted feet in the viewfinder, legs, a normal-seeming trunk, two arms, a head—

Donovan gasped, his fingers tightening on the camera. He'd expected differences, and there were none! At first glance, the alien appeared to be a normal human male of middle years, with thick gray hair and keen blue eyes. He was wearing high black boots, looking for all the world like ordinary English riding boots, and a reddish-colored coverall that was cut much the same as a pilot's flight suit. It had five diagonal black stripes across the breast.

Kristine's commentary was analytical and precise: "Roughly six feet tall . . . I'd estimate one hundred sixty pounds . . . He seems to have some difficulty seeing in the glare of the floodlights here . . . He's stopping now, halfway down the ramp . . . I think he's about to speak . . ."

The man's voice reached them clearly, but its unusual timbre—sort of a vibrating resonance—was even more apparent live, like this, than it had been over the airwaves.

"I trust you will forgive me . . . but our eyes are unaccustomed to this sort of brightness . . ." Reaching into a pocket of the coverall, he took out a pair of surprisingly normal-looking dark glasses and put them on.

"As the secretary general has told you, we have come in peace to all mankind on Earth . . . Our planet is the fourth in distance from the star which you call Sirius. It is some 8.7 light-years from your Earth. This is the first time we have journeyed from our system, and you are the first intelligent life form we've encountered." He paused, then a very warm smile brightened his features. "We are very pleased to meet you!"

Donovan could hear the murmur of relief and welcome rising audibly from the assembled journalists and dignitaries. He continued shooting, zooming in for a closeup as the man took a few strides toward him before resuming: "Our names would sound peculiar to you, so we—my fellow Visitors and I—have chosen simple names from Earth. My name is John."

The Visitor smiled again. "The secretary general referred to me as a 'Supreme Commander.' Actually, I'm just sort of an admiral. I'm responsible for this small fleet around your planet . . ."

*Small fleet?* Donovan tightened his fingers on the camera, suddenly conscious that his hands were sweating.

"We've sent other unmanned craft before us, some of which have monitored the Earth for quite a while, so we could learn your languages—but some of us are not as skilled as others, so we hope you will be patient with us. We have come here on behalf of our Great Leader . . . who governs our united planet with benevolence and wisdom . . . We have come because we need your help."

*Benevolence and wisdom,* thought Donovan cynically. *Sounds like a real party hack. They ought to do just fine down here. John may end up our next president . . .*

"Our planet is in serious environmental difficulty. Far, far worse than yours. It's reached a stage where we will be unable to survive without immediate assistance. There are certain chemicals and compounds which we need to manufacture—

which alone can save our struggling civilization. You can help us manufacture these. And in return, we'll gladly share with you the fruits of all our knowledge."

*The fruits of all our knowledge . . . Who the hell have they got for a speechwriter?*

"Now that contact is established, we would like to meet with individual governments so that we may present requests for certain operating plants around the world to be retooled for manufacture of the compound we need . . ."

Donovan thought fleetingly of his stepfather's plant, could visualize his mother, Eleanor, goading that poor SOB Arthur to try and land a Visitor contract. *Wonder what kind of compound they're talking about?*

"And we'll reward your generosity, as I have said, by educating your industrial and scientific complex to the limits of our knowledge—helping solve your environmental, agricultural, and health dilemmas—then we'll leave you, as we came, in peace."

*Talk about offering us heaven on a silver platter—what would they do if we told them to stick it in their non-pointed ears?*

"I know that if circumstances were reversed, and you had come to visit us, I'd feel a burning curiosity to see the inside of your spacecraft right away. With that in mind, we'd like to have the secretary general and five of your journalists accompany us back aboard our Mother Ship, for what will be the first of many opportunities to get to know us better."

Donovan felt a tap on his shoulder, and looked up from his camera's viewfinder to see one of the secretary general's aides at his side. "Your card came up, Mr. Donovan," the man said in accented English.

"Hot damn!" Hastily Donovan checked his equipment, then ducked under the rope at the man's signal. As he began walking toward the ship, Kristine and Tony fell in beside him.

"What'd he mean, my card came up?" Donovan asked them in a low voice as they crossed the rooftop.

"They chose the journalists by lot," Kristine explained. "Sam Egan and Jeri Taylor got it too."

"We really got the luck!"

"Yeah," Tony agreed dryly. Donovan turned to ask him what he meant, but Leonetti was already mounting the ramp. Donovan hastened after him.

The Visitor leader, "John," was waiting for them at the top of the ramp. Donovan was the last to climb it as he hung back to get a good shot of the other journalists meeting and shaking hands with the alien. Then he sprinted up the ramp for his own turn, hastily resting his camera on his left shoulder so he could free his right hand. *God,* he thought, impressed in spite of himself, *I'm getting to shake the hand of someone born under a different sun . . . even though he looks human, he's not . . .*

John's hand was markedly cool, the skin firm and smooth. He nodded pleasantly. "Mr. Donovan. I saw your films of the underside of our Mother Ship. Most impressive . . . and quite daring."

Donovan felt like a kid receiving a chuckle and a pat on the shoulder from an adult. "That's right, you said you monitored our television. How long have you been doing that?"

Behind the Visitor's dark glasses Donovan could see the man's blue eyes appraise him coolly. John smiled. "For several of your solar years, now. I promise you we'll satisfy your curiosity, Mike. We'll have lots of time to communicate during our visit here."

"I'm glad to hear it." Donovan moved along. He stepped into the shuttle, grabbing a closeup of John's face as the man smiled graciously at Kristine, before sitting down beside the newswoman.

*The guy wears authority like a shroud,* Donovan thought,

wrenching his eyes away from the leader with an almost physical effort.

The interior of the craft was disappointing. It looked like a cross between the Learjet and one of those shuttle vehicles that transport passengers to planes. Seats lined the walls, cushioned seats covered in what appeared to be (and probably was) very ordinary dark brown fabric—*A good color choice,* Donovan thought, remembering his own carpet shopping when he'd set up his apartment last year after the divorce. *Doesn't show dirt.*

Thinking of his divorce made Donovan recall—with a guilty start—that he hadn't called Sean in almost three days. *Since before this thing started. The event of the century, and you haven't phoned to see how your only child is reacting.* He made a swift mental promise to call first thing tomorrow morning, and to visit over the weekend. He wondered if Sean had seen him walk up those stairs and enter the alien shuttle—then smiled. He knew he had. Sean was his Dad's biggest cheering section. *Even Marjorie's bitterness can't change that.*

Kristine Walsh was sitting across the cabin from him, still deep in conversation with John. Donovan wondered what they were talking about—she was smiling that wide, candid grin that Mike knew she reserved for people she really liked. He felt an irrational stab of jealousy. *Cut it out, idiot. You're here for a story, not a romantic interlude.*

Quickly he panned the camera around the inside, wishing he had more light. The Visitors evidently kept their illumination levels at what most humans would think of as "late-night television" dimness. Donovan could see clearly enough, but reading would have been uncomfortable after more than a few minutes.

*But I thought Sirius was a really bright star . . . Have to check it out with the observatory when I get back . . . I suppose their planet could have a heavy cloud cover or something . . .*

Two other Visitors, young men about Donovan's age, stuck their heads into the main cabin, and John nodded. Moments later, Donovan felt a slight movement as the craft evidently took off. He wished the windows weren't darkened—what a shot it would make to catch the UN Building rooftop receding, and that giant saucer drawing closer!

The alien craft was silent and seemed nearly motionless. Donovan wondered how the Visitors powered their ships. Jargon from *Cosmos* episodes and science fiction stories zipped through his mind—*matter/antimatter, ion drives, tesseracts, space warps*—

Tony turned to him. "Scared, Mike?"

"Are you?"

"Yeah, a little maybe. This is a big day for the whole planet."

"It's funny how you start thinking of this place as a planet—only one of God knows how many—since they came along."

"I've noticed that. What you'd call a cosmic consciousness-raiser, I guess."

"Yeah. But to answer your question—yeah, I'm a little scared too."

There was an almost imperceptible bump, then the craft stopped. Donovan gathered up his camera, setting it to compensate as much as possible for the anticipated lack of lighting. "Here we go."

They stepped out into a large, open area. Rows of shuttles like the one they'd arrived in were lined up on either side. The large docking bay looked very similar to those Donovan had seen aboard the biggest of the Navy's aircraft carriers. The white craft gleamed faintly, reflecting a dim blue from the overall lighting and the painted floor. John explained that each docking bay held about three dozen shuttles, and that there were two hundred or more of them scattered through the great Mother Ships that made up the fleet. Donovan heard Kristine relaying this information in her voice-over recording as he wheeled slowly, panning his camera.

The Visitor leader touched Kristine's arm. "This way. I'll take you to see the Main Control Room."

Donovan trailed behind them so he could shoot the overhead catwalk with the journalists climbing up to it. Then he hurried to catch up.

As they moved above the docking bay, a dark-haired, extremely attractive woman entered from a side door and stood waiting for them. Donovan zoomed in on her. Even with the low lighting level it was impossible to mistake the authority in her dark eyes, an authority which seemed as much a part of her as her sculpted cheekbones and generous mouth. Kristine's voice reached Donovan as they walked toward the Visitor woman.

"You have both males and females in your crew?"

John sounded faintly surprised. "Well, yes, of course. This is Diana . . . she is second in command."

The brunette nodded pleasantly at them. Donovan gave her another closeup. She turned to accompany them on the tour.

The control room looked faintly like the conning tower of a nuclear submarine, but larger, with perhaps a dozen men and women busily working at large multilighted consoles before viewscreens. A few showed glimpses of Manhattan below, but most were filled with instrument graphs and readouts. All the crewmembers were dressed in the reddish coveralls, with slight variations in the breast designs that apparently designated rank and station. Mike panned the camera quickly, for the admiral did not pause, but kept moving.

"Next we'll see what you'd call our engine room."

"Does that screen over there keep you in touch with the other ships in your 'small fleet'?" John turned to see which readout Kristine was pointing to.

"Yes, Kristine." Diana's voice, barring the alien reverberation, was a husky contralto. "Most of the others monitor and activate the functions of the ship. It's quite routine and unspectacular, really."

*Sure,* thought Donovan, zooming in for a shot of the two women. *If you happen to be from another star . . .*

They moved along the catwalk until it led into a tunnel. The dark walkway extended for nearly forty paces—Donovan counted them. He realized, with a prickle touching the short hairs at the nape of his neck, that he was behaving as if he were scouting enemy territory. *Don't be paranoid, Mike. They've come in peace, remember?*

The only features worth noting in the tunnel were several doors painted a brilliant, chromatic yellow. Donovan examined them through the viewfinder, but saw nothing beyond their color to indicate that they were special.

"And those doors we just passed?" Kristine was asking Diana.

"Restricted areas—a lot of radioactivity. Our gravity drive, as you've seen, is quite effective, but it takes up nearly half the ship."

"How fast can this baby go?" Donovan asked. It was the first time he'd spoken, and Diana looked over at him.

"We can travel at speeds close to that of light itself."

Donovan thought of asking if they'd proved or disproved Einstein's theory, but stopped when he realized they might well not know who Einstein was.

They emerged onto a catwalk high above a considerable number of gleaming, golden-hued cylinders. The place looked vaguely like a refinery, with tracings of pipework running everywhere. A few technicians moved among the giant cylinders, examining and recording information from readouts and dials.

Diana was continuing, "The other half of the ship contains the living quarters for the crew, as well as storage areas to hold the chemicals we'll be manufacturing here on Earth. They'll be contained within enormous cryogenic tanks to keep them—"

"Cryogenic?" Kristine paused in her voice-over.

"Super-cooled. For maximum efficiency in storage."

John chuckled. "You'll have to forgive Diana, Kristine. Like all scientists, she tends to forget at times that not all of us are as well-versed in technical language as she is."

"Now, you also mentioned living quarters for the crew," Kristine continued her voice-over. "How many of your people are on this ship?"

Diana hesitated for barely a second, but Donovan didn't miss her quick, sideways glance at her commander. "It . . . varies . . . Several thousand."

*On this ship alone? How many does that make on all fifty or so ships?* Donovan bit his lip, glancing over at Kristine, but she was intent on her next question.

"Can we talk to some of them?"

John smiled. "You can. You'll have a lot of opportunity for that."

The tour ended a few minutes later back in the docking bay. Diana, not John, accompanied the journalists and the secretary general back down to the UN Building.

Sitting aboard the Visitor shuttle (as far as Donovan could tell, it was the same one they'd come up in—but it was impossible to be sure), Donovan stretched, rubbing the muscles at the back of his neck.

"What time is it?" he asked Tony, seeing his friend check his watch.

The soundman grinned. "About nine thirty. The night is still embryonic, Mike old buddy."

Donovan fought back a yawn. "'Zat *all*? Christ, why am I so tired? I feel like I've been awake for *days*."

"You have been. Unless you sacked out on the plane back from El Salvador."

"Nope. I was too busy playing nursemaid to you."

"Bull. I saw those closeups of the Mother Ship. You were playing daredevil pilot and hotshot cameraman again."

"That's me." Donovan acknowledged the ribbing with a grin. He patted the camera. "I can hardly wait to get this on the air."

"What do you think it'll be worth?" Tony, the practical one in the partnership, wanted to know.

"Just about anything we want to ask for it, old friend. I'll leave the extent of our greed up to you, as the business manager."

Tony nodded thoughtfully, then, taking out a pocket calculator, busied himself with the pleasant task of figuring out the profit margin this venture would net them.

The five journalists and the secretary general were relatively sheltered from the press until they'd turned their tapes and films over to the networks. Donovan, Tony, and Kristine watched their story air in a "Special Bulletin" broadcast by satellite.

"Do you think we'll place first in the Nielsens?" Tony studied Donovan's films of the docking bay with a wide grin.

"Maybe . . ." Kristine grinned back. "What about it, Mike? Do you think we managed to beat out *Dallas*?"

"I dunno." Donovan took a slightly tipsy swig from his third can of Coors. "You're talking about tough competition, lady. I mean, this is *only* the news event of the *century*."

As soon as the broadcast was finished, somebody brought out bottles of champagne. The corks popped with almost the

same frequency as the machine-gun bullets had just—
yesterday? The day before? Time seemed to Donovan to have
swerved, looped, gone sidereal.

He thought about traveling at the speed of light—what
that might be like. What would it be like to pilot one of those
big Mother Ships? Probably it would be such a group effort
that you wouldn't get the thrill of handling the ship yourself.

"Mike?" He looked up a little blearily to see Kristine standing in front of him, realized he'd nearly dozed off.

"What time is it?" He looked around. The party was in full
swing.

"Almost midnight. Want to come over to my place for a
nightcap?"

He almost said no, that he'd better go find a hotel, that he
was tired, but found himself agreeing. "Sure. You got a
VCR?"

"Of course. You bringing the tape?"

"Of course!"

It had been several months since he'd been up to Kristine's
apartment. The view was breathtaking here on the Upper
East Side. He looked out at the glimmer of the water, watching the play of headlights far below. And above, of course,
there was the floodlit enormity of the Visitor ship. Donovan
stood looking at it, hardly able to believe he'd actually been
up there, just a few hours ago.

Kristine emerged from the kitchen with several green bottles and two delicately stemmed glasses. Donovan grinned.
"*More* champagne?" The cork went off with a pop, and wine
foamed out. He hurried to get his glass under the bottle as
they sat down together in her luxurious velour conversation
pit.

Kristine laughed. "Sure! How often do we get to celebrate
our coverage of the event of the century?"

"Yeah." Donovan shook his head, then sipped carefully at the champagne. "I can't believe how the three of us just lucked into it!"

Kristine giggled. Mike had never seen her before when she'd had this much to drink. "Luck had nothing to do with it. I stacked the deck they drew from, so we'd get the pool!"

"Oh, come on!" He didn't know whether to believe her or not—or whether to hug her or give her a lecture. Stacked the deck?

"Yeah, I really did." She laughed, kicking off her shoes. She'd shed her businesslike tan blazer, and the white blouse she wore looked soft, feminine. He noticed that she'd unbuttoned it at the throat.

Donovan turned away from her, sipping his champagne. She edged back into the pit beside him, picking up the remote-control device for the television set. "Did you put the tape in, Mike?"

"But you saw it on the network . . ."

"Yeah, wasn't it terrific! Play it again, Sam. One more time!"

She turned on the unit, reaching for the bottle at the same time. Donovan felt something cold splash on his leg and yelped. "Kris! Try to get it into the glass, for Chrissake!"

She made a face at the newsman on the screen. "We don't want to listen to *you*. Fast forward!" The television screen blurred and rippled.

Donovan laughed. "Your *life* is on fast forward, honey."

They watched their tour of the Mother Ship, as captured by Donovan's camera. Kristine turned a mock-accusing face on Mike as Diana appeared on the screen. "There she is. Your girlfriend. You gave her more closeups than me!"

Donovan grinned at her, making no attempt to deny it. "She's got everything . . . brains . . . looks . . ."

"And a figure that doesn't quit." Kristine laughed, watching Diana in profile. "But would you want your sister to marry a Sirian?"

She punched the fast-forward button again, then when the screen resolved, Diana was looking straight at them, at close range. "See!" Kristine turned to Donovan, her glass held threateningly aloft. "*Another* closeup!"

Donovan, laughing, tried to fend her off, but she was too quick for him, splashing a cold spatter of wine down the back of his neck. He made a grab for her, trying not to spill his own wine, finally managing to snag one of her wrists. Her empty glass dropped, falling onto the thickly sculpted carpet.

Both of them were laughing as they struggled for the remaining champagne glass. Somehow Mike found himself sprawled on the couch, with Kristine pulled down on top of him—and the champagne still in his possession. The glass was still—miraculously—full, but Donovan had lost interest in drinking any more of it. He was too conscious of Kristine's gaze. Their eyes were only inches away.

Her voice was husky. "Mike . . . why didn't it work for us before?"

He shook his head, shrugging wordlessly, realizing that if he didn't intend to spend the night here, he ought to call a halt to this right now. It wasn't fair to Kris otherwise. But somehow, he couldn't summon the words.

"I'd like to try again, Mike." She leaned toward him. Her mouth tasted sweet from the wine.

Donovan kissed her back, closing his eyes. Her body was alive and warm against his as he pulled her down beside him. One hand caught in the soft tumble of her hair as he drew her even closer. His other hand searched for the end table. He managed to set the glass down without spilling it.

# 3

ROBERT MAXWELL FROWNED AT HIS WIFE, KATHLEEN. "I THOUGHT Robin had to be there by now!"

Kathleen was clearly rattled, but made an effort to project her usual calm confidence. "Take it easy, honey. She'll be ready in just a moment. Did you back the car out?"

"Yes!" Maxwell knew he was being bearish, but couldn't help it. His first chance to get a close look at the Visitors, and his daughter was holding him up. Teenagers! "What's the delay, Kathy?"

"She found a spot on her band uniform, and she's trying to get it out. Calm down, honey."

Their twelve-year-old, Polly, came down the stairs carrying her three-year-old sister, Katie. Maxwell gathered up his youngest, giving her an affectionate kiss, enjoying her soap-and-water cleanliness. "Mmmm, you look pretty, sweetheart. Thanks for getting her ready, Polly."

"That's okay, Dad. She sure didn't want to wear that pink dress and those ruffled panties, though." Polly grinned at Katie, who shared her older sister's rough-and-tough ideas of apparel.

Kathleen shook her head at Maxwell as he stooped to put his little girl down. "Don't. Just keep hold of her. If you put her down she'll be filthy inside of thirty seconds."

Maxwell straightened, Katie giggling in his arms. "Your mommy's pretty smart, isn't she, Punkin? You, the World's Champion Dirt Magnet? Huh?" Katie grinned unabashedly at her father and planted a moist kiss squarely on his upper lip.

"Mother, where's my hat?" Seventeen-year-old Robin erupted down the stairs in a flash of white and maroon, trimmed liberally with black braid. Polly picked up her sister's flute case and handed it to her.

"Here it is, dear." Kathleen picked up the furry scarlet hat.

"Let's *go*, gang! We were supposed to be there five minutes ago!"

Maxwell drove the station wagon quickly, surely, toward the plant managed by their neighbor, Arthur Dupres. In the three weeks since the Visitors had arrived, they'd selected a number of plants to be retooled for the production of their urgently needed chemical compound. The Richland Chemical Corporation owned the first such plant to be declared operational by the Visitor Scientific Commander, Diana. Consequently, the place was thronged with news media and crowds awaiting the landing of the Visitor shuttle. Luckily Maxwell was able to park the station wagon near the school buses transporting the band equipment.

Hurriedly he handed Robin her flute case, as Kathleen adjusted the furry uniform hat on her daughter's dark head. "Do I look all right?" Robin squinted at the station wagon's outside mirror.

"You're gorgeous, kid," her father said, thinking that his habitual answer was becoming more truthful every day. With her blue-green eyes, fluffy dark hair and pretty features, his daughter had most of the boys in her class at Rosemont High

School vying for her attention. Unfortunately, Robin was only too aware of this—a fact Maxwell found disturbing.

Watching her race over to where the band was forming up its lines, he sighed. *There's still a child in there,* he thought, *but not for long.*

Carrying Katie on his shoulder, Maxwell, his wife, and Polly headed for the reviewing stand. Late as they were for band formation, they were still earlier than the majority of the crowd, so were able to get good seats. Maxwell unslung his binocular case and took out his glasses.

"Bob!" Kathleen frowned, pushing her dark blonde hair off her forehead. "You're not going to use those things, are you?"

Maxwell focused the glasses, squinting, so he'd get the best view of the raised platform that had been set up for the opening ceremonies. "I sure am," he said.

"Doesn't that strike you as rather rude?"

"Nobody will even notice me. And we're sitting too far away from the platform for anyone to look up here."

Kathleen looked troubled. "Well, I still think—"

Maxwell put the glasses back in their case. "Honey, nobody's going to be looking at me! Everyone's going to be craning their necks for a glimpse of the Visitors! Arch Quinton told me last week that the telephoto shots of some of the Visitors showed some 'interesting anomalies,' as he put it. I want to see if I can spot what he was talking about."

"Why didn't you ask him?"

"You know Arch when he's got something on his mind. He was about as informative as the Stone of Scone."

"Maxwell!"

Both Maxwells turned at the hail, to see a balding man dressed in an expensive suit waving to them from the other side of the viewing stand. As they watched, a woman dressed in a quietly elegant hat and suit joined him.

With Polly and Katie in tow, Robert and Kathleen picked their way down the bleachers. At the bottom Maxwell held out his hand, "Hello, Arthur. Congratulations on the big day. The eyes of the world are on Richland today, eh?"

"They certainly are." Eleanor Dupres took her husband's arm proudly. "*I* was the one who suggested it. The very first night, when John first mentioned they needed chemicals, I said to Arthur that he ought to call up Richland and volunteer his plant for Visitor use. I pointed out that it was his civic duty, in a way. So he did, and now all this is happening . . . I think it's wonderful!"

"It certainly is," Kathleen said hastily, deliberately brushing Robert's arm with hers as she reached out to clasp Eleanor's hand warmly. Maxwell took a deep breath and manfully managed to smother the broad grin that Eleanor's speeches invariably invoked in him.

"Oh, and by the way, Robert and Kathleen," Eleanor said, oblivious to the Maxwells' byplay, "I'm giving a little party tonight to honor the Visitors. Several of them have consented to join us, and I wonder if you could come too."

Maxwell tried not to let his excitement show. "We'd love to, Eleanor. What time?"

"About eight. Nothing too formal . . . just evening wear required. See you then."

Eleanor and Arthur departed in the direction of the reviewing stand. Maxwell waited until they were out of earshot, then let out a whoop. "All *right*! I'll get to meet them close up!"

Kathleen gave him a mock glare. "You and your big mouth, Bob." Her light tones dropped into a deadly imitation of Eleanor's effusive ones. " 'Just evening wear required.' What the hell am I going to dig up to wear on six hours' notice?"

"You'll look gorgeous, honey, you always do," Maxwell said automatically, his mind already filling with visions of conversations with the Visitors about their evolutionary origins. So far, no scientific observers had been invited aboard the Visitor ships—just journalists and politicians. What a chance for him!

"And even if I *do* manage to scrape something up for myself, I can't figure what *you're* going to wear."

"What about that new sports jacket we got this past spring?"

Kathleen snorted rudely. "Did you even *notice* what you did to the cuffs that day you and Arch stopped off to visit the dig for 'just a few minutes'—when the few minutes turned into *three hours*? Talk about the original absentminded professors!"

"Oh, yeah." Maxwell looked chagrined. "Maybe I should go out and pick up a new one this afternoon, after the opening ceremonies."

Kathleen shook her head. "Sorry, hon. We can't afford it. But don't worry. I think the old navy one is clean, and it will do."

Maxwell dropped an impulsive kiss onto her forehead. "Thank you, honey. I don't deserve you, you know that?"

Her clear green eyes softened a bit. "Sure you do. I love you, Bob."

"And I love you." They exchanged a fond look—a look which was interrupted by Polly's shout.

"Mom! Can Katie have a soda?"

"Later, Polly." They turned to climb the bleachers again.

"But *Mommy*, I'm *thirsty*!"

Kathleen sighed. "I said later, Katie. You can have some of those grapes Mommy brought."

The band began tuning up, and the bleachers filled rapidly. Maxwell saw a white van pull up, and several technicians began setting up gear. Several people got out of the van, and Maxwell, who was using his binoculars again, recognized two of them immediately.

"Look, honey, it's Michael Donovan and Kristine Walsh!"

"Let me see!" Kathleen took the binoculars eagerly. "Hmmm . . . Somehow they look shorter than when you see them on television."

"She's an attractive woman," Maxwell said, squinting at the journalist.

Kathleen gave him an amused look. "Who would you rather meet? Ms. Walsh, or Diana?"

"Diana." Maxwell grinned. "Preferably with a specimen glass behind my back."

She laughed. "The anthropologist to the end. Are you trying to tell me you haven't noticed how gorgeous she is?"

Maxwell chuckled. "I didn't say *that*."

The band struck up a wavering but recognizable rendition of the *Star Wars* theme. Someone in the bleachers shouted, "There it is!"

Maxwell looked up to see one of the Visitor shuttlecraft approaching from the giant ship that hovered over Los Angeles. The Mother Ship was such a normal sight by now that the L.A. skyline would have looked odd without it.

"What are they using to provide the raw materials for their chemical, do you know?" the man sitting next to Maxwell asked.

"I understand that they're using garbage and other wastes," Maxwell answered. "But I've never heard much of an explanation of what the chemical *is*, or what they're going to use it for."

The man, a heavyset black man in his late fifties, grunted. "That reminds me of a really bad joke I heard. 'Bout aliens that eat garbage and piss gasoline. Do you ever—I dunno— worry 'bout all this?"

Maxwell frowned through the binoculars as the shuttlecraft door opened and the Visitor technicians began filing through and assembling in ranks. Each carried a large, cumbersome- looking container of some kind. His mind distracted by his attempts to study their features under the caps and dark glasses, he almost forgot the man's question until Kathleen nudged him. "Worry? About what? They've shown their peaceful intentions."

The black man rubbed thoughtfully at his salt-and-pepper moustache. "I dunno. What *have* they really shown us? Where's all this scientific jazz they're supposed to be showing us? They've been here three weeks now, and we barely know any more about them than the first day they talked to us."

Maxwell squinted, recognizing Diana in the crowd. The Visitor technicians continued to file from the craft. Now a second shuttlecraft settled down and began disgorging red-garbed Visitors. Polly nudged him. "Hey, Dad, I just heard a joke."

"Ummmm?" Maxwell tried to focus the binoculars on the troops of Visitors. How many were out there now? The band continued to labor through the *Star Wars* theme—Maxwell winced as he heard a flutist hit a sour note and hoped fervently it wasn't Robin.

"How many Visitors does it take to change a lightbulb?"

Maxwell craned his neck. "I don't know. How many?"

Polly laughed with all of a twelve-year-old's enthusiasm. "None! They *like* the dark!"

Maxwell laughed politely, heard the black man chuckling at his side. Visitors continued to file out of the craft, the band continued to play.

"How many of them *are* there, Robert?" Kathleen asked.

The black man turned to her. "I been wonderin' that myself. How many you counted?"

Maxwell stared at the growing sea of red coveralls, frowning. "I don't know. A lot."

"Yeah," said the black man. "A helluva lot."

ROBIN MAXWELL WAS DOING HER BEST TO KEEP PLAYING IN TIME with the band while her head turned to watch the Visitors file past her. She wasn't going to miss the chance to see them this close! She hit a sour note and winced—hoping the rest of the band had covered up her mistake. Still, she couldn't look away from the Visitor technicians walking past her.

There were a lot of them—Robin wondered what the various black stripes and insignia on their uniforms meant. What had Daniel Bernstein said? Something about the markings denoting rank and type of work.

She wrinkled her attractive nose, thinking of Daniel. He'd been acting so *dumb* since the Visitors had come. They were all he could talk about. Used to be that all he'd wanted to talk about was whether or not she'd go out with him . . . not that Robin had any intention of *that*. Daniel was a nice kid, good-looking too, but that's all he was—a kid. True, he was almost nineteen, nearly eighteen months older than Robin herself, but he acted like a kid.

In the six months since Daddy had allowed her to go out on real car dates with boys, she'd already decided she wasn't going to waste her time going out with kids. Why, the last time she'd driven over to the University library with Daddy, two really cute freshmen had tried to pick her up as she walked across the quadrangle.

Robin smiled around the mouthpiece of her flute, remembering. *Star Wars* continued around her. Mr. Elderbaum, the bandleader, didn't look particularly pleased by the performance. But heck, they'd had less than a week to rehearse!

For sure, there were a lot of Visitors going by her, Robin thought. She wondered vaguely how many, then she hit a flat note without even noticing, and a second later she lowered the flute and simply stood there, staring.

He was the most gorgeous boy she'd ever seen—hair the color of bronze, and eyes—it was hard to make out behind the dark glasses, but Robin squinted until she was sure. Blue. A beautiful sky blue. He was standing beside the shuttlecraft hatch, evidently directing some of the Visitor technicians as they formed their ranks.

For long moments Robin stared, unaware that she was smiling. Just before he turned to move on, the Visitor's eyes met hers for a second. Robin felt the quick flush in her cheeks as his gaze touched hers.

Then he was gone, and she was alone once more with the band, and the seemingly never-ending *Star Wars*. Robin put the flute back to her lips, picking up her place, but her playing was completely automatic.

*What a* fox *he was,* she thought. *A bitchin'* fox. She hoped that somehow, someday, she'd see him again . . .

ON THE CATWALK OVERHEAD, TWO MEN WEARING HARDHATS stood, watching the red-coveralled forms file by. One, a heavy-shouldered black man, shook his head. "Damn!"

His companion, a wispy-haired white man whose stomach proclaimed his fondness for beer and armchair football, turned to him. "What's the matter, Caleb?"

"What's the *matter*?" Caleb Taylor pointed indignantly. "Look at them, man! There's so many of those suckers they can hardly fit onto the parking lot! First we got to fight you honkies for jobs, then the Mexicans—and now these creeps have come to work with us, and they ain't even *from* this planet!"

Bill Graham laughed. "Don't be so paranoid, Caleb!"

After a second Taylor chuckled wryly. "If you'd had to worry 'bout layoffs as many times as I have, Bill, you'd be paranoid too. You know black people are most often the first to go, don't try and tell me any different. In the days when I had a wife and two kids to feed, I used to sweat every time things got a little slow here at Richland."

"Well, it's sure different for you now," Bill pointed out. "Ben's doing so well at the hospital that you won't have to touch your pension from this place if you don't want to."

"I don't know 'bout that," Caleb said thoughtfully. "I've never lived off another person, and I'm not about to start. Even if Ben *is* a doctor. Shit, he could get married and move to Boston or something, and what would Elias and I do then?"

"Is Ben finally getting serious about someone?"

Caleb Taylor snorted. "You kidding? He's so wrapped up in medicine that the only time he ever *looks* at a woman is when she's stripped an' lying on an examining table!"

Graham made a juicy noise with his lips. "Hey, for all I know, that's as good a way as any to get some—"

"Shit, don't you ever suggest that to Ben! He's so dedicated to that Hippocratic oath of his that he wouldn't even know you were jokin'. He'd probably nail you one before you could explain it to him!"

Both men laughed. "Speaking of Elias, how's he doing?" Graham asked.

Caleb Taylor turned back to stare morosely down at the Visitor ranks. "Hell, Bill, I don't know. He barely even sleeps at home anymore. He ain't worked in months, yet the other day I asked him if he could pay the paperboy, and he whipped a roll out of his pants you could choke an alligator with!"

"Uh-oh."

"That's what I said, believe me, man. I don't know where he goes durin' the day, what he does—and I'm scared to ask for fear he'll tell me, and then what would I do?"

"I'm sorry, Caleb. Funny about those two boys—Ben's such a success, and Elias—"

"Yeah. Don't I know it."

They watched the presentation ceremony for several minutes in silence. Graham changed the subject. "Did you hear that about half of the plants they've arranged for will be used to desalinate the seawater, not to produce the chemical?"

"Yeah? Which will they be doin' here at Richland?"

"Both."

"How many plants they going to be using?"

"I don't know. They're still negotiating. A lot of them. Almost every seacoast plant in the world was contacted, I understand. How many of them they'll pick is anyone's guess."

Caleb frowned, staring intently down at the Visitor ranks, his lips moving soundlessly. "What're you doing, Caleb?" Graham asked, trying to follow his friend's gaze.

"Countin' those suckers. *Damn*, there are a lot of 'em!"

JULIET PARRISH LOOKED OVER DENNIS LOWELL'S TANNED, MUSCU-lar shoulder at the television screen, which showed one of the Visitor leaders, "Steven," talking to the well-known television reporter Kristine Walsh. He was explaining that most of the Visitor plants chosen would be located on the Earth's coastlines.

As Juliet watched, her fingers continued their rhythmic knead and pull at Lowell's back. "Look at that mob, Denny. I'm glad we decided to stay here and watch this on the set. We wouldn't be able to see a thing if we'd driven over there."

Denny, absorbed in the *Wall Street Journal*, merely grunted assent. Juliet smiled down at his dark head, continuing her massage. Her fingers moved downward and together, rubbing in short, circular motions over the *vertebrae lumbaris* area. She had a sudden, insistent urge to kiss the back of his neck, but resisted. Denny didn't like being interrupted while he was studying the market—and although stocks and bonds frankly bored Parrish, she went out of her way not to let him know it.

"Mmmmm—that's good," mumbled Denny.

Juliet smiled again. "Well, after five years of anatomy, it *should* be."

"No—I meant the market. It's really surging up. The Visitors have been good for the economy. I think we've got some good times ahead."

Juliet sighed, smiling ruefully. Denny loved his work as a

stockbroker as much as she loved medicine. Someday, no doubt, he'd be very, very rich, he was so good at what he did. If they married—*if*—she'd share that with him. Though she'd never given a damn about money. If it hadn't been for that scholarship she'd gotten, she'd be in debt far worse than she was . . .

If she had her choice she'd join Vista or the Peace Corps—or maybe WHO—after her internship was complete. Or go back to China, where she'd studied on an exchange program for six months. But if she did, she'd lose Denny. She knew it, even though she'd never brought up the subject. Denny wasn't the kind to wait two or three years. She grimaced. Few men were, these days. Most guys she'd ever been attracted to had faded into the woodwork after learning she was a med student, at the top of her class. Her biochemistry research with Doctor Metz had only worsened matters. Then she'd met Denny . . .

He was one of the few men she'd met who enjoyed being with a woman who he acknowledged was probably smarter than he was. And Juliet, after the months and years of dedicated study, had found herself liking the changes he introduced in her life. Quiet homemade meals and intimate restaurants, instead of TV dinners and textbooks. Parties with a few congenial friends. Backpacking and camping when she had a free weekend. Old Bogart and Gable movies on his VCR.

She studied the face of the Visitor on the television screen through slightly narrowed eyes, wishing she could meet one of them, talk him or her into donating some blood samples. What did their DNA look like? Assuming they *had* DNA . . .

They probably did. After all, they looked so *much* like us. Except for their voices, you could put one in a business suit and drop him or her on Wall Street and nobody would bat an eye.

*In a way,* Juliet Parrish thought, *I'd have liked it better if they had purple tentacles or something.* She noticed a black face among the hordes of Visitors ranked beside the shuttle, and frowned. *Weird. They even have the same racial differences. Wonder if Ben Taylor's watching?*

Her eyes roamed the rows and rows of red coveralls, searching for any anomalies, noting the lack of visible facial scars or blemishes. *There are so many of them, and each one is perfect.* She didn't realize that her fingers had tightened on Dennis Lowell's back until he gasped and jumped. "Hey, watch it, honey! That's too hard!"

She kissed the back of his neck, feeling with relief the solidity and warmth of his flesh. "Sorry, Den. Let's turn off the television, okay?"

"Why? This is an historical occasion."

She reached for the remote control, clicked it off, her hands then sliding around his body very slowly. " 'Cause I've got something better than making mere history in mind."

" 'Zat so?"

Neither of them noticed they were crumpling the *Wall Street Journal.*

THE NIGHT AIR WAS BRISK AND DELICIOUS, JUST COOL ENOUGH TO make Robert Maxwell forget his usual distaste for a coat and tie. He held Kathleen's arm as the two of them walked up the street and through the gate to the Dupres house. The house itself was mostly dark; laughter and conversation were emanating from the garden out back. They took the flagstoned path around the side of the house.

The garden was festooned with outdoor lamps, mosquitoes, and people. Maxwell sniffed appreciatively at the good smells—he'd gotten home from the ceremonies too late to eat.

He scooped a couple of glasses of wine off a tray as the

waiter passed him, handing one to Kathleen. "Thanks," she whispered, her green eyes traveling around the guests, evaluating the women's clothes. "Do I look all right?"

"Gorgeous. That dress really suits you, honey." It did, too. Red was one of Kathy's best colors—and that shimmering shawl he'd brought home from Pakistan set it off perfectly.

A chiffon wave of blue that turned out to be Eleanor with both arms spread wide engulfed them, seemingly from out of nowhere. "Robert, Kathleen! *So* glad you could make it! Do come meet our guests of honor!"

"Nice party, Eleanor," Maxwell said, brushing unobtrusively at a mosquito.

"Delightful," murmured Kathleen.

"Didn't the ceremonies go off *splendidly*? Steven was saying to me a few minutes ago that the ceremonies and the party have been among the nicest they've encountered. I told Arthur we must do this again."

"Mother," said a male voice almost in Maxwell's ear.

He turned, as did Eleanor and Kathleen, to find himself facing the journalists he'd seen that afternoon—Mike Donovan, Kristine Walsh, and an Asian man. At the latter's side stood a slender, brown-haired woman.

"I beg your pardon?" began Maxwell, but Eleanor, with a moue of annoyance, cut him off.

"What is it, Michael?"

"Kris and Tony and I have a special interview with Diana to tape, so we'll have to be going."

"Oh. I'd hoped to be able to introduce you around, Michael." Eleanor was obviously displeased. Just as obviously, Donovan was unaffected by her pique.

"Sorry. The shuttle is supposed to pick us up at nine, over at the plant parking lot." For the first time the newsman seemed to notice the Maxwells standing awkwardly before him, and extended his hand. "My name's Mike Donovan. Kristine Walsh, Tony and Fran Leonetti. Nice to meet you."

Maxwell shook hands, nodding. "Robert Maxwell. My wife, Kathleen. Our pleasure."

Murmured greetings filled the air, until they were replaced almost without pause by murmured farewells. Maxwell watched as the three journalists left the party, stopping briefly to speak with Arthur Dupres. Robert turned back to his hostess.

"Eleanor, I had no idea that Michael Donovan the newsman is your son. Why, he's one of the most well-known cameramen in the country!"

Eleanor sniffed. "You'd think he could have stayed long enough to meet the rest of my guests."

"Uh, yeah." Maxwell, discomfited, looked sidelong at Kathleen, who gallantly rose to the occasion.

"Speaking of guests, Eleanor, isn't that one of your guests of honor over there? Robert and I would *love* to meet him!"

Eleanor brightened. "Yes, that's Steven. He brought a young woman with him—quite an attractive girl. I'll introduce you."

They threaded through the crowd in their hostess's blue wake until they reached the dark-haired, slenderly built man in the red coveralls. In the gentle illumination of the patio torches, he'd removed his dark glasses. He was nodding and smiling as Arthur introduced him to guests.

Eleanor took the Visitor's arm. "Steven dear, here are two people you simply *must* meet. Robert Maxwell and his wife, Kathleen Maxwell. Robert is quite a prominent anthropologist."

Maxwell extended his hand, felt his fingers gripped firmly by cool, resilient flesh. *Markedly cool*, Maxwell thought, shaking hands. *Body temperature about 85° or so.*

Kathleen, smiling warmly, also shook hands. Steven smiled, then spoke in that resonating near-echo voice that sounded so strange coming from such human lips. "An-thro-polo-gist? What kind of work do you do, Mr. Maxwell?"

"Robert," Maxwell said. "Please call me Robert, Steven. An anthropologist is a scientist who studies the development of man from his earliest hominid ancestors to our current version of *Homo sapiens*."

As Maxwell spoke, Steven stiffened perceptibly, his smile fading. *Now what the hell did I say wrong?* Robert wondered. He cast a sidelong look at Kathleen, only to realize from her anxious expression that she, too, had noticed the Visitor's reaction.

A moment only, then the alien was smiling graciously again. "You must forgive us—we have studied your language very closely, but inevitably there are words we do not know."

"No problem," Maxwell said, brushing at a ubiquitous buzzing near his ear. "Damn mosquitoes . . ."

Eleanor, who had vanished a few seconds earlier, suddenly reappeared, brandishing a tray of hors d'oeuvres. Maxwell thanked her, trying not to seem too greedy as he helped himself to several. As he chewed on a water chestnut, bacon, and chicken liver concoction, Steven, with a polite smile, carefully selected a carrot stick and munched cautiously on it. He shook his head graciously as Eleanor proffered meatballs, chicken wings teriyaki, and sausage—each time her offers were met by Steven's headshake and polite smile.

*Totally avoids cooked foods and meats,* thought Maxwell, slapping unobtrusively at another buzz. *And we're being eaten by mosquitoes—but he's not . . .*

Edging back through the crowd until he was again beside the Visitor, Maxwell cleared his throat. "Are there many scientists aboard your ships?"

Steven nodded. "Yes. What you would call engineers of all sorts—chemical, cryogenic, structural—plus many other specialties."

"Do you have any scientists that would be the equivalent of anthropologists?"

"Yes, of course. But they were not needed for this mission, which required technical skills."

"Well, do you mind if I ask you a few questions about your culture?"

Steven smiled. "Not at all."

"What is your planet like?"

"Much like yours. It is somewhat larger, as our star is larger. It is made up of many of the same kinds of minerals."

"And your evolution? Did your people evolve from a common ancestor with other anthropoids? You know—manlike apes and monkeys?"

"Oh, I see. Well, I am no anthropologist, you understand, but I think our anthropologists have concluded that our evolution was quite similar to yours."

"Great!" Maxwell nodded eagerly. "What kind of government do you have?"

"We have no nations, as you have. Just all the peoples of our world, united under the leadership of our Great Leader."

"How does he govern?"

"By divining the will of the people, and using it to lead us effectively."

"I see. What kind of social unit, then?"

"Social unit?" Steven cocked his head questioningly.

"Well, our basic social unit is the family. A male and female, pledged to live and work together for their mutual benefit, plus any resulting offspring."

"Matings with outsiders are considered undesirable?"

"That's right. Monogamy."

The Visitor nodded. "Monogamy is also our way. One male, one female, children, living together."

"I really appreciate getting a chance to talk to you, Steven."

The Visitor's eyes moved past Maxwell to fix on a table in the middle of the patio near the pool. Kathleen sat at the table, smiling at a young woman with long, fair hair in a red coverall.

"Your wife?" asked Robert, thinking how attractive the Visitor woman was.

"No." Steven smiled. "Barbara is a subleader in the unit I command. She was assigned to assist me. We work together."

"I see," said Maxwell. He was trying to sort through the questions jumbling through his mind. "What sort of—"

"Hello, Robert!" Arthur Dupres boomed, shaking hands fervently. "I see you've met Steven. Do you mind if I steal him from you?" He winked broadly at the Visitor. "Got some folks from Richland who just arrived, and they're dying to meet you. And if I know old Bob here, he was plying you with questions on your social structure and habits, eh?"

Maxwell forced a grin. "Can't blame me for being curious, Arthur. First time I ever met a gentleman who also happened to be an extraterrestrial!"

Taking Steven's arm, Arthur led him over to a group of men and women standing near the entrance to the garden. As they walked by the cage containing Eleanor's prize lovebirds, the creatures fluttered desperately, dashing themselves against the wire bars.

*Now* that's *weird*, the anthropologist thought, watching the birds' agitation subside. *What caused* that? Frowning, he walked over to study the birds, wondering if there were a cat skulking in the bushes. But the bushes at the corner of the garden were empty of anything except fallen blossoms and cigarette butts.

Arthur was coming back his way, and Maxwell quickly

stepped aside as his host, Steven firmly ensconced at his side, passed him.

This time Robert Maxwell kept his eyes on the lovebirds the entire time, and there was no doubt what was causing their panic. No doubt at all.

It was Steven, the Visitor.

# 4

ARCH QUINTON FROWNED DOWN AT THE FOLDER ON HIS BATTERED old desk in the university anthropology department, then picked up the phone. Punching buttons with quick, nervous fingers, he waited impatiently as the connection was made. A ring! He gave a quick grimace of relief—the line had been busy for nearly an hour. *Probably Robin. Teenagers,* thought Quinton sourly.

After four rings, he heard a surprised voice. "Hello?"

"Robin, this is Doctor Quinton. I apologize for calling so late. Is Robert in bed?"

"No, I'm sorry, Doctor Quinton, he and my mom are out for the evening. They went to a party over at the Dupreses'. You want him to call you when he gets home?"

"No, that's all right, lass. I'll be headin' out now, since it's—" He checked his watch. Good Lord, it was after midnight! "It's late," he said. "I'll call him tomorrow, if he's not reached me first."

"Yes, sir," said Robin. "I'm leaving a note you called. Is it important?"

"Sort of," said Quinton, not wishing to alarm her, "but

nothing that can't wait for tomorrow. I've something in my current files he'll find interesting. Good night, lass."

" 'Night, Dr. Quinton."

With a sigh Quinton cradled the instrument, then turned back to the folder labeled, simply, "John."

He turned over the large, blown-up glossies of the Visitor leader, some of them marked with a numbered grid, to the infrared shots at the back of the folder. These were his prizes. A photography major on the university paper had taken and developed them using special equipment and a telephoto lens during one of the Visitor leader's many press conferences.

Quinton shook his head slowly, thoughtfully, as he studied the heat patterns the infrared photos revealed. *They're not right,* he thought. *Something about the skull ... misshapen ... bone too thick ... especially at the top of the head ... Wish they were clearer, then I'd really have something ... Maxwell may say I'm crazy.* He frowned, taking out a magnifying glass and examining the grid-patterned shot with painstaking attention.

*Even in this shot, the shadows indicate anomalies in the bone ... I've got t' have an X-ray. Then there'd be no doubt ...*

Picking up his ancient pipe, he tamped and lit it, staring thoughtfully at the folder. Then he pushed the photos back into it and shut it, dropping it into his "current" box with the happy face and the slogan his godchild, Polly, had presented him with: "Archeology: can you dig it?"

As he sat there, he felt weariness settle over him like a muffling blanket. Best to go home, get a good night's rest, think about it tomorrow, he decided. Knocking his pipe out in the ashtray, he stood up, feeling the hours of intensive study in the cramped muscles of his neck and back. His stomach rumbled, reminding him that the cheeseburger his grad assistant had brought him for lunch was now almost twelve hours in the past.

Wondering if he was too tired to stop for something to eat, he slung his coat across his shoulders and left, carefully locking the office door, then the back gate. The parking lot was silent and deserted. Quinton stopped for a moment by the back gate, looking up at the stars. It was a clear night for Los Angeles—they were very distinct. He could even make out the densest part of the Milky Way stretching overhead. His eyes shifted to the eastern part of the sky, but Canis Major wouldn't be visible for a month yet, at least. The Great Dog, containing the brightest star in the heavens, Sirius, with a magnitude of $-1.58$. A white scorching star, some 8.7 light-years away, a back-fence neighbor, as galactic distances go.

Arch Quinton's eyes began to blur, and he rubbed them wearily. Sirius. Just a local star a month ago. Now . . . what?

His hands were cold in the night wind as he fumbled with the keys to his Granada. Opening the door, he swung in, started the engine, then turned to back the car out of its space.

Sitting in the backseat was a man wearing a red coverall. The dash lights reflected an eerie green from his dark glasses. Quinton opened his mouth to scream . . .

# 5

THE VISITOR WAS NOT HAVING A GOOD DAY. THIS MORNING HE'D awakened to find that his original assignment of a chemical plant near Saudi Arabia had been changed: he was now assigned to the Richland plant in a place called Los Angeles. Even his name, Ahmed, had been changed—he was now William.

Now, the bulky cryo storage unit held before him like a heavy shield, he clutched his orders in his fingertips and staggered, blinking, from the shuttle.

The lights were so *bright*! He'd been warned, but with everything else that had happened, he'd forgotten. This was his first time down on the surface of this new world. Blinking, he stumbled forward until he could set the gray unit on the pavement and find his dark glasses.

Thanks be to the Leader, he had them. Blinking, William slipped them on. The glare became manageable. His back muscles complaining, William picked up the c-unit again, starting off in search of his assigned area, mentally struggling to remember the snippets of English he'd picked up from hearing the officers talk among themselves. John had given the order that crewmembers must practice their assigned

Earth languages at all times in order to gain proficiency as quickly as possible. Ahmed—no, *William*, he must remember *William*—had learned to think in Arabic.

And now this! William found a flight of metal stairs in front of him and began cautiously to climb them. The gravity of Earth was slightly lower than that of his native planet—one hardly felt it on a straightaway, but the difference could cause stumbles on an incline.

He peered again at the assigned station on the card inscribed with his technician's data and personal background. The plant seemed a warren of steel-gray and orange piping and hurrying people. He realized he'd have to ask directions—

An impact jarred him backward. "Hey! Watch out where the hell you're going!"

William almost slipped on the foot-polished treads of the stair, but managed to keep his balance. Looking up, he saw a dark-skinned man (the humans called that shade of skin "black," though to William it looked like a warm brown) wearing a yellow hardhat with "Taylor" stenciled across it. The Visitor struggled for words. "Uh . . . Oh, excuse, please. Uh . . . help, please."

William wasn't very familiar with human expressions, but he thought he remembered this one. It was termed a "frown," and if the Visitor wasn't mistaken, it was a way of displaying displeasure. "Help what?" the human growled.

"Please," said William, thinking furiously and finally hitting on the right word—he hoped. "I am just."

"Just what?" asked the man, still frowning.

"Yes." William nodded emphatically. "Just."

The man growled again. "Aw, get out of my way!" He pushed William roughly aside. "Damn stupid alien!"

The Visitor watched him leave, trying to translate the man's words. Directions to the Cryogenics Transfer Unit?

Somehow William was pretty sure not. He even suspected that Taylor's words constituted an insult of some kind.

Sighing, William looked around, hoping from this elevation to spot some sign of his destination.

Nothing. Another whistle blew from a nearby speaker, making him jump. He "heard" the raucous blast throughout his body, and it "felt" even more unpleasant than it sounded.

He abandoned the stairs and wandered forlornly across the cement, looking over at the shuttles for some sign of someone he could talk to. He was even beginning to consider disobeying orders and asking directions in his native language (though that would definitely be a last-resort tactic), if he could find another of his people. He rounded a series of cylindrical containers that appeared to be used as repositories for waste (a notion which puzzled him—why simply store waste? It was a valuable energy source).

Ahead of him he saw several larger transports parked, and made his way toward them. His back ached, and, to his distress, he realized he was beginning to feel hungry. He would not be able to eat until after his shift, back in his quarters. Those were the rules.

He trudged around to the nose of one of the transports, peering at the vehicle. Nobody inside. He turned, growing ever more frustrated, conscious now that he was *very* late for his work shift. Everyone said that Steven, who was in charge of operations here, was someone to avoid angering. What was he going to do?

Hesitantly he rapped on the black opaqueness of the viewscreen, hoping that someone might be in the back of the shuttle.

A voice spoke from behind him. "Hi there. Are you okay?"

Turning, he saw a human standing behind him. The blue dress and the rounded protuberances beneath the front of it told him this one was female. Her hair was dark gold and blew around her head in fluffy profusion. Her eyes were almost exactly the same color as her planet's lower atmospheric regions in favorable weather conditions. She smiled—William was quite sure that was what she was doing, and was also sure, although why he couldn't say, that he vastly preferred this expression to the one Taylor had treated him to.

"I am just," he told her simply.

"Yeah?" She cocked her head inquiringly. "What?"

"Just," William repeated as clearly and meaningfully as he could.

Her smile faded slightly. "Just . . . just?"

William had the distinct impression he wasn't communicating properly. "Yes. *Just*."

She frowned—though not in the same way Taylor had. "Just what?"

William had been hoping so strongly that she'd understand that he'd been holding his breath, willing her to. Now air puffed out of him in a hiss of frustration. He turned to leave.

Her hand caught his sleeve—the first time he'd ever been touched by a person from another world. "Now wait," she was saying, and William struggled to comprehend her quick, easy speech. "Don't let it get you spazzed. I'll help you out."

William seized with gratitude on the one word he recognized. "Yes, help. Help to go. To *this* place." He showed her the English translation printed above the concept blocks of his own language. "I am *just*."

She scanned the card quickly, then turned to him, plainly guessing. "You don't know where to go?"

"Yes," agreed William fervently. "I'm just."

Sudden understanding so blatant that the Visitor had no trouble seeing it brightened her features. "You're *lost*."

*Lost!* The word linked in his memory, and relief flooded him. William nodded eagerly, putting the cryo unit down. "*Lost!* Yes, lost." He peered at her through his glasses, and for some reason risked the morning glare to take them off so he could see her more clearly. "Thank you . . ." He fumbled to explain. "English . . . not well to me. Learned Arabic . . . for going there."

She nodded sympathetically. "And they screwed up and sent you to L.A.?"

"Yes," agreed William, remembering his entire miserable morning. "Screwed," he repeated, wondering what the new word meant. He felt fairly sure it was a colloquialism. He'd have to ask someone.

"Well, L.A.'s not so bad. Beats Fresno, lemme tell you. What's your name?"

"Ah—" he began, then remembered. "William."

"Well, hi. I'm Harmy." She smiled. "That's short for Harmony . . . can you believe it? I work here." She shifted the tray she was carrying, which was littered with empty paper cups and plates. "Food service, y'know." She scanned the card he held out. "Cryo—Cryogenics Transfer Unit. Well, c'mon, Willy. Let's go find it."

William tried to match her expression to show his gratitude. Smiling wasn't as hard as it looked. They wended their way through the maze of pipes and holding tanks, each with attendants and gauges, until they looked upward at a series of catwalks spanning a huge pressure unit.

William recognized Steven as one of the men standing at the foot of the massive installation.

The officer was shouting, "No, the pressure's still not balanced! Must be the inner seal that's bad. Someone will have to go inside."

Harmy called out, "Is this the Cryogenics Transfer Unit?"

Steven looked over at her. "Yes—" Then his eyes fixed on William, who remembered guiltily that he was *very* late, and he snapped, "William! Where were you?"

He looked over at Harmy, who smiled encouragingly. "Uh . . . I was lost."

Steven shook his head, but obviously held back from any further remarks in the presence of the humans. "Well, get up there." He pointed to the catwalk overhead. "You'll be working with that man."

William looked upward, to see a dark face he remembered, wearing a disgusted expression he knew, looking back at him. The man wearing a hardhat and business suit supplied, "Caleb Taylor is one of our best men. Caleb, meet William."

William was not surprised when Taylor did not speak. He couldn't think of anything to say either.

JULIET PARRISH LOOKED UP TO SEE RUDOLPH METZ ENTER THE door of the laboratory, with Ruth only a pace behind him, looking upset. Juliet guessed quickly what the problem was. "Don't tell me they've canceled again!"

Doctor Metz nodded. "Yes. We've been asked to be patient. Their scientists have been too busy setting up the processing at the plants to finish their introductory presentations for us. I just spoke to Vasily Andropov, who was chosen for the Soviet team, and he told me in confidence that their team's visit has been postponed too!"

Juliet was profoundly disappointed, making no attempt to hide it. "But this is the *second* time! When did they say they'd be able to do it?"

Ruth shook her head disgustedly. "They didn't. 'A week or two' was the only thing we could get out of the Visitor who delivered the message. His name was Martin, and he seemed genuinely sorry, but he said Diana had personally given the order to postpone."

"Damn!" Juliet stared morosely at one of the rat cages. "Everybody *else* is going up there! Did you hear that they're even giving kids special visits to the Mother Ships if they join up with this youth organization they're sponsoring? They call it the Visitor Friends."

Doctor Metz nodded heavily. "I heard Kristine Walsh's broadcast earlier. Still, we mustn't be too disappointed. We must remember that the Visitors' primary reason for being here is the production of their chemical. Giving seminars for us is merely a courtesy."

Juliet made a face. "Not the way I heard it that first night. They were going to share 'all the fruits of their knowledge' *in exchange* for our help with processing their chemical."

"You're right," Ruth said. "I remember those were their exact words."

All three scientists turned as Benjamin Taylor poked his head in the door. "Doctor Metz . . . glad I've found you. We've had another requisition from the L.A. Mother Ship for more lab animals."

"But we gave them a shipment just last week!" Doctor Metz exclaimed. "They need *more*? Did they say what for?"

"Of course not," said Ruth sardonically.

"No," admitted Taylor. "They did say, however, that they've been breeding their own, and expect in a month or so to be able to supply their own stock."

"Well, send them what they've asked for, of course," said Metz with a worried frown.

"Of course," mumbled Juliet, so softly that nobody but Ruth heard. "I'm getting curiouser and curiouser to see that Mother Ship."

ROBERT MAXWELL UNLOCKED THE DOOR TO ARCH QUINTON'S OFfice, then stood in the doorway for a moment, his eyes roving its familiar features. The "current" box was empty. Frowning, he opened several file cabinets, searching with quick, impatient movements, then, frustrated, slammed the gray drawer back into its casing with a bang.

Reaching for the phone, he dialed quickly. "Kathy? Let me talk to Robin for a second."

A pause. "Robin, this is Daddy. Are you sure Doctor Quinton said the stuff he wanted me to look at was in his current files?"

His frown deepened. "Okay. Thanks, hon. See you later."

Almost as soon as he hung up the phone it began to ring. Maxwell picked it up. "Hello? Doctor Maxwell here. Yes, this is Doctor Quinton's office. I'm one of his associates."

He listened intently for a moment. "No, I've been trying to reach him. Nobody's seen him today. I called his landlady—he didn't come home last night, as far as she knows. He called about midnight last night, and spoke to my daughter. Said he was working late."

Absently, he began searching Quinton's top desk drawer, then lifted the blotter and peered underneath it. "Listen, Officer—Robeson, did you say? Have you checked with the L.A. police? Any sign of his car?"

He paused. "He drove—" He corrected himself quickly, with a grimace of worry, "*drives* a gray Granada. A '78, I think. Yes, it's got a campus parking registry."

His breath hissed sharply. "I'll meet you there. The parking lot behind this building?"

Maxwell was running by the time he erupted into the sunlight. It was Saturday, and this early the parking lot was nearly empty. Quinton's car stood off by itself.

Robert Maxwell felt strangely reluctant to approach the vehicle—somehow it looked abandoned, forlorn. He swallowed, forcing himself to walk numbly toward it.

The door gave easily beneath his hand—not locked. He

reached out, past the steering column, then moved away with Quinton's worn leather-tab key ring in his hand. There was an odd smell hanging about the automobile that sickened and repelled Maxwell, making the fear mounting in the back of his throat turn to nausea.

He swallowed again, fighting not to breathe too deeply, turning to look around the interior. Empty. Clean, just as Quinton had always kept it.

His eyes turned to the door. The handle on the driver's side hung askew, and an oily black stain marred the red vinyl. Maxwell realized he was shaking with deep tremors that twisted his gut. His heart seemed to be directly between his ears, throbbing.

Putting out an unsteady hand, Robert touched fingertips to the stain, then sniffed them cautiously. Bile flooded his mouth, and if his stomach hadn't been empty, he'd have vomited. He spat on the cement, then spat again, then leaned back against the Granada's rear door, feeling dizzy, emptied.

Footsteps . . . quick, heavy. The campus cop Robeson. "You Maxwell?"

Robert swallowed, scrubbing the foulness of that oily stain off on the roughness of his jeans. "Yes, I'm Doctor Maxwell."

"This Quinton's car?"

"Yes, it is. I found his keys in the ignition."

Robeson took the key ring with a reproachful *tchh* of his tongue. "Shouldn't have touched it, Doc. There might be fingerprints."

"Sorry." Maxwell's shock was turning to grief now, a paralyzing sense of certainty that he'd never see Arch again. He tried to think rationally, convince himself that Quinton would have called to explain everything by the time he got back inside, called Kathy, but he couldn't.

The cop was inspecting the interior of the car. "Never saw

anything quite like this. I'd better call L.A.P.D. right away."
He peered at Maxwell. "You gonna be okay, Doc?"

"I'm all right," Maxwell said, untruthfully.

"This is *weird*," Robeson said. "You got any idea what
might have happened to him?"

"No." Maxwell found he was shaking again as the breeze
brought that smell to his nostrils again. "God, no."

"I'll call L.A.P.D.," Robeson said, then added kindly, "you
better sit down, Doc."

THE AFTERNOON SUN SLANTED THROUGH AND SPATTERED ITSELF IN
a yellow haze against the oyster-white wall of Kristine Walsh's
Los Angeles loft apartment. Mike Donovan sat on the sofa,
checking and packing his camera equipment. Kristine, in bra
and half-slip, was in the other room, putting on her makeup.
Her monologue was broken into uneven bursts of speech and
pauses as she squinted in the mirror, daubing carefully at her
eyes and mouth.

"...and then Diana said that she was pleased with the
progress at the Richland plant. Said it was representative of all
the others around the world." She widened her eyes, touching
sable mascara to her lashes in quick brushing gestures.

Donovan's voice reached her from the living room. "Did
she mention that she'd postponed the seminars for the scientists a second time?"

"Yes. She said they'll be beginning them shortly."

Donovan made a rude noise. "That's what they said the
other time."

"But wait, Mike, I haven't told you the best part." Kristine
tilted her head, examining her blusher critically. "Then Diana
said, 'The other thing I'm pleased with here, Kristine, is *you*.'
I didn't know what to say, what she was getting at, you know.
Then she explained that of all the journalists they've met
since they've been here, the Visitors feel most comfortable

with me. She said, 'Our research also shows that your people have a lot of confidence in you. You're trusted and respected . . . attractive—' "

"So is Lassie," snapped Donovan. "What's that got to do with anything?"

"Well, she told me those qualities were essential in the person they selected as the official Visitor spokesperson—and then she offered *me* the job!"

"Huh?"

"Or press secretary . . . She said I could call it what I wanted. Which do you like?"

There was a long pause. Donovan's voice, when he finally spoke, sounded tight. "I don't much like the sound of either one."

Kristine gave a final pat to her hair, then pulled on her tan wool skirt and the dark brown striped blouse. "Come on, Mike. You're jealous."

"The hell I am. Don't be a jackass, Kris! I don't understand why you'd even consider it!"

"They want someone the public trusts . . . and *I* think it's an excellent career move." She walked past him into the living room, and, picking up her purse, began checking the contents.

Donovan looked over at her. "What about your objectivity?"

"What?" *Notebook*, she thought, *tape recorder . . . lipstick . . . where's my pen?*

Mike's tone was hard, one she'd only heard a few times before—usually when someone asked him a question about his divorce. "Don't you think you're compromising your objectivity by sucking up to those—"

She whirled to face him. "I'm not sucking up to anybody!"

His eyes were troubled. Kristine came over and knelt in front of him so she could look directly at him. "Don't you see? It's the perfect opportunity to really get the inside stuff!

Exclusive stuff . . . material that no one else has access to! I'm
sure to get a *book* out of it, at the very least!"

She took his hands in hers. They were limp, unresponsive,
and his face still wore that shocked, puzzled expression. She
tried to reassure him. "I'm going to stay objective, Mike. After all, I'm one of us, not them."

He looked down, stubbornly refusing to meet her eyes
again. Kristine gave his hands a squeeze—then a shake. "Oh,
come on, Mike! Any good reporter would be crazy not to
jump at this!"

His green eyes, when they met hers again, were full of challenge. Kristine bit her lip. "I'd like to think I had your backing, honey. You know how I respect you." Her hand moved to
brush his cheek, lingering for a moment against the freshly
shaven smoothness. "More than respect . . ."

Donovan looked down at his hands, slowly extricated them
from her fingers. "You'd better put the steaks back in the
freezer, Kris."

Her mind flashed back to the conversation with Diana.
"Oh yeah. Tonight's a problem—the last thing Diana men-
tioned was that she'd send a shuttle for me so we could meet.
How did *you* know?"

He stared at her for a long moment, and slowly his meaning dawned. Kristine moved blindly to look for her pen, eyes
blurring, holding her shoulders stiffly erect. After a second he
closed his camera bag, then went back into the bedroom. She
heard him packing.

"Damn," she whispered, and was horrified to hear her
voice crack. "Damn, damn, damn . . . *damn!*"

She didn't turn around until the apartment door closed behind him.

# 6

WILLIAM THE VISITOR LOOKED OUT ACROSS THE CRYOGENICS SEC-
tion to see a familiar blonde head halfway across the compound. He smiled, the expression coming unconsciously now.
His bootheels rang on the steel catwalk as he trotted down
the stairs and over the pavement. Harmy had apparently seen
him coming, and stood waiting, the familiar tray in her hands.
William nodded shyly. "Hello."

"Well, hello yourself. How are you doing?"

"Fine, fine." He smiled. "I like to thank you again for your
help. Without you, I would have stayed 'just'—probably
forover."

She giggled. "Forever, Willy. But listen to you! Only a week
here, and your English is better than mine! You guys really
learn fast."

William nodded. "We are told to practice all the times.
How are you today?"

"Okay—same old, same old. How are you getting along
with that guy? He didn't look any too thrilled t'see you, the
other day."

William shrugged—another gesture he'd picked up from
the humans. "Caleb Taylor is good worker. He knows a lot

about refinery equipment. But I don't think he lives us being here."

"Likes. He treating you okay?"

William shrugged. Harmy's face fell. "That's too bad. I know what it's like t'work with people who are down on you. I had a boss once who—"

An explosion rent the air, and the ground shook beneath their feet. A Klaxon screamed. William instinctively jumped between the human and the blast, but they were too far away to be hurt. One quick glance told William that it was his own work area!

He began to run, shoving past panicked workers and Visitors alike. Shouts and screams challenged the alarm Klaxon's shriek. He'd been working with Caleb Taylor and Gus Jennings—and they weren't among the crowd!

"Caleb!" he shouted.

White clouds of frozen vapor and supercooled gases poured out of the hatch as William reached the stairway to the catwalk. A shape darkened the opening—Gus Jennings! The burly worker staggered out, his mouth working as though he was screaming, but the whoosh of the gas drowned out even the alarm. Jennings was covered with white frost, clutching his arm above the wrist. Even as William started up the stairs, the human lurched, his hand smashing into one of the steel pipes.

Both William and Jennings stared unbelieving as the impact *shattered* the flesh like so much glass. Jennings was left clutching a bloody stump. William was close enough now to hear his screams.

Even as he reached Jennings, shouting "Caleb?" the man collapsed. Bill Graham, another worker, caught him.

"Caleb's still in there!" He eased Jennings onto the catwalk, shouting down to the men on the ground, "Get an ambulance, for God's sake!" Graham turned back to William.

"The liquid nitrogen blew through the inner seal—there's no way anyone can get past it to reach him!"

William stepped over Jennings, heading for the hatch and the billowing frozen gases. Behind him he could hear Graham's shout. "William! Stop! For God's sake!"

William hesitated for a brief second, filling his lungs with a deep breath, then plunged inside.

Graham watched him go, torn between trying to stop the Visitor technician and tending to Jennings. He turned as a hand grabbed his shoulder. "What's happening?"

It was Steven. Graham gestured helplessly. "William went in there after Caleb!"

"*What?*" Steven glanced into the frozen darkness of the hatchway, his features hardening.

Graham stripped off his coat and laid it over Jennings, who was still unconscious, but moaning now. "It's got to be three hundred below zero in there—they're both goners. Nothing human could—" Graham broke off in confusion as he stared into the Visitor officer's eyes. They were flat and cold—shards of ice in that otherwise handsome countenance.

Shouts echoed around them, and both Graham and Steven turned to see what was happening. William emerged from the hatchway, supporting Caleb Taylor. The older man seemed barely conscious, his dark skin and hair frosted white. He twitched uncontrollably as bouts of shivering hit him.

Bill Graham moved quickly to help William lower Caleb to the catwalk. The Visitor technician seemed unharmed, except for his face and hands, which were covered with large, bumpy blisters, whitish in color. Dark cracks seemed to furrow the skin around the raised areas. Graham glanced quickly at Jennings—then at Caleb. Though both men were rimed with frost, their skins roughened by the frostbite, neither displayed those disfiguring blisters.

William, catching Graham's eyes on his face, turned away,

ducking his head. Steven leaned over him, blocking Bill's view of the technician.

"The ambulance is coming!" The shout was followed almost immediately by a wail, then the screech of brakes below the catwalk. Graham looked over to see the paramedics pile out. "We'll need three stretchers up here!" he shouted.

"You'd better sit down, William," he said. "The ambulance is here. Are you in much pain?"

The Visitor technician didn't raise his head. His voice sounded even stranger than usual—a high-pitched, muffled tone accompanied the usual reverberation. "No. I am okay."

"I'm taking him back to the shuttle," Steven said. "Our doctors will deal with this."

"Don't you think—" Graham caught the Visitor officer's eye and stopped abruptly. Perhaps it was a blast of the frozen vapor from the open hatchway behind him that made him shudder suddenly, violently.

DOCTOR BENJAMIN TAYLOR SAT AT A MICROSCOPE, PEERING IN-tently into the eyepiece. Ruth Barnes sat across the laboratory from him, labeling specimen dishes. The door banged open to reveal Doctor Metz. "Where are those cultures, Ruth? I can't proceed without them!"

Ben glanced over at the middle-aged woman, saw pain, quickly hidden, shadow her eyes at Metz's brusque tone. "They're not back from pathology, Doctor."

Taylor saw Metz's frown deepen—hastily spoke up in Ruth Barnes's behalf. "They're running way behind there, Doctor Metz."

She nodded. "I heard that two of the top technicians didn't show up for work today. They didn't even call in!" Ruth, who hadn't missed a day of work since Ben had first known her when he was still a med student, sounded scandalized.

Metz pursed his lips. "That's odd. Who are they?"

"Morrow and Prentiss."

"I must say, with their work records, I'd never have expected such a cavalier attitude from them." Metz shook his head.

"Maybe there's a good rea—" The laboratory phone interrupted Ben. He picked it up. "Doctor Taylor here."

He recognized Juliet Parrish's voice, but couldn't recall ever hearing it so strained and anxious. "Ben—get down to the ER, stat. They just brought in your father."

When the three reached the emergency room, Caleb was conscious, barely. Ben clasped his father's hand, shocked at how dreadfully cold it was, while he listened to the ambulance technician summarize the accident at Richland. "How did he get out of there?" Ruth asked.

"One of the Visitor technicians carried him out, apparently," answered the paramedic. "He was damn lucky. Those supercooled gases are kept at temperatures hundreds of degrees below zero. I don't know how the hell the guy managed to get in there and keep moving—he should have been a Popsicle within seconds if he had to pass through blasts of liquid nitrogen."

Ruth leaned forward, peering intently at Caleb's jacket. Whitish flakes adhered to it—*Some residue of the chemical?* she wondered, scratching at one cautiously. On impulse she picked up a sterile specimen case and a pair of forceps, and scraped several of the larger flakes into the glass. She'd examine them later, under the microscope.

*They almost look like skin*, she thought, stepping back from the rush of monitors and doctors that surrounded Caleb Taylor. *But not quite . . .*

She remembered the paramedic's statement that it had been one of the Visitors who had rescued Caleb. *Visitor skin?* she thought excitedly. *Rudolph will want to know about this!* She turned to mention her suspicion to him, but he was no longer in the room. On impulse, she decided to analyze and examine the samples herself first, before telling him. No sense in getting him all excited unless she was sure what she had . . .

Caleb moaned, then spoke. "Ben?"

"I'm here, Pop. You're going to be okay."

Quietly, Ruth turned and tiptoed from the room, slipping the sample case into her pocket.

ABRAHAM BERNSTEIN AMBLED SLOWLY ALONG THE STREET, THE AF-ternoon sun baking his shoulders beneath the worn old sweater. His companion was Ruby Engels from across the street. She was a widow, and each day the two walked the two miles to the neighborhood shopping center and back. They rarely bought anything—Social Security checks barely paid for the necessities. But it was a nice walk.

Abraham glanced up as a Visitor squad vehicle cruised by overhead. "More of them every day," he commented.

Ruby nodded. "You get so you don't even notice them on the street anymore. It's like when my husband and I first moved here from Germany. I had never seen a black, and it was all I could do not to stare. Within a couple of months several of the ladies I rode to the market with were black, and I never gave it a second thought."

Abraham shook his head. "It's not the same, though. These people are from a totally different world, one you and I, at least, will probably never live to see. They aren't human." He looked over at two Visitors standing casually on a street corner. "All those uniforms. And more every day. I don't like uniforms."

Ruby took his hand in hers, giving it a little shake. "Abraham, it's been nearly forty years." Her fingers pressed the inside of his forearm, where she knew the faded tattooed numbers were. "This—and everything it represents—belongs to the past. You have to let it go."

Bernstein shrugged. "Maybe you're right, Ruby. Still—I don't like uniforms. And there *are* more of them every day."

With a sigh, Ruby changed the subject. "What is your grandson doing these days?"

"Nice try, Mrs. Engels. But you picked the wrong subject. Daniel . . . Daniel." Abraham kicked desultorily at a pop top on the concrete. "He lost the job at the supermarket. When the register came up short, he thought they were blaming him, so he quit before they could say anything. I've lost count of all the jobs he's quit."

"Abraham." Ruby didn't look at her companion. "Is it possible that Daniel was . . . guilty?"

Instead of the hot denial she expected, Abraham sighed again. "I don't know, Ruby. He's my own flesh and blood, and of course I don't think he'd steal. His father and I have done everything we could to teach him what's right in this world. But—he just never has fit in."

She touched his bent shoulder quickly. "Don't be so hard on him, Abraham! He's only eighteen."

"But he's been this way for years! No good in school . . . hardly any friends . . . can't keep a job, or stick to a task . . ."

"Didn't you tell me that he's gotten involved with this Visitor Friends group?"

Abraham was obviously less than thrilled. "Yes."

"Well, maybe this will be just what he needs. He hasn't found his niche yet. You wait. This may be it."

Abraham Bernstein didn't look reassured. Another squad vehicle whispered by overhead, its shadow blotting out the sun for a second.

MICHAEL DONOVAN SAT IN THE PASSENGER SEAT OF THE VISITOR shuttle, looking down on the streets and the people below. He saw an elderly man and woman, then they were gone. He glanced over at a large, imposing house with a beautiful, professionally landscaped garden. Eleanor's house. Another Visitor craft rested on the front lawn.

His pilot, a Visitor officer named Martin, also glanced over at the shuttle. "That's Steven's vehicle below." He adjusted a control without glancing up. "I hear the supervisor visits there a lot."

Donovan smiled wryly. "She *can* be charming." He wasn't sure if Martin knew that Mrs. Dupres was his mother. It was possible—Martin, from Donovan's uneducated reading of his insignia, seemed to have a fairly high rank. If the Visitors were anything like humans, they probably gossiped among themselves.

He busied himself watching the pilot handle the controls. The craft seemed simple to fly. A bar with a handgrip controlled the direction, a lever set within a notched slot regulated the speed. The slot nearest to the pilot was the slowest—cruising speed. Donovan wondered idly what the top acceleration on these babies was . . .

Something shiny behind the pilot's seat caught his eye and he bent over to pick up a small implement. It was about three and a half inches long and perhaps a half inch thick, made from some crystalline substance with what appeared to be a golden metal handle. Small indentations dotted its narrow sides—Donovan had the sudden impression of a key, though why, he couldn't have said.

He straightened, half opening his mouth to speak to Martin, tell the pilot what he'd found—then found himself, instead, putting it in his pocket. *Sean,* he thought. *I don't have anything for him—this will knock him for a loop.*

"Where does your son live?" asked Martin.

"In a small town just ouside of L.A.," Donovan answered.

"Is that your home, also?"

Mike found his mouth tightening, but realized Martin's question was merely polite conversation. "Not anymore," he said, trying not to sound too abrupt. "My wife and I are divorced. My son lives with his mother."

"Where is your home, then, Mike?" Martin asked.

Donovan looked out the window—at his request, Martin had un-opaqued the viewports. "I don't really have a permanent base. I follow the stories, I guess you could say. I was staying in downtown L.A. with a . . . friend."

"I see. I have our heading coordinates in view. Where would you like to be set down? At your son's house?"

"No, I want to rent a car. I'm taking Sean camping for a couple of days, and I'll need something to drive." He peered out. "That looks like a car lot down there—" He pointed. "Can you set down in that parking lot?"

"Of course." Donovan watched closely as the pilot maneuvered the craft in for a landing. *Compared to a plane, these things are a snap,* he thought.

They set down with nary a jar. "Thanks a lot, Martin. I appreciate the lift." Donovan hastily gathered up his gear. Martin helped him carry it out, looking curiously at the backpack, the sleeping bag in its nylon covering.

"I was glad to do it, Mike. I wanted to meet you." They shook hands. Donovan was used to the coolness of Visitor flesh now—it barely registered in his mind.

He watched the vehicle lift silently away, before turning around to find the owner of the rental car lot standing behind him, his mouth open. *That's right,* Donovan reminded himself, *most people still haven't seen one this close up. Bet he doesn't have many customers who drop in out of alien spacecraft.*

A few minutes later Donovan turned the little yellow sports car onto a tree-shaded avenue. Even as he swung the wheel he heard excited shouts. "Dad! Hey, Dad! Dad!"

Donovan grinned, waving. "Hiya, Sean!" Two boys stood waiting for him, and Mike recognized Josh Brooks, Sean's best friend. "Hi, Josh!" He swung into the curb and parked. He'd barely opened the door when Sean swarmed into his arms. Donovan hugged his son, realizing only when he held him in his arms just how much he'd missed him. He hugged Sean tightly, fiercely, and knew from the boy's grasp that Sean was equally glad to see him.

After long moments he straightened, grinning, to tug at the boy's Dodger cap. "Hiya, kiddo. Who are you today? Fernando Valenzuela or Steve Garvey?"

Sean straightened proudly. "Just Sean Donovan." Then, remembering, he caught his father's arm, pulling him toward the lawn. "Come see what Josh's got!" With barely a break, he demanded, "Hey, did you know how many Visitors it takes to change a lightbulb?"

"No, how many?"

"None. They *like* the lights out."

Donovan grimaced, then laughed. "Right. How are you doing, Josh?"

"Hello, Mr. Donovan."

Josh was about thirteen, a year older than Sean, and half a head taller. They were often mistaken for brothers—both had dark hair and freckles. Sean waved a proud hand at a model of a Visitor shuttle. "See, Dad?" Sean said excitedly. "Check it out! The squad vehicle . . . and the action figures." He picked up two tiny red-garbed and capped figures. "Here's the admiral, and Diana—"

Mike shook his head, grinning ruefully. "Wonder if they get a royalty?"

Sean carefully tucked the little action figures into the pilot's seats in the squad vehicle. "He's got a Mother Ship at home!"

Josh sounded a bit smug. "I got 'em *all*."

Sean looked up. "Can I get 'em, Dad? Mom said we didn't have the money . . ."

Donovan tried to keep his face from hardening. He hadn't contested his child support or alimony payments, and he'd never been even a day overdue. And any time he'd known that Sean wanted something extra, he'd always seen that the money was there. *Damn Marge,* he thought. *She could have told me—I'd have brought him a set.* He forced a smile. "Well, I'll talk to her about it. But in the meantime," he pulled the little crystal and gold key from his pocket, "this is for you."

Sean took the implement, turning it over wonderingly. "What is it, Dad?"

Mike shrugged. "Just a little something I picked up in a squad vehicle." Behind him he heard the front door open and close, and out of the corner of his eye was aware that Marjorie stood on the steps, watching them. He didn't have to turn to guess her expression—it was always the same.

Sean's eyes widened. "In a *real* squad vehicle?"

"Yeah."

"You mean it came from the Visitors themselves?"

Donovan couldn't help sounding a little smug himself. "That's right."

"Hey! Check it *out!*" Sean held the implement up reverently. Josh leaned forward avidly.

"Wow! Lemme see it, Sean!"

Sean pushed his hand away. "In a minute, Josh."

Donovan heard Marjorie's voice behind them, tight, angry. "Boys, your pizza's ready. Come on in."

Sean stood up. "You coming in, Dad? I've still got some stuff to pack . . ."

"In a second, kiddo. You fellows go ahead." Donovan followed the boys as they raced up to Marjorie. She was looking good, he thought, seeing that she'd shed a few pounds. Her blonde hair was a little longer than the last time he'd seen her, curling softly about her jaw and neck.

Sean held out the Visitor key to her. "Look, Mom! It's from a squad—"

Her voice splintered like a fallen icicle. "Your dinner's getting cold."

Sean's animation dimmed. He turned and trudged up the steps, looking back once at his father. Mike winked and nodded at him encouragingly.

Marjorie barred his way, and even from the sidewalk Donovan could feel the tightness of her body. He was angry at the way she'd treated Sean. All he'd done was bring his son a little present—you'd think he'd stabbed her, the way she was acting. He tried to control his voice. They couldn't keep tearing at each other like this—it was hell on Sean. "Hi," he said.

She didn't answer, only stood there, arms folded over her breasts. Donovan had a sudden, vivid memory of touching those same breasts but repressed it savagely. *It's over. Over.*

He sighed. "So what's wrong now?"

She gestured helplessly, her voice breaking. "Oh, nothing. It's just that it's a little tough competing with someone who flies around in spaceships."

Donovan felt equally helpless. "Margie, what am I supposed to do? Give up my work?"

Tears glimmered. "And what am *I* supposed to do? Sprout wings and fly him off to never-never land? How else can I compete? With *pizza*, for God's sake?"

Mike was exasperated. The old, old problem—would they ever get past it? "Why compete, Margie?" He'd asked her this same question so many times. He realized he was feeling guilty again, and his anger flared. "It's insane! Why do you always feel diminished if I do something successfully? Why not do something of your own? Something you can feel proud of, someplace where nobody has ever heard of me. What about your college plans? You know I'll lend you the money—hell, I'll *give* it to you! What about—"

She held up her hand, cutting him off. She sounded as weary as Mike felt. "Please. Don't start. Okay?"

Donovan stared at her, words jumbling in his throat. He realized that there was nothing left to say, and that was the most painful thing of all.

JULIET PARRISH GUIDED HER WHITE VOLKSWAGEN CONVERTIBLE TO a halt in front of Ruth Barnes's brownstone. Overhead both women could hear the faint whispering passage of a squad vehicle. Juliet set the parking brake with an excited jerk. "You're kidding! You really got a Visitor skin sample? *How?*"

Ruth smiled at her eagerness. "When they brought Ben's father in, there were some whitish particles clinging to his shirt and jacket. I just picked them off."

"Did you get a chance to look at them?"

"For just a minute, then Doctor Metz came in with some cultures he wanted mounted on slides immediately. I had a lot of extra work today, since two people didn't show up at the lab."

"*Well?*"

"They didn't look like skin, Julie. Not human skin, anyway. There didn't seem to be any cells—it was all smooth. Too smooth."

"Damn!" Juliet thumped her fist softly against the steering wheel. "Wish I'd known earlier, then I could have had a look! Now I'll have to wait till tomorrow!" She looked over at Ruth and smiled. "Doctor Metz will love you for this, you know."

Ruth's expression froze. "I'd better go. Thanks so much for the ride, Julie."

Juliet put out her hand, catching the older woman's arm. "Ruth . . . what's wrong? It was something I said, wasn't it?"

Ruth shook her head, turning her face away. Juliet remembered her words, and a sudden flash of insight surfaced. Why hadn't she ever noticed before? "Ruth, it's Doctor Metz, isn't it? You . . . really love him, don't you?"

Ruth bit her lip, managed a wan smile.

"Does he know?" Juliet asked.

The lab assistant shook her head. "No, honey. I'm just another piece of lab equipment to him."

Juliet patted her sleeve, then slid her hand over the older woman's gently. "Well, starting tomorrow morning, we're going to go to work on him. We'll make him realize that 'Nobel' isn't the only prize he's got."

Ruth smiled gently. *It's been a lot of years since things looked that simple to me, Julie*, she thought, but the younger woman's words awakened a bittersweet optimism nevertheless. She patted the young woman's cheek, remembering when her own skin had felt that smooth, that soft. "You're a darling, Julie. Thanks. Thanks for everything."

Ruth got out of the car, waved Juliet a quick good-bye, heard the VW accelerate away. Fumbling for her keys, she walked slowly up the steps to her home, thinking what a long day it had been. She wished suddenly that she'd remembered to tell Juliet where the skin sample was hidden . . .

The door clicked open beneath her fingers. Ruth Barnes stepped inside, turning to close the door behind her. Her motion brought her face-to-face with the man who had been standing, hidden, behind the door.

Ruth had barely a moment to take in the fact that he wore a Visitor uniform and cap before her horrified eyes focused on the weapon in his hand. It didn't look much like any gun she'd ever seen before—but she knew, from the way it swung to follow her, what it was.

All the breath seemed to have deserted her lungs. It was like one of those hideous childhood nightmares where you try to scream and can't. Ruth gasped, seeing his finger move—

There was a muffled pulse of high-pitched sound, and a blue light. For a moment Ruth thought he'd missed, for she felt no pain. Then she realized she was falling, falling, twisting in midair, uncontrollably—

There came a burst of red-tinged blackness, then nothing. She never felt the impact of her body on the floor.

# 7

CALEB TAYLOR HISSED WITH PAIN AS HE CROSSED THE THRESHOLD of his apartment door and one of his bandaged hands brushed the jamb. "You okay, Pop? A little shaky?" Ben Taylor reached out to steady his father.

Caleb shrugged off his son's ministrations impatiently. "I'll be okay. You let me do it by myself."

Ben Taylor grinned wryly as he watched his father walk carefully into his bedroom. *He may be one terrific father*, he thought, *but he's sure as hell one lousy patient*. From the rustling sounds in the bedroom, he realized Caleb was obeying orders and resting. Ben turned to straighten up the small apartment. Usually his father kept it neat as a pin—a holdover from his dead wife's training—but it was a mess at the moment. That meant Elias had been here. Ben made a face as he tugged a pair of dirty sweat socks from between the couch cushions.

A second later he heard a key in the lock, turned to see his brother bounce into the room, a wide grin on his face. "Say, man! What it is, Ben?"

Ben shook his head. " 'What it is' is bad grammar, brother.

Elias, when are you going to quit this poor man's Richard
Pryor act?"

Elias stared for a second, his smile hardening into a fixed
grin. "What you talkin', man? This here ain't no *act*. This
here is pure-D *Elias*."

Ben was disgusted and showed it. "It's pure-D *something*,
that's for sure. Pure-D shit, if you ask me."

Elias did a mock shuffle, his hard, cocky grin never dim-
ming. "Look here, man, can't all of us be Doctor Kildare,
dig?" His voice hardened. "Or *Uncle Tom*."

"Oh, drop that sixties jive, Elias! You can be anything you
want, but first you've got to dump that tap dance and two-bit
crook routine, and *grow up*."

Ben could tell he'd scored. Elias laughed, a short, forced
explosion of sound that sounded anything but amused. "Well,
once again we thank you, *Mr. Sidney Poitier*." He turned
away angrily. "Hey, Pop!" He headed for the bedroom, his
strut plainly put on now. "How you doing?"

Ben watched him go, then resumed his cleaning. He was
tired, tired of Elias, tired of work—tired of worrying. His
eyes felt as though they were bulging out of his head from
eyestrain—he'd had to work on the microscope nearly all
day, except when he'd made his rounds. All of them were doing double duty on lab work ever since Ruth had disappeared.

He felt a heaviness inside, remembering that it was now a
full three days since anyone had seen her. Doctor Metz was
inconsolable, shutting himself up in his office for hours and
chain-smoking (he hadn't had a cigarette, Doctor Larraby
had told them, since he'd quit in 1963), staring stonily off
into space.

*Where did she go?* Ben wondered. *The police conducted an
investigation, but I've seen people search for lost dogs with*

*more energy. There have been so many disappearances—what the hell is going on?*

Angrily he slammed half of the mountainous pile of dishes into the sink, ran hot water, rolling up his sleeves. *Damn Elias,* he thought. He remembered what Juliet Parrish had told him: that Ruth had been examining a Visitor skin sample the day she vanished.

He glanced out the window as he scrubbed, saw a portion of the Mother Ship suspended overhead. Wherever you went, it was there, hanging over you. The Visitors had given an "introductory seminar" for some of the scientists, and Ben and Juliet had gone. Doctor Metz should have been the representative from their campus, but he hadn't even roused himself to reply to the invitation.

*What a bunch of shit that turned out to be,* Taylor thought, wincing as he stabbed his thumb on something sharp. *They spoon-fed us maybe ten minutes' worth of real information about themselves in half a day's time. The rest of it was either doubletalk or stuff that Kristine Walsh has already released.*

Ben rinsed his bleeding thumb under the cold water and went looking for an adhesive strip.

NIGHT HAD FALLEN, CARRYING JUST A HINT OF LOW-LYING MIST. Robin Maxwell paced in her yard, talking to her friend Muffy (née Abigail) on the cordless phone. From inside she could hear her parents talking quietly as they loaded the dishwasher together. "Oh, it's been grody, Muf, really. My Dad's been so *down* since Professor Quinton left. Or got kidnapped, or whatever. I even had to talk to the police, tell them what he said that night he called, y'know. Yeah, really!"

Her feet slid through the lawn's soft green with a tiny wet swish as she walked back and forth. "But you know about that. I wanted to know if you saw him! Daniel said he was in the neighborhood today . . . What do you mean, who am I talking about? *You* know who! The Visitor Youth Leader!"

"Daniel said he'd be by tonight?" She grinned ecstatically into the phone. "You're kidding! You *saw* him? Isn't he a *hunk*? Just a fox, right. Totally. I knooow . . ."

She sighed, listening so intently to her friend that she was unaware that a uniformed figure was approaching from behind her. "Couldn't you just *die*! Did you see his *eyes*? Gorgeous!"

She nodded vigorously. "Sure I saw them! When I was playing in the band. He looked at me for *quite* a while, for sure. Real meaningful, too, y'know. Like two ships in the night—so romantic . . ." The silent figure was nearly behind her. "I think he really likes me, but is just afraid . . . shy, y'know. Yeah, *totally*."

"Excuse me." Robin whirled, startled, to see the young Visitor she'd just been discussing standing behind her. She moaned softly, then turned away from him for a last agonized whisper:

"My life is *over*, Muf!"

She clicked the phone off, wondering whether to run or just die where she stood. He smiled uncertainly. "Excuse me. Did I startle you?"

"No!" she squeaked, then cleared her throat. "No."

"I'm Brian," he said, holding out his hand. Robin took it, feeling the blood race in her ears. She felt the cool pressure of his fingers for just a second, then dropped her hand. It tingled.

"I'm Robin," she said.

He cleared his throat, the sound very different because of the strange reverberation. "Uh . . . hi. Sorry, I'm a little nervous."

"*You're* nervous?" Robin said blankly.

"Well . . . it's not every day that I meet somebody from another planet."

She relaxed slightly. "Y'know, I never thought of that. It must be just as weird for you. Not that you're weird, I mean, y'know."

Brian smiled again. "Which one is Daniel's house?"

Visibly deflated, Robin pointed. "The one over there, on the right."

"Thanks." He turned away.

"Sure," Robin whispered, watching him leave. *He doesn't care*, she thought. *My life is over.*

He stopped, hesitated, then turned back to face her. "Uh . . . would you like to take a walk?"

Robin hesitated, trying to control the grin surging inside her, threatening to burst onto her face. "Okay," she said, following him.

WILLIAM THREADED HIS WAY THROUGH HURRYING WORKERS, RE-sponding to the blast of the noontime whistle. He could see Harmy's truck standing just ahead of him. As he approached, she looked up, waving. "Hey, hero! Willy!"

William smiled. "Hello, Harmony."

"Everybody's just *raving* about the way you rescued Caleb." William ducked his head, shrugging, unable to think of anything to say. "You seen him yet? Caleb, I mean."

"Yes," William said, "I have seen Caleb. He said he was fun."

"Fine," corrected Harmy automatically. "Did he thank you for saving his life? He ought to, seeing how mean he was acting."

William nodded. "He has been talking to me, since this morning. He shooked my hand."

"Well, that's more like it!" Harmy turned to her lunch wagon. "You want a burger or something? It's lunchtime."

He shook his head. She peered at him intently. "Say, don't you guys ever eat?"

He nodded, feeling uncomfortable, wondering how to change the subject. "Sometimes."

She took a bite of a sandwich, chewed thoughtfully. "You ever go to movies?"

"No, I do not . . ." William said, wondering what "movies" were. Like television, he thought he remembered, only larger. He smiled shyly at her. ". . . Yet."

She chuckled, and after a second, he found himself echoing her. It was his first laugh.

JULIET PARRISH WAS FEEDING THE MICE WHEN THE ANNOUNCEMENT came on the television. "We interrupt this program to bring our listeners an urgent special report."

*What now?* she thought. Aloud she called, "Ben? Doctor Metz? There's a bulletin on the television . . ."

She listened to Howard K. Smith explain that this story was being brought by satellite from Belgium. A picture of a distinguished-looking man came on, facing a steel bouquet of microphones. Doctor Metz exclaimed, "That's Leopold Jankowski! What is going on here?"

"He's with the Brussels Biomedical Institute, isn't he?" asked Ben. Metz nodded tensely as the man began to speak.

"I have called this press conference today to reveal a shocking discovery. There exists, in this world, an organized conspiracy of some of our best scientific minds. The aim of this conspiracy is to harm—possibly destroy—the Visitors."

Juliet and Ben gasped, their reactions mirrored by the hub-bub of reporters' voices in the crowded room. Doctor Metz stared incredulously. "Impossible!" he muttered. "That's insane—has Leopold lost his mind?"

Jankowski was speaking again. "This organized effort to harm the Visitors came to my attention first approximately two weeks ago, when Doctor Rudolph Metz in California called me and asked to speak with me on what he called 'urgent and confidential matters.'"

"*What?!*" Juliet grabbed Ben Taylor's arm.

"I did no such thing!" Doctor Metz said indignantly. "I haven't spoken to Jankowski since—"

"Others of my colleagues here in Belgium have also been approached by scientists," Jankowski continued. "Primarily those scientists in the fields of biomedical studies or anthropology seem to be involved. But we cannot be sure of how far this insidious contagion among some of our best minds has spread."

"*How can he say this?*" Doctor Metz was shaking with rage and hurt. "Jankowski was a good man—I have known him for years. What is he *talking* about?"

Juliet patted his arm. "Take it easy, Doctor. Maybe you'd better sit—"

"Scientists of many nations are apparently part of this insidious conspiracy. Their plan, quite simply, is to seize control of several of the Visitors' Mother Ships . . ."

Cries of "Why?", "To what purpose?" rang out from the assembled reporters.

Jankowski shook his head gravely. "They tried to convince me that it was to protect the human race and keep the military from learning advanced Visitor technology secrets. However, I am sure that their true motivation was far more personal than their avowed purpose."

Jankowski ceremoniously lifted a piece of paper. "On this statement I have listed the events exactly as they transpired, and the names of all those who tried to enlist my help in this dreadful conspiracy against those who had proved themselves our friends. I now authenticate this statement with my signature. Copies will be released to the appropriate authorities that they may deal with each of the scientists on this list according to their local laws."

Jankowski solemnly signed the statement. Ben, Juliet, and Doctor Metz looked at each other speechlessly.

WITHIN HOURS, SCORES OF OTHER SCIENTISTS FROM AROUND THE world had come forward, admitting that they had been approached by representatives of the "conspiracy." Some, like Doctor Jacques Duvivier, a Nobel laureate like Doctor Metz, admitted that they had belonged to it, signing statements similar to Jankowski's.

The entire world scientific community was in an uproar. In the United States, the FBI began investigating the records of those named by Duvivier, Jankowski, and others, trying to determine whether such a conspiracy indeed existed. They were assisted in their efforts by Visitors, who helpfully chauffeured them from lab to lab, standing by impassively as the record searches implicated scientist after scientist.

Doctor Metz's office was searched the day after Jankowski implicated him in his statement. Juliet Parrish and Ben Taylor stood by helplessly as Doctor Metz, incensed, challenged the FBI representatives to search his files—he had nothing, *nothing* to hide! Search they did—with the result that one of the men discovered a folder taped to a false panel inside the cabinet containing Metz's personnel files. The folder contained notes from meetings, lists of names, coded messages, maps showing the location of the Mother Ships . . .

Metz was dumbfounded, insisting the "evidence" had been planted. The FBI appropriated the files, plus several others they discovered in the office, and told Metz that no policy had yet been determined to deal with those discovered to be conspirators, but that he was not to leave Los Angeles without notifying them. Juliet and Ben received several hard looks, but no overt warnings. The FBI representatives left in the squad vehicle their Visitor pilots had landed on the roof.

Kristine Walsh, the press secretary for the Visitors, made a

sorrowful statement to the effect that, as a result of the conspiracy, the Visitor-proposed scientific seminars would have
to be postponed.

Many scientists who had been implicated in the conspiracy
charges simply vanished, lending credence to the allegations
of their guilt. Police departments were flooded with missing-
persons reports—thousands of them. Law enforcement agen-
cies were at a loss to explain what was happening, much less
investigate even a significant percentage of the cases.

Finally, when evidence found in the implicated scientists'
files showed that some groups in the secret cabal had even
planned violent takeovers of Visitor shuttles and weaponry,
John, the Visitor admiral officially requested the United Nations to intercede with its member nations to demand that all
scientists and their family members register their names and
current addresses with local authorities. The information
would be verified by computer against local address listings.

When first told about the United Nations' request, most
national authorities were reluctant—the president of the
United States was openly skeptical of the entire "conspiracy"
notion. But within a few weeks, in the face of mounting evidence of a secret scientists' cabal, resistance to the UN and
Visitor requests began to crumble. Key people, one by one,
began to reverse their stands, almost overnight in some cases.

Finally, by special act of Congress and the president, the
registration commenced.

ABRAHAM BERNSTEIN CAME OUT OF THE HOUSE FOR HIS DAILY
walk just in time to see his neighbor Robert Maxwell walk
down to his station wagon. Maxwell carried a sheaf of papers,
holding them so tightly they were wrinkled. "Good morning,
Mr. Maxwell," called Abraham.

"Not to me, it isn't," Maxwell said grimly, getting into his
car. "I've got to take these damned forms down to the post

office for this idiotic registration! I *still* don't understand how they got that passed in Congress! And you know something that's *really* weird?"

Abraham shook his head.

"Russia's doing the same thing. Of course it won't be as hard for them, since they kept their scientists pretty much under official Party observation anyway. But they're going to open their files to Visitor observers! I can't believe it!"

Bernstein realized he was trembling as he watched Maxwell start his car and drive away. Ruby Engels came over to him, having caught the end of the conversation. She put a comforting hand on her friend's arm as they started their daily walk. "Abraham, don't get so wound up! Nothing's going to happen. This will all blow over, you just watch."

"Yes, watch," said Abraham through gritted teeth. "Watch while they destroy everything I've come to hold dear."

"Nothing's going to happen," insisted Ruby. "After all, it's not as though you or your family are scientists. You won't be involved with this. And anyway, it's going to pass."

Abraham looked at her for a long moment. "That's what I said in 1938. In Berlin."

Ruby looked upset for a moment. "But this is different!"

"Is it?" Abraham glanced back at the squad vehicle which had just landed in front of his house. Brian, the Visitor Youth Leader, got out, followed by Daniel. They shook hands. Abraham's grandson wore a brownish-orange coverall, similar in design and cut to the Visitor uniform, a cap, and a wide grin.

Abraham slowly turned to Ruby. "*Is* it?"

She had no answer for him. Fear awakened in her eyes.

DENNIS LOWELL TRIED FOR THE FOURTH TIME TO PULL THE corkscrew out of the bottle of Liebfraumilch. He tensed his muscles, straining, and slowly . . . slowly . . . the corkscrew came forth—along with nearly half the cork.

"*Shit!*" Lowell slammed the cockscrew down on the kitchen counter, then glanced at the clock. *Forty-five minutes late,* he thought furiously, flicking on the small portable television that sat on the counter. He dug in the drawer for a sharp, thin-bladed knife while he listened.

"In other news, while international police have scoured scientific files for facts on the conspiracy, some startling evidence is being uncovered that many scientists who specialize in medical research in life sciences may have actually had major breakthroughs in research which they've *suppressed*. The Senate Medical Affairs Committee chairman, Raymond Burke, had this to say . . ."

The scene switched to the Senate stairs, where the senator was surrounded by the press and flashing cameras. Denny dug another piece of cork out of the bottle, watching morosely as Senator Burke spoke.

"Yes, indeed. I do have evidence that new and revolutionary cancer treatments *do* exist, and *have* existed for some time—along with many other breakthroughs of enormous potential benefit to the world. Apparently our scientific friends have seen fit to keep quiet about them."

Shouts of "Why?" echoed around him. He shrugged grimly. "Well, I won't speculate, except to say there's a lot of money to be made on research grants." "*Damn,*" said Dennis aloud, not sure himself whom he was addressing—or about what. He dug another sliver of cork out of the bottle, then had the dubious pleasure of seeing the remainder of the cork disintegrate into tiny pieces and slither down the neck into the wine.

The scene switched back to the newsroom just as he heard Juliet's key in the apartment door. The newsman looked grave. "A groundswell of resentment has begun to build around the world against the scientific community. In Stockholm, where the Nobel Prizes are awarded each year, a crowd of angry demonstrators—"

"I'm *sorry* I'm late, Den. Everything is a mess!" Juliet bustled into the kitchen, hastily pulling off her lab coat. Rain glistened in fine little glimmers on her blonde hair. "Doctor Metz
can't seem to pull himself together now that Ruth's gone, and
he heard about another associate who's been implicated just
as he was, and I—"

Dennis snapped off the television with a final click. "Take
your time. They called to cancel dinner."

Juliet looked dismayed. "Oh, Den! You must be disappointed."

"Yes," he agreed, shortly.

"You don't think you'll still get the account." She sounded
as though she wished he'd tell her something reassuring.
Dennis poured himself a drink, swallowed it in a gulp.

"No, I don't think so. They were *too* polite, y'know."

Juliet hung her lab coat over the back of the kitchen stool.
Her fingers smoothed it for a second, then stopped abruptly.
"Denny . . . do you think it's *me*? They know I'm a bio-
chemist, and a med student."

Dennis knew he'd waited a second too long to speak. "No.
How could it be you?"

She looked at him for long moments. He could feel her
eyes on his face, but couldn't raise his own to meet hers.
"Now *you* sound a little too polite, Den."

He couldn't think of anything to say. He poured himself another glass of wine, then went into the bedroom, leaving her
there, staring at the lab coat.

MIKE DONOVAN WATCHED TONY LEONETTI INTENTLY AS HIS FRIEND
flicked the switch to start the VCR unit. Doctor Leopold
Jankowski appeared on the screen, bending to sign his damning
statement. "Yeah?" Donovan turned to his partner. "I saw this. I
think it's all a load of shit. So?"

"You don't notice anything?" Tony punched up another

tape. "When we saw this when it originally aired, it bugged me for *days*—I couldn't figure out what the hell was wrong with the picture. Finally, I woke up the other night with the answer. Look. This is a tape we shot of him last year at that international science fair. You remember when I asked him to autograph that book for my old man?"

The second image appeared beside the first as both signings played simultaneously. Donovan stared, then nodded suddenly. "Yeah!"

"You see it, don't you, Mike? He used his right hand last year—yet when he signed the conspiracy statement, it was with his *left* hand."

Donovan shrugged, his eyes wary. "So? He's ambidextrous."

"No, he's not. And neither is Duvivier. I checked. Both men are now signing their names with their left hands, where before they were right-handed."

Donovan met Tony's eyes, his own speculative. Tony nodded. "Something very strange is going on, Mike. And I'll bet you a steak it's connected with the Visitors somehow. Everything's turned so damned *weird* since those guys showed up."

"Yeah." Donovan frowned. "Somehow we've got to get a look at the Mother Ship, and soon. And not just a guided tour. I mean a look at the whole thing. I'd love to see that area where they're storing the chemicals."

Leonetti nodded. "Just like old times, huh?"

Donovan nodded slowly. "Yeah. But at least Nam and Cambodia weren't over a mile in the air. We're going to have to be careful."

Tony Leonetti slapped a hand to his forehead, rolling his eyes expressively. "As I live and breathe, the fearless Michael Donovan, the greatest 'cowboy' photographer of all time, is going to be *careful*. These guys got you scared, Mike?"

Donovan's laughter held an edge—he didn't like being

reminded of some of his more reckless photographic exploits. Then he sobered, looking back at the stilled images of Jankowski Number 1 and Jankowski Number 2. "Yeah, Tony," he mumbled, his voice so quiet Leonetti had to strain to hear him. "I gotta admit, I have a feeling about this . . . There's not going to be any room for slip-ups this time . . ."

Leonetti forced a grin, jabbing his partner with a muscle punch. "What you're feeling, Mike, is hunger. Been a long time since lunch, old pal. Come on. The steaks are on me."

Donovan turned, punching playfully back at Leonetti, glad his friend had broken the tension. "I'm game. When do you want to do it?"

"Eat? Right now!"

"No, I meant sneak aboard a squad vehicle."

"Tomorrow?"

"Sounds good to me. Think Fran will let you out? The last time we went out together you dropped a bundle at that casino in Atlantic City."

"Now, *that's* where I'll have to be *careful . . .*"

# 8

BRILLIANT FLOODS TURNED THE PARKING LOT AT THE RICHLAND plant into a garish semblance of day. One of the large Visitor shuttles stood, cargo bay doors open, as Tony Leonetti and Mike Donovan crawled carefully through a maze of ground-level piping to crouch, hidden, behind a trash receptacle. Insulated pipes led from the large cryogenic tanks overhead to smaller tanks on board the shuttle craft. Two Visitor technicans stood by, along with two humans wearing hardhats.

"Pretty crowded, Mike," Tony whispered. "Don't you think maybe we ought to call for a squad vehicle and go up like we usually do?"

Donovan shook his head, judging the distance involved to the open cargo bay, hefting the Sony Betacam. It was his smallest and lightest VTR. "This way they won't know we're on board, and we'll have a better chance to find out stuff." He glanced quickly at his partner. "I hope this thing will produce broadcast-quality film. What about the sound?"

Tony shrugged. "It's state-of-the-art, Mike. It'll have to do."

Several Visitors began to uncouple the insulated pipe. Donovan tensed. "Okay, they're finished with the chemical— get ready."

Tony swallowed with an audible gulp, earning him a reproving scowl from Donovan. The human technicians walked away as the two Visitors climbed into the pilot's compartment of the shuttle. "Now!" Donovan hissed.

He climbed out of the piping, dashing forward, leaping over a ground-level pipe hidden by the shadows and the incandescent glare. Tony came after him, but, not seeing the pipe, caught his foot and went sprawling. Donovan, already at the cargo entrance, heard his muffled "Oooof!"

"Damn!" Tony scrambled for the cargo door as its two halves began to rise toward each other. Mike reached out, grabbing for his wrists.

Leonetti leaped gamely. "Can't—get my—leg—up—"

"I've got you—" hissed Donovan, but a second later had to admit defeat as the doors continued to close. He had one last second to see Tony scuttle away from the vehicle before the doors locked together. "Shit!" He crouched behind some containers in the cargo hold, hugging the Betacam. The darkness was complete.

He felt the now-familiar lift and swoop of the craft and knew they were on their way.

The shuttle bay of the Mother Ship was as he'd seen it before. He could hear a woman's voice announcing landings and departures—in English—as the cargo doors began to widen. Donovan scuttled through, almost before the opening would admit him, and in seconds had ensconced himself behind a barricade of the cryo units he'd seen Visitor technicians toting about. He listened to the announcements, wondering suddenly why here, where there were no humans present (except Kristine, probably, he reminded himself bitterly), the Visitors wouldn't use their native language.

"Prepare for venting operations," announced the voice.

*Venting operations?* Donovan frowned. *What the hell is that?*

He peered out cautiously, saw Visitor technicians attaching yet another insulated hose to the chemical storage tank in the shuttle's cargo hold, then screwing the end of it into a nozzle in the floor of the landing bay. Donovan was puzzled—according to the many views he'd had of the landing bay as he'd approached it in the squad vehicles, there were no pipes or storage containers on the outside of the huge Mother Ship. And from this angle, if the nozzle did indeed point straight through the landing bay floor, then there was only empty air outside.

He watched, filming now, as the technicians turned a valve, and there came the whoosh of escaping gases. One of the techs stretched. "This is what the humans would call a royal pain," he commented, the reverberation in his voice echoing throughout the cavernous landing bay. "Dragging this stuff up to the ship, then dumping it out again—what a waste."

"Yeah," his companion agreed. "I can't figure out why we're doing this day and night."

"Who knows why the Leader orders most of the things he orders?" said the first. "But I'm not going to question it; that's too unhealthy."

"You're right," agreed his companion, glancing around to make sure they hadn't been overheard.

Donovan squirmed lower behind the cryo units, his hand grazing an accordion-like structure that looked amazingly like an old-fashioned radiator. The silvery-gray metal quivered under his arm. Donovan glanced at it, then tugged experimentally, and it swung open to reveal a rung ladder leading down to a shadowy catwalk and stairs. *Some kind of service access*, he thought, crawling through, *or that trusty standby of all spies and adventure-bound heroes, a ventilator shaft . . .*

Pulling the strange-looking grille nearly closed behind him, Donovan climbed quickly, one-handed, down the ladder. He found himself in the shadowy walkway. He could almost stand erect, but had to be careful not to bump his head on the piping hanging down.

Light filtered in from grilles set into the walls, and from tiny lights implanted in the walkway floor every couple of feet. Donovan began walking along, feeling a distinct chill. The Visitors must keep parts of their ship colder than human beings would consider comfortable.

Part of the chill came from swiftly circulating air. Donovan grinned wryly as the gust tugged at his hair. *Damn! It is a ventilator shaft!*

He began walking, his soft soles echoing slightly on the metal floor. He wasn't too concerned with noise giving him away; the whoosh of air and the thud of machinery would muffle any sound.

He reached the grille and peered out cautiously, hearing voices. Two Visitors stood by one of the yellow-marked doors he'd seen earlier—the ones Diana had said were inaccessible due to radiation. One of the Visitors produced a crystal-and-gold key like the one Donovan had given to Sean and inserted it into a slot. Light washed outward, illuminating the crystal, then the door slid aside.

*Interesting,* thought Mike. *They weren't wearing any protective suits . . . if there's so much radiation in there, why wouldn't they need them?* He moved onward, then downward as the main duct sloped. He eased the camera along—Tony had said the thing was rugged, but he wasn't taking any chances. Another grating on the other side of the walkway showed him one of the Visitors—a woman, this time—reclining on a bunk, reading something that looked vaguely like a book—if a book were printed on aluminum foil and manuscript-sized paper. She wore a snug-fitting garment that left her arms and legs bare and looked rather like a bathing suit. Donovan, who had been without feminine companionship since he'd left Kristine's apartment nearly a month ago, gave her legs a quick once-over.

*Not bad. A little chunky, but nice . . .*

Silent-footed, he moved on. He was careful to memorize the route as he went—it would never do to be caught in these walkways without being able to get back. *Like a rat in a maze,* he thought, appreciating the analogy grimly as the walkway turned again and he ducked to avoid more overhead piping.

He heard voices ahead—and something about them was familiar. Donovan crept carefully to a larger grille, peering through. Diana walked by, clad in a long red robe open down the throat. Mike's pulse quickened a little at the way the silky garment clung to her breasts and thighs. She was talking to a man Donovan recognized as Steven—the Visitor officer who divided his time between the Richland plant and Eleanor's house.

"You must be pleased, Diana," Steven was saying. "We're well on our way to completely securing most of the continents."

Diana smiled archly. "Well, let's just say that it pleases me to serve our Leader," her sideways look at Steven was so coy it nearly made Donovan gag, "with whatever minor talents I possess." She walked across the room to a plexiglass cabinet of some sort. In small compartments ranged across the wall, Donovan saw, were a variety of small animals—lab animals, he realized.

Thankful that the Betacam was nearly silent, he began filming the Second-in-Command. She reached into one of the compartments and extracted a white mouse. The little rodent squeaked frenziedly as she grasped it, then was still, its beady little eyes glazed in panic.

"The Leader must be very well pleased with your conversion process, Diana," Steven said. Still holding the mouse, Diana turned, walked across the room—and out of camera range. Mike could hear her talking.

"Yes . . . but you know how impatient our Leader can be." She paused for a long second.

Steven sounded amused. "Even with *you*, Diana? Given the *intimacy* of your relationship, I would think—"

Diana moved abruptly back into camera range, and even from the dimness of the walkway Mike could see her anger. She gestured with both elegantly manicured hands—Donovan wondered briefly where she'd put the mouse. "Be very careful, Steven," she hissed.

Steven spread both hands in a gesture both apologetic and mocking. "It's just that I hate to see you distressed."

Diana sounded frustrated. "He doesn't understand that my conversion process is still limited. It doesn't work the same on every human subject."

"No," Steven agreed, "but when it works—Duvivier, Jankowski and the others—it's remarkable."

"Yes, isn't it?" Diana sounded smug. She reached into one of the other cages, extracted a frog. She smiled brightly at Steven as she walked past him, out of Donovan's line of sight again.

"They actually *believe* that the conspiracy exists—some of them even believe that they were a part of it." Steven walked into Donovan's view, smiling.

"Of course the evidence we planted reinforces their belief," said Diana.

*We've* got *to get this on the air!* thought Donovan excitedly. Briefly he considered leaving, but when Steven came back into his view, heading for the cages on the opposite wall, he decided to see what else the Visitor officer might reveal. He didn't have long to wait. Steven stopped in front of the cages, but Donovan could hear every word.

"The operation's working wonderfully. The scientists are being ostracized—disorganized worldwide. And *they* pose the greatest threat. Once they're eliminated, or converted . . ."

He made a gesture with his fingers as of someone flicking away dust.

Diana sounded a bit rueful. "The problem now is that our Leader says, why not convert them all? He doesn't understand that human will is much tougher than we bargained for—converting all of them would take forever!"

Steven nodded, still standing with his back to Mike, then reached into one of the small cages, taking out a mouse.

"However, we'll continue to refine the process," Diana said.

"Yes, I'm sure you will," Steven said, holding the mouse up, apparently examining it. As Diana walked toward him, he turned back to her—and only years of training and experience kept Donovan's hands from dropping the camera. The mouse's hindquarters *protruded from the officer's mouth,* and as Donovan watched in horror, Steven jerked his head several times in a bizarre staccato motion. The mouse's wiggling legs and thrashing tail disappeared down his throat with an audible gulp.

Diana's words came in the same matter-of-fact tone. "Well, it's important that we learn the most effective and efficient methods to be used against them." The woman reached into another cage, then grasped a large, fluffy guinea pig. As the terrified creature squeaked and struggled, she opened her mouth—wider, *wider*—her jawbone seemingly dislocated at the last second, and she lowered the frantic animal between her lips.

Donovan clamped his teeth hard on his lower lip, his stomach turning over, as he watched Diana swallow the living animal whole. *Oh, God, what's happening to us? What* are *these things?*

The Second-in-Command's throat bulged outward, rippling with a downward motion. Steven spoke. "Well, I don't think our Leader could have chosen anyone who could do the job better than you, Diana."

Shaking, Donovan had had enough. Grasping the camera firmly, he turned, making a stumbling progress back along the shadowy walkway. In his mind's eye he saw again the squirming guinea pig—the mouse's tail—and suddenly he turned, braced himself against the wall of the walkway, retching. *Don't puke, you sonofabitch*, he told himself frantically. *You don't want them to know you've been here!*

It took him long seconds to gain control, but finally he was able to grope his way back down the walkway.

He passed the grille closest to Diana's room, which he'd bypassed before, and paused to peer in. A Visitor stood before a washstand of sorts, apparently doing something to his eyes. His pose looked familiar to Donovan, then he remembered. Kristine wore contacts, and from the rear at least, the Visitor's actions seemed to be nearly identical to those of a person removing or inserting contact lenses. In spite of the urgency which drove him, Mike hesitated, watching.

There seemed to be a case of some sort beside the alien. One rounded half-circle with a blue center sat on one of the raised surfaces inside the case. As Donovan watched, the Visitor placed another of the things beside the first. Seeing them together, Mike began filming again. They looked like eyeballs—as though the alien wore human eyes as Kristine wore her contacts. The Visitor turned, and even though Donovan had braced himself, he was unprepared for the shock—the man's eyes were reddish-orange, with black, vertically slitted pupils!

*And those hideous eyes saw Donovan right through the grille.*

The creature let out a hissing gasp of surprise, then, reaching for the grille, tore the metal frame from the bulkhead with one hand, grabbing for the cameraman with the other. Donovan dodged—but the thing moved with a blurring swiftness that was as inhuman as those eyes. It grabbed Mike, hauling him through the grille opening one-handed, throwing him across the tiny cabin onto the washstand.

Donovan landed badly, grabbing wildly for support. The Visitor advanced on him, his breathing a hissing gasp in the whoosh of air-displacement from the vent opening. Gathering himself, Donovan lashed out with his legs, catching the alien in the midsection, hurling him backward. The blow would have disabled a man, but the creature recovered immediately, advancing on Mike again—those terrible eyes glaring like bloody pools in the dimness.

It had been a long time since Donovan had been in a fight, but his early training as a reconnaissance pilot and sometime intelligence photographer had been thorough. He managed to toss his camera onto the bunk as the creature moved toward him, thanking all the gods there were that he'd been using the wide-angle lens to film Diana's chamber. Maybe it would pick up a shot of those eyes—

The Visitor lashed out, hitting Donovan's shoulder, though he managed to duck the worst force of the blow. He slammed a hard left into the Visitor's face, but the blow didn't even faze the creature. They grappled in the tiny cabin, bouncing off the walls, pushing and struggling. Donovan managed to work two hands around the creature's throat, but in turn felt the Visitor's hands groping beneath his chin. Ducking his own chin into his chest as hard as he could, Mike tried to block those squeezing fingers while he tightened his own grip.

The Visitor opened his mouth slightly—Donovan had only a second to realize that the mouth seemed to have *two sets* of teeth—when something lashed out at him. Dry—red—it flew from the creature's mouth, spattering drops of burning liquid—it was a foot long or more—

The tongue lashed again—forked—Mike felt a frenzy of repulsion. His reflexes took over, bringing his knee up in a vicious blow that landed true and hard.

*It didn't faze the thing at all.* Somehow that fact, more than anything else he'd seen yet, brought home the *alienness* of the creature. Panicking, he grabbed madly at the thing's eyes, seeking to blind it. His own vision was beginning to blur as his assailant's fingers groped ever deeper into his throat, nearing his windpipe.

His fingers sank *into* the thing's face. Stunned, Mike looked at the flap of skin that had torn away in his hand, leaving a large, greenish-black oily patch.

As its face began to rip, the creature partly relaxed its grip, half turning away—as though to hide the ripped place. Donovan renewed his efforts, grabbing at the torn place viciously, pulling with both hands.

The rest of the face sheared off in sticky, plastic-stretching strings, like mozzarella cheese off a pizza. Donovan was looking at a reptilian face—the false hair flopping back to reveal a crested head. The thing hissed at him slurringly, the tongue flicking in and out, and, even as he struggled with it, Mike realized the thing was calling out in its own language. *No wonder the bastards speak English! They can't speak their own language when they're wearing the masks!*

He managed to land two slamming punches to the thing's head, which staggered the Visitor. Donovan grabbed the Betacam from off the bunk in back of him, and, praying it was as tough as Tony had promised, clubbed the creature brutally on the side of its head, then again in the face. It slipped, falling.

Mike didn't wait to see if it got back up. Clutching the camera, he was through the grille before he could even take a decent breath.

Forcing his steps to come quickly, he moved back toward the shuttle bay, feeling blood trickling down his face from a cut above his eye, and, more painful still, the pinpoint smarting from whatever venom the thing had spit at him. It burned sharply, but luckily, he thought, feeling his head, it seemed mostly to have landed in his hair, missing his eyes.

He crawled back through the grille into the shuttle bay, only to see a craft being readied for immediate liftoff. Several Visitor technicians stood by the cargo doors. Somewhere overhead a pulsing sound began to reverberate through the landing bay.

"Emergency," said the announcer. "Emergency on level seventy-three. Emergency. Intruder alert on level seventy-three." The cargo bay doors began to rise as two of the Visitor technicians hastened away.

*Oh, shit,* thought Donovan, eyeing the slowly closing doors to freedom.

One of the Visitor pilots turned to the other. "I'm so tired of all these drills. Let's go, before we have to sit here and wait through another one." His companion nodded agreement, and they climbed into the pilot's compartment—leaving the bay, for the moment at least, deserted.

Mike crouched frozen for a precious second, unable to believe his good luck, then, diving forward, raced for the cargo doors. There were perhaps two and a half feet—no more—separating the moving sheets of metal. Donovan leaped, flattening his body in midair, launching outward in an impromptu racing dive.

One of the doors struck his shin with paralyzing force, then he was through, inside, hugging his shin, and blinking away tears of pain or thanksgiving—Mike wasn't sure which.

He felt the familiar lift of the shuttle, and hastily, dragging his leg, crawled behind the cargo tank. He crouched in the darkness, rubbing his shin, breathing deeply, trying to slow the blood racing in his veins. He was trembling violently from adrenaline overload . . .

*Don't kid yourself, Mike,* he told himself cynically, *adrenaline overload in this case is just another word for* fear, *and you're goddamned* scared, *admit it . . .*

"Okay, I'm scared," he mumbled, laying his head against the coolness of the Betacam resting on his pulled-up knees. *What the hell is going to happen to us? What have we gotten ourselves into?*

The shuttle tilted slightly as it landed. Favoring his leg, Mike crawled to the doors, peering out. He watched the two Visitor pilots walk away from the shuttle, then, when the area seemed deserted, limped out.

He'd barely reached the other side of the parking lot when a dark shape rose from a sitting position by a Dumpster. Donovan tensed, ready to swing the Betacam again.

"Mike!" Tony sounded horrified. "What the *hell* happened to you, man?" Hastily he took the camera out of Donovan's lax fingers. "You look like hell!"

"Feel like it too," Donovan admitted, staggering a bit with relief. "I'm glad to see you, buddy. Let's get over to the station. I've gotta see what I got on the tape."

"What—"

Mike shook his head. "If I try and tell you, you'll think I'm crazy. Or drunk. I hardly believe it myself. We've got to see this tape."

Reaching Tony's car, they climbed in. Donovan looked at the lighted digital clock on the dash, then, with a muffled exclamation, peered at his watch, wiping the blood off his eye with a curse. "Is this thing *right*? Can't be!"

Leonetti started the car. "What?"

"You mean I was only up there *twenty-five minutes*?!"

Tony checked his watch before putting the Toyota in gear. "Yep. Seem longer?"

Donovan leaned back against the seat cushions, letting his breath out in a long, long sigh. "Yeah. Forever longer."

Amazingly enough, he dozed off during the twenty-minute drive to the television station. When Tony stopped the car in the parking lot, he roused, sitting up with a jerk. "Wha—"

"Take it easy, Mike. We're here."

As he climbed out of the small car, Donovan groaned, feeling the stiffness of bruised muscles, and a dull ache in his back where the Visitor had thrown him against the washstand. He almost welcomed the pain as proof that he hadn't dreamed the whole thing.

They went in the back way, straight to the network president's office. It was after nine, and he had gone home, but the evening director was there, preparing for the eleven o'clock news broadcast. Leaving Donovan, Tony went over to speak to the man, a heavyset bald fellow. Mike remembered having met him a time or two before. Sitting down gingerly on the edge of one of the newsroom desks, Donovan tried to recall his name. *Martini? Gibson? Some kind of drink*, he thought fuzzily. The back of his neck was killing him.

Leonetti came back with the bald man. "Mike, this is Paul Madeira. He's willing to put on a special bulletin, if your tape warrants it. Are you willing to do a live interview to accompany it?"

For all his years behind the camera, Donovan had never had one focus on *him*, except for the press that had gathered around following their first visit to the Mother Ship. He hesitated. "Okay. Just so long as you don't expect Barbara Walters's brand of poise out of me."

They went into one of the rear screening rooms, while Tony readied the tape. Donovan sat in the darkened room, his pulse racing, as the images began to unroll.

First the loading dock. "What's 'venting operations'?" Madeira wanted to know.

"They're evidently taking some of those chemicals up there, then dumping them into the atmosphere," Donovan said. "The chemical story may be just a cover-up."

"But why would they do that? Why present such an elaborate hoax?" Tony asked.

Mike shrugged, wincing as his back protested. "Don't know, buddy. But I doubt they're going to all this trouble just for a social call."

The shadowy walkway came next. "Cut that when we broadcast," Donovan suggested. "It doesn't show up well, and nothing happened there."

Then they heard distant voices. Donovan tensed as the scene with Diana and Steven replayed. When Diana reached into the chamber holding the mouse, Donovan gulped audibly, for the first time realizing what was happening to the creatures off-camera.

"Get set," he whispered quietly to Madeira and Leonetti. "This next part's a doozy. Hope you guys have strong stomachs."

"What?" said Madeira—then the big man froze as Steven gulped down the mouse.

"Holy *shit!*" Tony hissed.

Donovan swallowed. "The best is yet to come, boys and girls." He watched Diana raise the guinea pig, her jaw expanding—

Then, almost without realizing he'd moved, he found himself leaning over the trash can, vomiting. Tony stopped the machine with a curse, then turned on the light. "Mike—"

Donovan waved him away, then heaved again. "No—okay—I'm . . . okay." He straightened, gasping, then rinsed his mouth with the cup of water Madeira handed him. "Thanks. I feel like an asshole—I suppose better here than there, where they might've heard me."

"Believe it," said Tony. "I nearly whoopsed just watching the tape. What *are* those things?"

Donovan looked at him. "You'll see—at least, I hope you will."

"Start it up again, Tony," said Madeira.

Donovan could have kissed the Betacam. The tough little

camera had landed on the bunk, making the picture sideways, but by craning their necks, they could see most of the fight. One or two closeups of the alien, his human mask dangling off the side of his face, made both Madeira and Tony gasp.

Lights back on, the three looked at each other. "Reptiles of some kind," said Madeira. "It was like seeing a science fiction movie come to life. The things are evidently very strong, Donovan. You're lucky you're not hurt worse."

"Yeah," echoed Tony

"Let's get that bulletin on the air," said Donovan.

Minutes later, Donovan sat with the station's anchorman for the eleven o'clock news, listening to the calls throughout the studio.

"Lights! Give me lights, dammit. *Now!*"

"We're feeding bars and tone right now."

"Dan, check your patching."

"Get lavs on them. I want them double-miked." A technician came up and fitted them with small mikes. She offered to dab some antiseptic on Donovan's blistered and battered face, but he waved her away, seeing the director give the signal to begin.

Mike heard an off-camera voice: "We interrupt this program for a special bulletin live from our newsroom in Los Angeles."

Madeira's voice reached Donovan. "Stand by, one—take one. Cue, Charles."

The anchorman across the table from Donovan looked up. "An astonishing occurrence just took place aboard the Mother Ship. With us tonight is—"

"Hey! What the hell!" Madeira's voice interrupted. "Hang on, Chuck, we've just lost our line—"

The assistant director, a young black woman with long, dark hair, looked up in amazement. "We've lost our line. We've lost Ma Bell."

"*What?!*" Madeira looked frazzled. The studio lights glistened on his bald head.

"Somebody's pulled AT&T right out from under us! The whole damn network's off the air!"

"So are both the others!" shouted the technical director.

"And now I've lost New York," said the young woman in a hopeless tone.

The monitor flickered above Mike's head. "There's something!" shouted Madeira.

The screen filled with the Visitors' symbol.

# 9

"DAMN," DONOVAN MUMBLED, LOOKING UP AT THE MONITORS ON the newsroom wall. The screens flickered, then filled with Kristine Walsh's familiar features.

"This is Kristine Walsh. The Visitors' admiral, John, is here to make a statement."

Mike sighed, slumping on his spine behind the broadcast desk. *We were too late . . . too damn late, and now we're shit outa luck.* He didn't look up as John spoke:

"My friends throughout the world. First, I must thank the leaders of each of your countries, who have graciously and in the interests of peace, turned over all their broadcasting facilities to us to help avoid confusion in this crisis." Donovan heard the ripple of disbelief and growing anger as the broadcast room reacted to the Visitor leader's lie.

"I am sad to say that there has been a carefully coordinated, and quite violent attempt by the conspiracy of scientists to commandeer control of our facilities at many key locations around the world." Shots of several refineries in flames filled the monitors. "These scenes came from Rio de Janeiro, Tokyo, and Cairo, where our plants came under furious attack by terrorists—at least two dozen other places suffered similar

attempted assaults, but managed to partially or completely re-
pel them."

Shots of ambulances and stretcher-bearing paramedics appeared against a backdrop of flaming chemical tanks and
guerrilla-style warfare. The victims wore human clothing as
well as Visitor uniforms. John's words voiced-over the scenes:
"The loss of life has been enormous—both to your people and
ours. In addition, thousands have been wounded—and we're
fearful there will be more attacks."

John's image filled the screens again. "The outbreak is so
widespread and so dangerous that most civilian members of
your governments have asked us to extend them protection—
which, of course, we were happy to provide. They're safe
aboard our ships, and we'll take good care of them."

"I'll bet, you lying sonofabitch!" the assistant director
snarled. Donovan looked over at Madeira, who appeared to
be in shock.

John sighed, looking regretful. "I'm also sorry to report
that this man—a person in whom we placed considerable
trust"—a photo appeared on the screens, and with weary ex-
pectation, Mike looked up to see his own face—"Michael
Donovan, of the United States, has proved to be the biggest
traitor to the peace and well-being of the world. He is one of
the leaders of the conspiracy, and is responsible for engineer-
ing the violent attacks conducted today."

"Too bad they didn't get one of your best side, Mike," said
a disgusted voice, and Donovan looked down to see Tony
Leonetti crouched by his side. "Come on, you'd better get out
of here. This'll be the first place they'll look."

Donovan followed his partner to the videotape room. "Did
you get a chance to copy my tape?"

"Setting up to do it now. Man, we're in trouble."

"Tell me about it," said Donovan bitterly, hearing the last
words of John's statement: "Any person who gives information

leading to Donovan's capture will be handsomely rewarded by the UN General Assembly and the government of the United States.

"If you see this man, do not—I repeat, do *not* attempt to apprehend or speak to him. He should be considered armed and dangerous."

"*What?!*" Donovan turned to Leonetti. He'd never thought they'd go this far. It was like something out of the Middle Ages.

A scream broke from the newsroom, then the place seemed to erupt with the sounds of booted feet and strange, whining pulses of sounds. "They're here, Mike!" shouted Tony.

The locked door burst inward, and beyond it Donovan could see Visitors wearing strange protective helmets and carrying heavy-duty weapons. He yanked open the other door, just as Tony tossed him his tape. "Here!" Leonetti overturned a rack of video components in the path of the Visitors—effectively cutting off his own escape route. Donovan had no choice—it was run or be gunned down where he stood.

He bolted out the door, dashed across the corridor, hit the fire exit door with his shoulder, and, accompanied by the shriek of the alarm, hurtled out into the night. The stair railing caught him across the waist, as, unable to stop, he careened over it and down to the parking lot. It was a short drop—only four or five feet—but Donovan landed badly, the wind knocked out of him.

Bad landing or not, the fall saved his life. Almost before he'd landed, a bolt of energy cut the air above the railing like a lash, leaving a singed, ozone smell. Scrambling to his feet, Donovan stuffed the precious tape inside his jacket pocket and raced down the alley toward where he thought the parking lot lay.

He rounded a corner, running full-tilt into another trooper—

a California highway patrolman, this time. The man reeled back, then, seeing Donovan's face, made a grab for his sidearm. Mike's foot lashed out, and the weapon went spiraling away.

Panicked by this new evidence that his own people believed the Visitor report and would treat him like a criminal, Donovan raced on farther into the alley. With a sick feeling he realized he'd lost his sense of direction—instead of the parking lot ahead, there was nothing but a high wall.

Behind him came the beat of booted footsteps, then that strange whining pulse as the shock troopers fired their alien weapons. Realizing he had no choice, Donovan lengthened his strides, then, when he was only feet away from squashing himself on the bricks like a bug, leaped, arms over his head. His groping fingers closed over the top of the wall, and he hung there, feet kicking wildly, trying to get a toehold that would allow him to swing up—

A bolt singed the wall beside him, and Donovan felt sudden heat in his right buttock. As though the blast had been a whip to encourage a balky horse, Mike pulled himself up, his leg swinging up to hook over the wall. He hesitated for just a second, then another pulse nearly singed his hair, and he jumped outward, into the darkness below.

DANIEL BERNSTEIN SAT UP EXCITEDLY AS THE VISITOR LEADER, John, described the violent attempt to take over the chemical plants. "I wonder if they got Richland," Stanley Bernstein murmured. Abraham sat across the room, very still, only his eyes moving.

"Oh, God, Stanley!" Lynn whimpered. "Look at all those people they injured! What's going to happen to us?"

"Nothing, honey, nothing." Bernstein patted his wife's shoulders encouragingly.

"Quiet, Dad!" Daniel turned around. "This is important!"

John had just finished describing the manhunt going on for the photographer, Michael Donovan. Daniel's lip curled, watching the picture. *After all these guys are doing for us, this sonofabitch tries to screw it up? He'd better not get in my path . . .*

John smiled reassuringly from the television screen, and Daniel smiled back automatically. John would handle everything.

"Your national leaders have suggested that a state of martial law will be most helpful at this time, and we agree. Police at local levels will be working with our Visitor patrols—and we'll also ask the help of all our Visitor Friends units everywhere . . ."

"All *right*!!" Daniel sat up, squaring his shoulders, tugging at his uniform to straighten it.

"We anticipate that this crisis will pass relatively quickly. In the meantime, friends, I and my fellow Visitors will do our best to see you through it and help you maintain control. There will be more announcements later, giving you specific rules to follow during the crisis."

The television screen went black. Daniel stood up, his head held proudly. "Gotta go, Mom and Dad! You heard the admiral!"

He left, hearing his mother behind him. "Stanley, oh, my God . . ."

Then his father's reassurance. "It'll pass—you heard what John said. Right, Dad?"

But Abraham said nothing at all.

# 10

MIKE DONOVAN LAY ON HIS BELLY ON A WINDSWEPT HILLSIDE, sighting through the telephoto lens of his 35-millimeter reflex camera at what lay below: Davis Air Force Base—Strategic Air Command Headquarters for Southern California. He snapped off several shots of the Visitor sentries patrolling the entrances and perimeters of the base. Suddenly a puff of dust rose in the distance, and Donovan focused on a long black limousine approaching.

As the car came closer, he could see several high-ranking military officers in the vehicle's passenger seats, and—he narrowed his eyes to read the stripes—a captain was driving.

He swung the camera back, focusing on the base again, then saw something interesting—the Visitor shock troopers scattered, moving quickly inside the building, and suddenly several MPs clad in standard-issue uniforms appeared, taking up positions at the entrance gate. Donovan glanced back at the limo, frowning helplessly. The gate was too far away for those in the car to have seen what was happening.

The Lincoln pulled up in front of the gate, and the lieutenant colonel got out, gesturing at the inside of the car. Mike squinted again at the older man inside. He was a general.

Sick, he watched. The sentries stood helplessly as the Visitor troopers emerged from the building, heavy-duty weapons at ready. They ordered everyone out of the car, and when the lieutenant colonel made a move toward his sidearm, shot him without hesitation. The general, the colonel, and the captain were led away under guard, while the MPs, under direction of one of the Visitor troopers, picked up the lieutenant colonel's body and carried it away.

Donovan recorded the entire incident on film, wondering, as he'd wondered so often these past two weeks, if anyone would ever see this record he was collecting of the Visitor occupation. He changed film, stowing the record of the slaying safely in his jacket. His pockets bulged with film and the VTR tape—he'd have to try to get copies made and the pictures developed soon, but wasn't sure just how he was going to manage that. He fingered his week-old beard . . . Not really enough yet to cover his features.

He wished his beard grew faster, or that he hadn't worked so hard, that entire first week, to shave each day. It hadn't been easy—sleeping in flophouses, all-night movies, one night at the Y. He rolled over onto his back, letting the sun play on the now-gaunt planes of his face, appreciating its warmth. He'd had only fifteen bucks on him the night of his foray into the Mother Ship, and the money had soon run out. For the past two days he'd eaten at missions and soup kitchens— when he'd eaten. His thinking was a little fuzzy from hunger, he suspected.

Four days ago he'd picked up ten dollars from a woman living near Eleanor when he'd knocked on her door, asking for work. His nose wrinkled. The only job she'd been able to offer him was cleaning stalls in her backyard stable. He'd taken it—but if he didn't get his clothes washed soon, he didn't know what he'd do . . . There were always coin-op Laundromats, but when he only had the one set of clothes . . .

He pictured himself sitting buck naked on a wooden bench, watching his clothes spin, and found himself chuckling. The laughter had a desperate, zero-hour quality.

He wondered bleakly if Tony Leonetti had managed to get away. He hadn't seen a soul he knew, but he'd have to try and make some contacts. He couldn't go on like this much longer.

He scratched suddenly at his shin, then felt something nip his thigh. He'd been fleabitten before, when he'd been caught and interned briefly in Laos, but he'd hardly noticed then—fleas, compared to dysentery, lice, and torture, paled a bit. Now the little buggers were driving him crazy.

He'd have to take the risk of trying to phone Tony, he decided. He hadn't heard any news reports given by anyone but Kristine lately—he didn't think any of the networks were doing their own news anymore—but the situation was terrible, and getting worse. Visitor troopers were stationed on nearly every street corner. Others spent their time, along with the Visitor Friends, putting up propaganda posters showing Visitors hugging old folks, or toting babies on their shoulders. Prices had risen astronomically, and the curfew was still in effect. Donovan had overheard gossip in the flophouses that the police force was acting only on the written orders of the mayor—that the man hadn't actually been seen for more than a week. Donovan wondered bleakly which hand the mayor had used to write those orders commanding the police to cooperate in every way with the Visitor troops . . .

Wearily he climbed to his feet, stowing his camera in a battered plastic shopping bag. The camera represented his one foray to gain help—he'd broken into Eleanor's house one night, while she and Arthur were in the living room with Steven, talking. He'd left the camera there the night the Richland plant began producing the Visitors' "life-sustaining" chemical. The camera and some of the rolls of film—now used—were all he'd had a chance to grab.

Arthur, hearing a noise in the back, had come in just as Mike had put a leg over the sill in the spare bedroom and was climbing out. Eleanor's husband had stood in the doorway, his gaze locked with Donovan's, for seemingly endless seconds. Then Donovan had forced himself to move, waiting all the time for the shout that would bring Steven and the other Visitors down on him. But the man hadn't raised the alarm.

With a sigh, Donovan began the long walk back to the main highway. If he was lucky—and he admitted, fleas or not, he was incredibly lucky still to be free and in one piece—he'd be able to thumb a ride back to L.A. by late afternoon. Then he'd try and scrounge a few bucks, and maybe by night he could risk calling Tony . . .

His head filled with planning another night as a fugitive— plans that had become second-nature since he'd been on the run—Mike Donovan walked on . . .

TIGHT-LIPPED, JULIET PARRISH FOLDED A BLOUSE AND TOSSED IT into the open suitcase on the bed. Denny sat across the room from her, not meeting her eyes. "You going to stay with your folks in Manhattan?"

She swallowed, keeping her voice even with an effort that hurt. "No, I can't get through to them. You need a special permit for long distance now, and anyone in the life sciences doesn't have a prayer of getting one. It's better not to even ask." She picked up her hairbrush mechanically and put it into the suitcase. "Besides—maybe it's better if you don't know where I'm going. I'll get the rest of my things—I don't know . . . sometime later." She took a deep breath, forcing herself to breathe out through her mouth slowly, but not letting Denny see her effort.

Denny made a small gesture as he picked up a bag of Hershey bars—Juliet's chocolate addiction was one of the first things he'd discovered when she moved in—and handed it to her. "Here. You'd better take these. I'll never eat them, and they say it's getting hard to find stuff in the stores."

Blindly she took the plastic bag, careful not to touch his fingers. He shifted on the bed, still not looking directly at her. "I still think you're overreacting."

She shook her head, folding a skirt. "No. I don't want you losing any more accounts because of me."

"But Julie, we don't know that's it for sure."

She stopped, sobs rising, looking directly at his dark, handsome features. "No, that's the really nasty part. They're always *so* damn polite!" She slammed the skirt into the suitcase without looking at it. "But we know, don't we? We know . . ."

He didn't argue, and after a second Juliet realized she was waiting for him to. She shook her head and walked over to get her jacket out of the closet. Making an attempt to change the subject, she told him the news she'd learned that morning. "Anyway, another biochemist—Phyllis, you remember? Well, she didn't show today either. And no one's heard from her. Just like Ruth and all the others. Classes in the medical school are still suspended until the 'resolution of the current crisis.' If I'm going to go, I'd better make it now."

"Maybe Phyllis just went away," said Denny, not looking up. Juliet stared down at his bent head, resisting an urge to touch his wavy hair just once more . . .

She felt absurdly protective of him in his self-enforced blindness. "Denny. Have you ever thought that maybe she— and Ruth—were *taken* away?"

Denny looked uncomfortable, but still stubborn. "There's nothing to those rumors, Julie!"

She snapped the suitcase with a final click. "You think not? Shall I stay, then?"

The seconds dragged by, then she heard his voice, so low

she had to strain to pick up the words. "I think . . . you should do . . . whatever makes you happy . . ." His voice died away.

"No, Den," she said, picking up the suitcase. "Sometimes you can't do the things that make you happy. Sometimes . . ." she bit her lip, ". . . you have to do the things that make you *un*happy—because they're the things you *must* do." She turned away, the suitcase thudding against her blue-jeaned leg. "I'll see you, Denny," she whispered, and left.

DANIEL BERNSTEIN PROUDLY POLISHED HIS VISITOR SIDEARM, THEN took a swig from a glass of burgundy as he inspected the results. The bottle, half-full, sat beside him on the carpet. He looked up with interest as his father turned on the television set and Kristine Walsh's voice filled the room:

". . . and there were even fewer incidents of violence today. It seems that people everywhere are starting to report in to the authorities when they suspect someone might be involved with the conspiracy. This early warning will save countless lives, and the admiral urges—"

"Dammit!" Stanley angrily switched off the television set. "I'm so *tired* of her face, and only hearing *one* side of what's going on!"

Daniel didn't understand why his father was upset. Carefully he holstered his sidearm, and then poured himself more of the wine. "The truth's the truth, isn't it?"

"Then why not let some others say it?" Stanley peered at the level of wine in the bottle with some disbelief. "Don't you think you've had enough of that, Daniel?"

Daniel looked at the bottle as though he expected it to answer for him. "No," he said finally.

"Well, *I* do." His father reached out suddenly and snatched both the bottle and the glass away from Daniel, who glowered at him sullenly.

"You know, Stanley, there *is* the newspaper," said Lynn Bernstein placatingly.

The elder Bernstein gave his wife a disgusted look. "Yeah. It says exactly the same thing *she* says—sometimes word-for-word! And not just that! It's everything! Look at these bills!" He grabbed a handful of the bills Lynn was working on, shaking them at her. "The price is up on everything! Can't make a long-distance phone call without a permit—and when you get the permit, most times you can't get through!"

He paced angrily back and forth, ignoring Daniel, who watched him, narrow-eyed. "It's not even safe on our own block anymore! Dad told me that the Maxwells' kid, Polly, got beat up at school when her project won the science fair! That's crazy! And last night, when that carload of drunks rode by, yelling—well, they didn't just make noise over there. They smashed in their bay window. Dad told me Kathleen said she was scared to death. Crazy! That's what it is!"

"But Stanley, you know Robert is . . ." She trailed off apologetically.

"A scientist? That what you were about to say? Well, so what if he is? We've lived across the street from them for ten years now, and you couldn't ask for a nicer guy—the idea of Bob being involved with a conspiracy is ludicrous! This whole thing is nuts!" Stanley paused, breathing hard.

"You always said this would pass." Lynn frowned up at him, peering over the top of her reading glasses.

"Yeah." Stanley sighed. "Well, it'd better hurry up and pass before we sink. I want things back the way they were."

Lynn glanced around. "Where's Daniel?"

Bernstein made a face. "Well, he's not out looking for a job, that's for sure."

His wife lowered her voice. "Stanley, you have to be more careful what you say in front of him."

"*What?* In my own house?"

"But *he* lives here too, and you know how involved he is with . . . them."

He made an impatient, yet conciliatory gesture. "All right, all right . . . I know. But he shouldn't have the right to—"

Lynn watched the light flash on her wedding band. Her voice was soft as she interrupted, "I've heard stories . . ."

"Rumors, you mean."

"*Stories*, Stanley, that a member of his group had actually . . ." She twisted the ring, swallowing.

"Actually what? Informed, you mean?"

She nodded. "On his own parents—and then they disappeared."

Bernstein rubbed the back of his neck roughly, then dropped into a seat beside her. "Well, Lynn, I hardly think that *Daniel*—"

She shivered. "I don't think so either, but . . ."

"I mean, what's to inform on?" He tried to sound casual, but even to his own ears the words sounded unconvincing. "*We're* not scientists, and it's not like I said anything . . ." He frowned, trying to recall exactly what he *had* said. His mouth was suddenly dry.

"You were very critical. Of her—Kristine Walsh. Of them. The papers. Of him, also."

"Well, I don't think he ought to drink that much. Seems like every time I turn around, the liquor's disappearing faster than I can replace it! And with the prices so bad!"

"But that's not all that you said."

"Look, all I said was that I was tired of hearing—"

"One side of the news. *Their* side."

"Well, I meant . . . hearing only one opinion. No, I meant . . ." he trailed off, his eyes flicking around the comfortable room as though it were a place he'd never seen before. "You don't think he'd call them, do you?"

They both stared at the telephone. There were three additional extensions in the house—one in Abraham's room, next door, which they would have heard—but the other two were in the kitchen and their bedroom. On the other side of the house. Bernstein tried to think, to calm himself. In the middle of his effort, Daniel came back into the living room.

Lynn spoke with a pathetic attempt at normalcy. "Danny, honey, where have you been?"

Daniel sat down on the couch with the paper, not looking up. "To the bathroom."

Stanley turned to his wife, and moved his lips exaggeratedly, while barely breathing the words: "Do you think he's lying?"

She stared for a second at Daniel, then looked back at her husband and shrugged.

Bernstein leaned back in his chair, fighting back fear. *This is terrible. What am I going to do? Why is this happening to me?*

ROBIN MAXWELL TRUDGED SLOWLY UP THE STREET, HER ARMS filled with books. Usually she only did her homework to keep her parents from bugging her, but lately, the way things were going, even her textbooks had begun to feel more friendly than the school and the neighborhood.

The only boy she knew who wasn't acting like she had the plague or something was Daniel. Robin's pretty mouth thinned—she was angry at Daniel Bernstein. He'd managed to mention, in front of Brian, that Robin's dad was an anthropologist. She hadn't seen Brian in several weeks now.

Robin shook back her dark hair, and her indigo eyes were stormy. *Damn you, Daniel Bernstein!* The grody little creep must've thought that if he turned Brian off her, that she, Robin, would have no one to turn to but *him*. Well, she'd teach him to think again, that was for sure . . .

If it hadn't been for Brian's absence, Robin would have felt worse about the situation at school—but even the pain of having kids she'd known all her life treat her like crap was nothing to the ache she felt whenever she thought of Brian. Thoughts of the handsome Visitor tormented her dreams at night, and filled her mind's eye by day. Every time she looked at that great Mother Ship hanging in the sky—and you couldn't go anywhere without seeing it—Robin thought of him.

She was so deeply engrossed in her current visions of him that Robin almost walked by her house. Her father's voice jolted her out of a daydream where Brian was there, everywhere, his arms around her, smiling down at her— "Robin, get in the car!"

She looked up to see the family station wagon loaded down with clothing, camping gear, and valuables. Her father was lashing a large bundle to the luggage rack on top of the vehicle. "What?" Robin said blankly. "Where are we going, Dad?"

"To the mountain cabin, honey." Maxwell gave a final tug at the knots, then fumbled in his jacket for the keys. Robin looked beyond him to the cardboard-covered hole that had been their bay window.

"For the weekend?" Robin asked, somehow knowing the answer would be negative.

"Maybe, honey. But more probably we'll be staying there awhile. Your Mom and I packed for you. Hop in, unless you have to make a bathroom run."

"No," responded Robin, feeling something shatter inside her. *If I leave, I'll never see him again. I'll die.* She moved a few steps toward the car door, then suddenly balked. "But I don't *want* to go up to the mountains. Please, Dad. I hate our place up there. It's *boring!*"

Her father's mouth thinned, and Robin took an involuntary step back. But his voice was even. "Get in the car, Robin."

Her mother opened the car door and came around, the expression in her green eyes gentle, but unyielding. "Please, Robin, try to understand. Too many things are happening. A scientist your father works with was arrested for conspiracy this morning."

Polly poked her head out the open car window. "I think we ought to stay and fight, Dad! You haven't done anything wrong!"

Kathleen bit her lip in silent anguish, looking back at her home, then her chin came up. "It's not that simple, Poll."

"But Daddy's no conspirator!" Robin wailed. "Those others—"

Robert gave her a look. "They weren't either, Robin. Get in the car."

"But all my friends are *here!*"

"Yeah." Polly's voice dripped sarcasm. "Especially the one in the red uniform . . ."

Robin whirled on her sister. "Shut *up*, Polly!" She turned back to her father. "Please, Dad. I could stay with Karen and her—"

"*Robin.*" The girl had never heard that tone from her father before. "*Now.*"

Robin clenched her fists helplessly against her textbooks as she stalked around the car and jerked the door open. She climbed in, ignoring both Polly, who stuck her tongue out at her older sister, and Katie, who wanted to "sit in Binna's lap, Mommy!"

Robert put the car in gear and backed it out. His tension was reflected in the squeal of the tires as he gunned the motor. Kathleen recognized a figure watching them from across the street, leaning on a rake, and waved sadly. The man waved back. Robert glanced over at her. "Who was that?"

"Sancho Gomez. He came around a couple of months ago looking for gardening work, and I hired him for a couple of hours a week, on Fridays. He worked for a couple of families on this street . . . did a really good job with the roses . . ."

Robert frowned. "But I was just noticing that our roses really needed cutting back."

"They do . . . did." Kathleen brushed distractedly at her hair. "Sancho told me a couple of weeks ago that he couldn't work for me anymore—that his other customers, among them Eleanor Dupres, had told him if he kept working for us, he couldn't work for them anymore. What could he do? The guy's got a wife and kids . . ."

Maxwell nodded tightly. They drove in silence for nearly twenty minutes, until they reached the outskirts of L.A., and topped a small hill. Suddenly Polly pointed. "Look, Dad! It's a police roadblock!"

Kathleen made a tiny sound in her throat as she stared down the street to the Visitor squad vehicle that had landed across the highway, blocking all but one lane. A line of traffic sat waiting, bumper-to-bumper. Two police black-and-whites sat on the side of the road, lights flashing red-blue-red-blue-red . . . A helmeted Visitor shock trooper stood by the nose of the squad vehicle, his stun rifle carried muzzle-up. His helmet swung back and forth as he watched the L.A.P.D. officers check cars, two at a time.

Maxwell's fingers tightened on the wheel of his car, and he didn't dare look at his family, afraid they'd see the naked fear in his eyes. Without a word he swung the station wagon off the road, put on his blinker, then, as other oncoming vehicles slowed to take in the scene below, swung the wheel savagely in a U-turn.

*They can't have blocked every road*, his mind argued against his growing panic. *One of the smaller secondary ones . . .*

Ten minutes later they pulled over to the side of the road,

staring in dismay at the roadblock ahead of them. "Another one," Kathleen said tightly.

"Daddy, why don't you just drive through?" Robin asked. "You haven't done anything—"

Polly gave her sister a withering look. "Boy, Robin, you sure are *stupid*. Were you born that way, or did you have to study?"

Robin stared at her sister in shock, then flared angrily. "God, Polly, how can you be so *totally*—"

"Shut up," Robert commanded without raising his voice. "I have to think."

"How come they want to keep us in the city, Mom?" Polly asked.

"Makes it easier to find us," Kathleen said.

"Why do they want to be able to find us—and people like us?"

"We don't know, Poll." Kathleen cast a quick, frightened look at Robert.

Shouts broke the silence, and they watched a man leap out of the back of one of the cars stopped at the roadblock, running frantically down the road toward them. Horrified, they watched as the Visitor trooper sighted carefully at the fleeing man's back, then fired. A pulse of sound filled the air with a brief flash of blue electricity, then the smell of ozone. The man staggered on a few steps, then fell against Robert's door, his anguished face pressing briefly against the glass, then slid bonelessly down to the road, leaving a trail of saliva and mucus on the window.

The Maxwells sat frozen with shock, unable to move or think, as the Visitor shock trooper and the two police officers ran up to the fallen man. The Visitor got there first. Without a glance at the horrified Maxwells, he pushed the man's face brutally against the pavement. The first cop came up with the handcuffs. They heard the man whimper as they dragged his arms behind him, wrenching his back where a black burn showed the impact of the alien weapon.

Sickened, Maxwell recognized that oily blackness of charred cloth and singed meat—and knew, with a terrible certainty, what had happened to Arch Quinton. The other police officer approached, stood looking down at the injured man, his face expressionless, but something flickering in his eyes that might have been pity. "Another scientist?" he asked.

"No," answered the officer with the handcuffs. "He was *helping* one try and run the roadblock. So that makes him one of 'em, in my book. On your feet, pal!" He dragged brutally at the now sobbing man.

"Easy, Bob—" the first officer remonstrated. "He's wounded."

"That's his fault, Randy. He wants to break the new laws, he's gotta take the consequences."

Randy gave a quick glance over at the Visitor trooper, who was walking back toward the squad vehicle, to make sure the alien was out of earshot. "Come on, Bob! This is different!"

"No it ain't!" The man glared at his partner. "A crook's a crook, and don't you forget it. Ain't nothing different except the guys who give the orders."

Without a backward glance, he dragged the barely conscious man away. The officer named Randy looked after him, then back at the Maxwells, obviously troubled. "You folks coming down the road?" he asked, indicating the roadblock.

"Uh . . . no," answered Robert, thinking fast, pasting a fatuous grin on his face. "The . . . uh . . . little woman forgot her grocery list, can you believe it? We're gonna have to go back and get it." Heart threatening to erupt from his chest, he put the car in reverse.

The officer looked at him a moment, then nodded sadly. "Yeah, okay. Prices what they are today, you can't shop without a list, all right." He glanced back at the roadblock, then at Maxwell. "You all take care, now."

Robert backed up and turned the car around, and they started back toward town. Kathleen gave a choked, hysterical laugh. "Little woman! Oh, God, Bob, what are we—"

"Don't start, Kathy! Or we'll all be doing it!" Maxwell swallowed.

"Where're we going to go? Who's going to help us?" Robin wailed plaintively. Maxwell felt a strong urge to spank—or slap—her, but repressed it. *It's not her fault—this whole thing is as far outside her experience as it is yours*, he thought.

"I don't know, Binna," he said as gently as he could.

Kathleen suddenly straightened beside him. "*I* do. Head back for the house, Robert."

He looked curiously at her, but obeyed, turning on the blinker and swinging the car back onto the crosstown freeway, toward the house that, until this morning, had been his home.

# 11

JULIET PARRISH PEERED CAREFULLY THROUGH A CRACK IN THE VE-
netian blinds. A few blocks away, a police siren shrieked, but
as Juliet listened and watched, the sound began to diminish.
She dropped the slat back into place with a sigh of relief. "It's
all right, I think."

The others in the dry-cleaning shop also relaxed perceptibly. Ben Taylor, sitting beside a steam-pressing machine,
made an exaggerated gesture of wiping his forehead, producing a few wry grins. Then, sobering, he began to speak. "All
right. We know what's happening: censorship, suppression of
the truth—the whole United States ruled by a totalitarian dic-
tatorship under martial law. The military are apparently under arrest, or else they've made them disappear—"

"Talk about paranoia," a dark-haired woman in her forties
broke in, "all the scientists I know are scared to death. With
good reason."

"Yeah, they're still disappearing," said Brad, a young police
officer with curly brown hair and worried eyes. "Like my
partner and all the other cops who wouldn't go along with
their 'requests'—that's how they phrase it. A real joke, huh?"

Nobody laughed. The dark-haired woman—Juliet couldn't

remember her name—twisted her hands together. "Yesterday they took another family from my building. He was a doctor . . ."

Ben Taylor looked over at Juliet. "Why do you think they're so hot to arrest scientists? Especially life science researchers, anthropologists, and physicians? They haven't paid nearly the same kind of attention to theoretical physicists, for example, or astronomers."

Juliet nodded agreement, thinking. "They must think we're a threat. That people with expertise in the life sciences might . . . find out something about them—" She shrugged, her mind groping for an answer.

"Like maybe how to stop them?" Ben asked.

Juliet chuckled dryly. "I only hope we turn out to be as big a threat as they seem to worry we'll be!"

One of the women, a black receptionist who had announced that she worked for the telephone company, shook her head. "There's no way we're going to stop them . . . There's too many of 'em."

"No!" Ben glared at her. "There *has* to be a way!"

"There is." Juliet tried to sound positive. Her bluff was called when they all turned to her, their eyes hopeful. She thought faster than she ever had in her life. "We . . . organize," she said, feeling her way into the idea as she talked. "Look, any complex biological structure—our bodies, for instance—starts with individual cells. The cells will reproduce—expand themselves—join with others—"

Brad snorted. "That's great for a biology lesson, Julie, but—"

Juliet whirled on him. "*Listen*, Brad—" She took a deep breath, then started over. "Sorry. Look, I know we're embryonic. There are only a handful of us here in this shop. But you can be sure we're not the only ones who are meeting in darkened rooms at this moment! We can't be the only ones who have come up with the idea of fighting this thing!"

Mumbled agreements came from all quarters. Juliet nodded. "Now what we've got to do is *find* those others, and still
more after that. Then we'll need equipment—"

"Weapons," said Brad.

"Supplies," said the dark-haired woman.

"A headquarters," said Ben.

"Yes," Juliet agreed. "We're going to need all those things.
But I was especially thinking about laboratory equipment and
medicines—microscopes, culture dishes—all scientific stuff.
That way we can work on trying to figure out why the Visitors
want to eliminate the scientists first. We're a threat to them,
and we've got to discover that threat!"

"Right!" "Yeah!" "Good thinking, Julie!" they all chorused.
The former med student paused, waiting for some of the others to make contributions, but nothing was forthcoming. She
began thinking fast again. "We ought to also figure out who is
closest to the Visitors, and try to see if they'll join us. That
way we'd be able to keep an eye on their actions."

The black woman nodded. "Like that reporter—what's her
name? Kristine—"

"Walsh," Ben supplied. "Sure as hell, she's on the inside."

"Maybe too much on the inside," Brad said glumly. "Think
we could trust *her*? Maybe she's a hundred percent in favor of
what they're doing."

"How could she be?" Ben asked grimly. "If she is, she's the
worst traitor since—I dunno—"

"Judas?" suggested the dark-haired woman.

"I agree with Ben," said Juliet. "We ought to at least watch
her, see if she seems like the sort of person we should risk
contacting. Then, if the group agrees that she's okay, we'll ask
her for her help."

She waited, but nobody volunteered. Juliet decided that
leadership definitely wasn't all it was cracked up to be, and
stood up. "I'll find her, and watch her. See if she's someone

we can trust. Why don't we meet back here . . . uh . . . Thursday night. Eight sharp?"

"Okay by me," said Brad, who was the only one in the group assigned to work nights. The rest agreed.

"And everybody has to bring at least—" Juliet thought rapidly, "four other people with them. How about that? Agreed?"

"Agreed," they echoed.

"Good," Juliet said. "Guess that's it for now."

She stood in the dimness, the smell of cleaning fluid and steam all around her, watching them file out of the shop and into the alley, warily, one-by-one, exhibiting a caution none of them (with the possible exception of Brad) had ever needed before—and tears filled Juliet's eyes. *It's not fair*, she thought. *We shouldn't have to do this. It's not fair at all . . .*

MIKE DONOVAN DROPPED COINS INTO THE SLOT OF A PAY PHONE, then dialed the number scrawled on the back of a crumpled dollar bill. He counted rings, then, when it was picked up on the twelfth, sighed with relief. Anything but the twelfth ring, and he wouldn't have spoken. "Hello?" said Tony's voice. "Is that you, Uncle Pedro?"

"Uncle Pedro?" Donovan frowned, trying to remember if this was one of their old code responses. He didn't recognize it.

"Ah, it *is* you, Uncle Pedro! *¡Buenas noches!*"

"Tony, cut the—" Donovan stopped suddenly as another thought occurred to him.

"We've been having trouble with the phone. You comprende? *Uncle Pedro*? Trouble with the phone."

"Yeah?" said Donovan heavily. "*Pobrecito* . . . you must be all tapped out, eh?"

He could almost see Tony's careful nod. "You got it, Uncle. The 'repairmen' even came to check things out—a lot of 'em—and they smelled your cooking all around here. Boy, they sure would like to get their hands on *your* burrito—"

"Yeah, I'm sure they would."

"But I like *Italian* food even better than your Mexican cooking, Uncle . . . remember?"

Donovan grinned. "Yeah, I remember. You still owe me a steak, do you remember? A *twelve ounce* one. Pay up, amigo."

"Right, Uncle. Well, don't let me keep you standing there— I know you have to run. Good luck . . ." The phone clicked off.

Donovan started to hang up when suddenly, with no warning siren, a police car skidded around the corner, two wheels on the sidewalk, heading straight for him.

Mike took off, heading down the opposite street—but a squad vehicle swooped down, firing! Donovan zigged, and the powerful electric blasts rocked a nearby car. Donovan threw himself away from it just in time—it exploded, spraying deadly edged metal all over the street.

Donovan dashed down the nearest alley, one too narrow for the squad vehicle to enter. More and more sirens sounded like they were converging on the area. At the end of the alley was a board fence. *This is getting monotonous*, Mike thought, leaping to scramble over it. *I haven't had to get over so many obstacles since Basic—*

He hit the ground on the other side, and dashed away, grinning. At least he'd been able to reach Tony . . . the first thing he was going to do following their twelve o'clock meeting tomorrow was buy some new clothes and a bath—then for a real meal . . .

His mind filled with visions of steak, Donovan crouched behind a garbage-filled Dumpster, waiting for the onset of darkness, and safety.

SHADOWS LENGTHENED ON THE LAWN OF THE BERNSTEINS' HOUSE, but there was still a good hour of daylight left. Not that you could tell here in the pool house, Kathleen thought. Off to her right a broken barbecue leaned drunkenly against a wall, and the place was filled with old lawn furniture.

Abraham Bernstein nodded at her reassuringly. "Lynn and Stanley never use this old cabana—it's just for storage. Nobody comes here. You will be safe."

Kathleen smiled gratefully at him. "Thank you, Abraham. We can never repay you for this."

The old man smiled, waving aside her gratitude. "I will bring supplies, when everyone is asleep. Sheets, and soap, towels. There is a bathroom in there, used only when they have pool parties. And with this curfew . . . there are no more parties."

Kathleen had a sudden, vivid memory of Eleanor's party the night she'd first seen the Visitors, and sighed. Robin blundered into a cobweb and jumped back with a little shriek. "Daddy!" She lowered her voice, but Kathleen knew Abraham's hearing was excellent. "It's grody! Gross! We can't *live* here . . . It's filthy!"

"We'll clean it up," Kathleen said. "It will be fine."

"But there's no way it's ever gonna look decent—"

"Robin! That's enough!" Robert snapped, then turned to Abraham. "I apologize, Abraham. My daughter isn't usually so rude. It's just that . . ."

"It's all right, I understand," Abraham said graciously.

"I'm afraid *I* don't," said Stanley Bernstein, peering in. "Father, can I talk with you? Outside?"

They walked a few paces away from the cabana, but Kathleen could still hear the conversation, Abraham's low, accented tones contrasting with Stanley's shriller, accusing ones.

"I really don't believe you brought them here, Father!"

"They have nowhere to go. Their home is being watched, to see if they try to return there."

"But so is ours! Daniel's here whenever he isn't off with his alien buddies! Tell the Maxwells we're sorry . . ."

"Stanley, son, you don't understand. They have to stay. They need a place to hide, and we are the only place—"

"But Robert Maxwell is a *scientist*, and therefore suspect! And now he's a *fugitive scientist*! That makes him doubly dangerous."

Abraham's voice held a dogged, quiet persistence. "They have to stay."

"And I am telling you to get them out of here before—"

"I won't!"

Stanley turned back to the pool house. "Then *I* will!"

Abraham exploded. *"No, you won't!"*

Kathleen had never heard kindly little Mr. Bernstein use that tone before. She flinched back involuntarily from the fury in it—even though it wasn't directed at her. Stanley Bernstein stared at his father in shock.

Abraham began to speak in a monotone that was all the more passionate for its very lack of expression. "We had to put you in a *suitcase*. In a *suitcase*! An eight-month-old baby. And that's how the underground smuggled you out. But they couldn't help the rest of us . . ."

Stanley made an uncomfortable movement. "I know this story, Father."

*"No, you don't!"* His voice returned to a low monotone. "You don't, Stanley. Your mother . . . *auv shalom* . . . your mother didn't have a heart attack while we were in the boxcar. No. She made it to the camp with me. I can still see her . . . standing naked in the freezing cold, ice on the ground . . ."

He took a deep breath. "Her beautiful black hair was gone. They'd shaved her head. I can see her . . . waving to me, as they marched her with the others—all those people—to the showers. The showers with no water, you understand."

The old man's eyes were focused only on the past. "And perhaps . . . if somebody had given *us* a place to hide . . . she could still be alive today." He looked back at Stanley. "They have to stay, you see? Or else we haven't learned a thing . . ."

Stanley Bernstein rubbed wearily at his face, then made an inarticulate little sound in the back of his throat, nodding. He blinked, his lips moving, but there was no sound. Abraham nodded past him, reassuringly, toward the cabana. Kathleen smiled back, clutching Robert's hand, trying to blink away the tears in her eyes.

"BUT ELIAS, WE REALLY NEED YOUR HELP!" BENJAMIN TAYLOR SAID, lengthening his strides to keep pace with his brother.

Music, remotely of Hispanic origin, blared from loudspeakers along the row of shopfronts. The Visitors were sponsoring an International Day in the shopping district— festivities (food, dancing, and exhibits) were going on around the corner. Ben had noted grimly that the proportion of Visitor attendees to human was almost two to one.

Elias gave a shudder of mock shock and surprise. "What? The great big doctor needs *my* help? How come it is, Ben my man?"

Ben swallowed, realizing Elias was baiting him. "'Cause you've got contacts here on the street."

His brother's lips drew back in a wolfish grin. "Damn right I do! But listen, brother Benjamin, ain't you the one who is always putting down my 'street contacts' and how I come by them?"

"Yeah. Look, Eli, the times have changed." Ben tried to look as humble as he could, despite the anger bubbling inside him. Elias's help in this could make all the difference.

"Well, the streets ain't changed. There's just a different man to be The Man. Fact is, the streets is doin' fine right now, better than before. Man can make a whole lotta money out here right about now."

Ben nodded grimly. "Black market."

"You should pardon the expression, Ben," Elias said. "You know how much fresh fruit is goin' for? And beef?" He laughed shortly. "I make more sellin' hamburger these days than I do pushin' reefer!"

"Well, you can keep on doing all of that you want, Elias, but there's a group of us who're trying to fight this thing—"

Elias broke in. "That's no never mind to me, man. Why fight it? It don't affect me none—'cept to line my pockets."

Ben put a hand on his arm, swinging Elias around to face him. "Eli—what is happening to this country . . . this world . . . is wrong."

"Says who?"

"We *need* your help."

Elias glared at him, dropping the street jive in his intensity. "Where were you when I needed yours?"

"Elias, I was always there for you!"

"But just a *little* unapproachable . . . Golden Boy."

"That's only in your head, man!"

"Shit!" Elias's dark eyes flashed. "I heard once I musta heard a thousand times, 'Why can't you be like Brother Benjamin, da doctuh?'" He took a fierce step forward and Ben stepped backward in reflex. "*Huh*? And now *you* need *my* help?!"

Ben nodded, his voice low. "That's right."

Elias took a quick little shuffling step sideways, away from his brother, his "jivin' mask" dropping over his features again. "Well, gee man, I'd sure like to help you out, but I gots to go up to the *medical libraree*—study mah *anatomee* . . ." He turned away. "Catch you *later*, Bro!"

Ben watched his forced, jaunty walk, feeling tired, guilty,

and sad. He'd never realized before the depth of his brother's
jealousy and anger.

MIKE DONOVAN HESITATED IN THE DARKNESS, LOOKING UP AT THE
balcony of Kristine's loft apartment. A vaguely human shape
crossed the frosted glass of the window, deciding him. His
meeting today with Tony had been unsuccessful—Leonetti had
walked down the street toward their favorite Italian place just
at noon, right enough, but as Mike loitered on the street corner, then shuffled toward him, Tony's almond-shaped eyes had
flicked quickly to the side, his lips forming a silent "no." Then
Mike saw the shock troopers patrolling behind Tony—just before they'd seen him. He'd managed to elude them (thank
goodness the layouts of human cities seemed to baffle them
still), but at this point he was so famished that he knew another day without food would make him easy prey.

The rungs of the fire escape quivered beneath his weight as
he climbed, the metal harsh and cold beneath his hands.
Thunder muttered overhead, and then a quick flash of lightning showed him he was almost to the fourth floor. He
reached the balcony, swung over the rail, then crouched for
long seconds in the gathering threat of the storm. The shape
silhouetted by the light moved again, within, and Donovan
reached out and tested the balcony door. Locked—of course.
He crouched, then sprang, putting his weight against the bolt,
and the French doors sprang inward.

Mike went through them with a rush, hearing a horrified
gasp—a woman's voice, thank God, and human. Then,
blinded by the sudden light, he fell over a row of potted plants
sitting before the doors.

He looked up, heard Kristine's voice. "Mike! My God, you
scared the hell out of me!" She bent down to help him up,
and as his eyes adjusted to the sudden light, he realized she

was damp and wearing only a pale green towel, held loosely across her breasts. As tense as the moment was, Donovan couldn't help noticing that the view was impressive.

"What are you doing here?" she asked.

"I'd like to say it's just to take another shower with you, but I need help. You got any money? Please, Kris. I haven't eaten in two days."

"Jesus, you look it." She turned, went to her purse, and bent over, fumbling in it. The towel slipped further. She came back and handed him a wad of cash, which he stuffed in his filthy jeans. Her nose wrinkled.

Donovan grinned. "A mess, aren't I?"

"Yes," she agreed frankly, grinning, "but I'm so glad to see you I don't care." She leaned toward him and their lips met in a long, warm kiss. Donovan touched her shoulder, pulling her to him, and her arms went around him. With one part of his mind, Mike realized that the closeness of their bodies was all that was keeping the towel up at all. He checked the slippage factor again, his fingers gentle on her skin.

But even in his rising excitement, the reactions of a fugitive were still with him—his eyes roamed around the room behind her head, noting the furniture, the television set, the peacefulness, and he listened . . .

Sensing his distraction, she stepped back, grabbing quickly for the towel. "I've been so worried for you!"

Mike smiled grimly. "I've been worried for me too."

"Why are they so hot to capture you?"

He stared directly into her green eyes—oddly, they were almost the exact shade of his own. "Because I've seen their faces."

"What? What faces? What do you mean?"

"They aren't human, Kris. I shot a VTR of them eating small animals *whole*—alive. Then, while I was trying to get off the Mother Ship, one of 'em spotted me—their real eyes must be able to see farther into the infrared than we do—or maybe they just have better night vision—but this guy saw me, dragged me through a ventilation grille *one-handed*, and did his damnedest to kill me. During the fight I tore at his face—and the mask came off. They're reptiles of some sort, Kris." He shivered at the memory. "I got it on film. Greenish-black skins, and red-orange eyes. Tongues this long"—he measured off a space with his hands—"that spray some kind of venom."

She was shaking her head. "Mike, honey—"

"You don't believe me, do you?"

"Well, it's so incredible . . . *reptilian*? With tongues that— I want to believe you, but—"

"It's all true! I've seen it, Kris!"

"I really do believe you *think* you've seen it—"

"*Think* I've— Damn it, Kris!"

They glared at each other, and the sound of their breathing was loud in the quiet room. "Mike, I work so closely with these people, every day . . . It's hard to—" She hesitated.

"Be objective?" he said sarcastically.

For long moments they stared at each other, then he turned back to the window. "I guess this was just a waste of time. Thanks for the loan. I'll get it back to you someday—with interest."

She came after him, grabbing him by the arm. "No, don't leave yet, Mike."

"Why?" He turned back to her.

"If I could see the tape you shot . . ."

"It's hidden."

She moved closer to him, her hand sliding up his arm to his shoulder. "Listen, Mike. It's possible you're right. I may have gotten closer to them than I should." She grimaced wryly. "It's funny, *you're* the one I always wanted to get closer to . . ."

Her open admission took him a little off-guard. "You've got a funny way of showing it, Kris," he said.

"I'd really like another chance," she said, then laughed self-deprecatingly. "That seems to be my favorite line."

She kissed him again, and again Mike wanted to lose himself in the kiss—in her warmth—and again, that sentry inside him wouldn't sleep. He opened his eyes mid-kiss, seeing the darkened glass of Kristine's television set. And in it—the reflection of a uniformed shock trooper crouched on the balcony. The alien was taking aim with a stun rifle.

Donovan swung around, pushing Kristine away so roughly that her towel fell completely off. Donovan was too busy to look; grabbing a barstool, he swung it viciously at the French doors and they exploded outward, showering the Visitor with glass.

Simultaneously the apartment door resounded with a crescendo of thuds and reverberating demands to open up. Donovan gave Kristine a disgusted glance, wondering if she had set him up. "Thanks," he said, his voice harsh.

He headed for the shock trooper who was struggling to his feet on the balcony.

"Mike!" she called.

Donovan ignored her. Grabbing the still-dazed alien's weapon, he headed for the fire escape—when suddenly he felt arms grasp him from behind. Whirling, he brought the butt of the alien weapon up, chopping hard at the trooper's head. The alien went staggering backward, hit the balcony rail, and went over.

Donovan felt vaguely sick, but had no time to spare. He swarmed down the ladder, hearing the ruckus in Kristine's apartment above him.

A shot from a stun rifle struck barely two feet from him, flaming and slagging the ground where it hit. Donovan looked up, saw a figure momentarily outlined by a sullen flare of lightning, stationed on the roof of the opposite building, then awkwardly tried to aim the weapon he held. He pressed a stud, saw a flare of blue from the muzzle, smelled the ozone. A clean miss—but the bolt sheared off a metal air duct on the roof, which fell, striking the Visitor on its way down. Mike heard the creature give a peculiar ululating cry as it staggered, lost its balance—then the thud as the trooper hit.

Donovan raced for the gate of the apartment complex, still clutching the Visitor's gun, as several shots resounded from Kristine's balcony. Reaching the gate, he bolted through, turning and twisting to avoid the shots—but the aliens were losing his range. His breath choking in his throat, Donovan forced himself to keep running, and soon even the faint echoes of his footsteps were gone.

A DARK-GARBED FIGURE WITH A GLEAM OF BLONDE HAIR ROSE from the bushes beside Kristine's building, slipped through the gate, then closed it behind her.

Juliet Parrish darted off into the night, hearing the pulse of a stun gun behind her. Looking back, she saw the latch on the gate sizzle and flame brightly. One of the Visitors was taking out his anger at missing his quarry on the wrought-iron fence. Juliet shook her head. She'd recognized the man who had darted away from Kristine Walsh's balcony—his picture had been flashed on wanted bulletins often enough lately. Mike Donovan.

Why had he climbed the ladder to Kristine Walsh's balcony? Juliet grinned sourly to herself. She was fairly sure his actions weren't attributable to a romantic interlude—Donovan was hard to cast as Romeo, the balcony to the contrary. No, Donovan must have gone to Kristine Walsh for help. The man had been a fugitive for several weeks now—he must need money, a place to hide . . .

She wondered what had really happened up there. The two

silhouettes against the French doors had merged into one—and then the troopers had arrived. Of course it was possible that Kristine was completely innocent, that the Visitors had staked out her place without her knowledge, figuring Donovan would go there. But it was equally possible that Kristine Walsh had betrayed Mike Donovan, almost to his death.

Juliet gave a small, dismissing shrug. Whatever had happened up there (and they'd probably never know) was academic. The point of the matter was that they couldn't risk betrayal by contacting Kristine Walsh . . .

A sudden, brutal gust of wind whipped Juliet's hair off her forehead, and as she hurried on into the night, the storm broke, soaking her within moments.

DANIEL BERNSTEIN FUMBLED WITH HIS KEY, MISSING THE LOCK several times before he managed to insert it and open the door. He stumbled into the hall, lit only by the watery glare from the backyard security light, a bit unsteady on his feet. He saw a figure standing by the French doors leading out to the backyard and the pool. He peered blurrily. It was Robin! Robin Maxwell!

Funny. Daniel frowned, trying to think clearly, without a great deal of success. He'd thought the Maxwell family had run away. What was Robin doing here? The lightning from the storm outside silvered her features as she looked out the doors, turning her hair into a dark cloud. She looked awfully good to Daniel. He smiled at her, said, "Hi."

She turned with a start, then giggled nervously when she recognized him. "Oh, hi, Danny. You startled me."

"What are you doing here?" He went over to her, enjoying the way the security light shadowed the full, rounded curves of her breasts. She was wearing those tight designer jeans, the ones he'd always liked, that her mother had raised such a fuss about her buying.

She sighed. "I know I'm not supposed to be here, but I just couldn't stand it in your pool house for another minute." She smiled at him. "So I took a walk."

Daniel focused slowly on her words. "Our pool house? What are you doing there?"

"Living there—if you can call that living." She made a face. "It's too small for *one* of us, let alone *five*! It's totally outrageous . . ." She sniffed audibly. "Oh, hey Danny. You've been drinking."

He shrugged. "Yeah."

A touch of eagerness entered her voice. "With Brian?"

"He wasn't there. He doesn't drink," Daniel told her. "I don't think he can hold it." He snickered.

"Did he ask about me?"

"No." Daniel frowned. "Why should he?"

She shrugged. "I just thought he might, that's all . . ."

Daniel dismissed Brian with a gesture. "Well, not tonight he didn't. I'm real glad to see you. You look real pretty in that sweater . . . and those jeans. I always liked them."

Hesitantly, he touched her arm. She didn't appear to notice. "Other nights, though?" she asked.

Daniel looked blank. "What?"

"He asks about me other nights, then?"

"Who?"

"Brian, Danny! You really *have* had too much to drink!"

He stroked her arm, but still she didn't seem aware of his fingers, only watched his face avidly, waiting for him to answer her. He summoned words, almost at random. "Well . . . sometimes . . . yeah . . . I guess he does. He wondered where you went. We both did." He gave her his most meaningful look. "Me especially. Until I found out you were in my pool house, that is."

She turned back, staring out the window at the rain turning the pool into a multitude of silver ripples. Daniel continued to stroke her arm. "'Member that day when the Visitor ships first came? When we didn't know yet they were going to be our friends?"

"Hmmmm?"

"You said that day that you didn't want to die without having made love. You still feel that, Robin?" The curve of her breast beneath her sweater was so close to his fingers that he felt dizzy just looking at her.

"Sure," she said, still not turning around. Daniel leaned closer, his lips readying for the kiss, then she spoke again. "Is he a virgin, do you think?"

"Who?"

"Brian."

He looked at her abstracted face and dropped his hand from her arm. She didn't even notice . . .

# 12

DOCTOR BENJAMIN TAYLOR PUSHED A LINEN CART HEAPED WITH
dirty sheets and towels along the loading dock of the Stamos
Pharmaceutical Company. With quick, nervous movements,
he swung the cart sharply into the back of a waiting industrial-
sized van, then gave it a sharp push. Juliet, waiting in the
back of the van beside several similar carts, darted forward
to catch it. "Terrific—with all this stuff we should be able to
set up a lab that can do just about anything. Including finding out enough about those guys to uncover some weak-
nesses." She picked up a pile of linen, peering underneath it.
"Good! You managed to snatch that high-powered microscope!"

Ben looked around nervously. "Yeah. We better get a move
on. I'm not sure they bought my act completely. There was
one guy looked kinda suspicious."

She nodded, heading for the driver's side of the van. Brad
McIntyre, the cop, was waiting in the passenger seat, wearing, like Juliet and Ben, a delivery coverall. Climbing in, Juliet
started the van, listening for the sound of Ben shutting the
rear doors. The sound came—but at the same moment, they
heard running feet. Brad and Juliet looked out to see several

Visitor shock troopers burst through the doors onto the loading dock.

Ben pounded the rear of the van. "Go! Go GO *GO!!*"

She looked back to protest, saw Ben running away from the truck, drawing the Visitors' fire. "*Go, Julie!*" screamed Brad. "*We've* got *to save this gear!*"

Juliet gave a cry of protest, but rammed the truck into gear, popping the clutch so hard the big van fairly leaped forward. She hit second with a squeal of rubber, then drove swiftly down the long service drive, past the ramps of the enclosed parking lot next to the warehouse. A few troopers fired at them, but none of their shots even came close.

Juliet drove for several minutes, snaking the big truck through a complicated series of turns and double-backs, until Brad announced that he thought they'd shaken off any possible pursuit. Juliet nodded numbly, turning back toward their headquarters. Brad, looking over at her, saw tears streaking her face, but she made no sound.

Finally she pulled the truck to a stop beside her little white VW convertible, then set the parking brake with a jerk. Brad looked over at her as she swung the door open. "What are you doing, Julie? You don't need your car now!"

She looked up at him, then at her watch. "It's been ten minutes—with any luck they still haven't caught Ben. I'm going back for him. I have to."

"*Julie!*" But she was gone. Cursing, Brad slid into the driver's seat as she swung the little car in front of the truck and shot back down the street in the direction from which they'd come. Slamming both hands into the steering wheel in frustration, Brad watched her go. Then, reluctantly, he drove away in the opposite direction.

Juliet turned back onto the driveway leading up to the loading dock, her blue eyes scanning desperately for a running figure in a navy blue coverall . . .

She gunned the VW up the driveway, then saw movement on the top deck of the huge parking garage, three stories above the driveway. She squinted against the sun—it was Ben!

Juliet beeped the horn to attract his attention, saw that he was running, aiming for a service ladder running down the rainspouts along one of the massive concrete pillars supporting the outside wall of the garage. But even as he leaped to grab the ladder, a blue bolt struck him from the side, spinning him around and over the edge of the three-story drop.

"*BEN!!!*" Juliet slewed the car into a seemingly impossible U-turn, tires protesting, then braked beside her friend's crumpled body. He'd fallen into a heap of rubbish beside the driveway. There was blood everywhere.

She heard the pulsing sound of another stun rifle as she jumped out of the car, ran around it, jerking the passenger door open. Then a distant voice shouted, "Capture them! Diana wants some of them alive to question!" The sound of distant booted feet began to echo inside the garage.

"Ben, Ben!" Juliet knelt by the young doctor, her med school training demanding that the man not be moved—but she had to, there was no alternative. She tried not to see the blood, the white shard of bone peeping out of the arm of the torn blue coverall. Grasping her friend around the chest, she began dragging him backward, toward the car.

The movement roused Taylor slightly, and he tried to speak. "Julie?"

"Easy, Ben," Juliet panted. It was taking every ounce of her strength to drag him—she didn't want to think how she'd manage to boost him into the VW.

"No, Julie. Go on . . . no use . . ." Juliet could barely hear him over the drum of the approaching booted feet.

"God, please . . ." she sobbed, heaving the injured man halfway up, bracing his body on the running board as she took a second, lower grip to complete the job.

Something struck her right hip, and suddenly Juliet found herself lying on the road beside Ben's legs—smelling charred meat. Then the pain connected in her stunned brain, and she gasped and choked in agony—searing flames seemed to be devouring her right side!

With what seemed like agonizing slowness, she managed to get her hands under her body, levering herself up. The pain flooded back in a wave of black flame, and she forced herself to breathe deeply, closing her eyes. *Please, God . . . please. Help me . . .*

With an effort that left her coverall soaking with sweat, Juliet climbed to her feet, then, with a strength she'd never known she possessed, dragged Ben the rest of the way into the seat. Hobbling, she staggered around the car to the driver's side, leaning one hand on the metal for support.

"Hey! She's getting away!" exclaimed a surprised voice, and there came another stun bolt behind her. Starting the car and putting it into gear brought more waves of agony, but she managed it. The little white car roared down the driveway— as a Visitor trooper appeared in the middle of it, having leaped the barrier wall from inside the garage.

With more hatred than she'd ever known, Juliet aimed the VW at the alien, flooring the accelerator. The Visitor jumped wildly aside, dropping his stun rifle, and Juliet felt the thud as the bumper struck his leg. Then she was past, turning the wheel, driving away.

She slowed slightly after the first block or two, wondering where to take Ben. The hospital? Out of the question—there were sure to be troops stationed on every floor and at every entrance and exit. Besides, she didn't know if there were any doctors left. She heard a groan, turned to see Ben's eyes open. She pulled the car over into a parking space, fumbling in her glove compartment for the little first aid kit she carried.

Tenderly Juliet wiped the blood off the young man's face,

feeling the curly softness of his short beard. The touch of her hands seemed to revive him somewhat. "Julie . . ."

"Ben, I don't know where to take you. Can you think of a place where I can get you some help?"

"No . . . good, honey," he said, closing his eyes as though it took too much strength to keep them open and talk at the same time. "I've had it . . . can tell . . ."

"*No*," Juliet said, refusing to believe him. She checked his arm—compound fracture of the radius, but, thank God, the artery wasn't involved. "Your arm is broken, Ben. Are you in much pain?"

"None," he said clearly, then opened his eyes to see Juliet's startled surprise at his answer. "Julie . . . honey . . . my back . . . it's also broken . . . Can't feel . . . anything . . . neck down . . ."

Juliet bit her lip, fighting back sobs—she'd suspected it, from the way his body had hung in her arms, but hadn't wanted to acknowledge the probable truth. "God . . . God, please, Ben—"

"Don't . . ." His eyes closed. "Not . . . much time . . . Want to see my Dad . . . Elias . . ."

"Okay, Ben." Juliet controlled her sobs, feeling the stab of agony in her hip as she restarted the car. "I'll get you there, I promise."

He nodded, then coughed—only his head moved. Flecks of red sprayed onto his face. Juliet wiped them away as she drove, then used the bloody rag to wipe her eyes—tears kept welling up to blind her, and she needed clear sight. She pulled up to a stoplight, taking time during the red to tilt Ben's seat back so it reclined somewhat—she suspected a punctured lung, for his breathing was becoming hoarse and labored. A passerby looked over at them as they idled waiting for the line of traffic to move. She saw the woman's eyes widen, then the woman looked straight ahead again, walking faster. The shadow of a squad vehicle enveloped them, and the craft passed by.

Five minutes later—it seemed like five years—Juliet swung the VW around to the back of Caleb's house, to the garage. Loud rock music blared, so she knew that Elias, at least, was home.

He sat outside with his portable radio, carefully inspecting eggs, then placing them into cartons. He looked up, grinning, as Juliet swung the VW up beside him. "Hey, Julie! Looka-here! Six bucks for a dozen clucks—ain't they beauti—" His voice died as he looked at his brother, sprawled bonelessly in the passenger seat.

"Is Caleb here?" Juliet looked around frantically. "Ben's hurt."

Elias came over to the car, shaking his head in response to her question. Ben's breathing, without the sound of the engine to mask it, was loud, rasping. "What happened, mama?"

"We . . . we were trying to steal some equipment for a lab." Juliet bit her lip as she turned to check Ben's pulse. Her own wound throbbed with ever-increasing pain. She could feel cold sweat starting out on her forehead—clinically, she recognized the symptoms of shock. Ben's pulse was thready and irregular beneath her fingertips. "They shot him."

Elias shook his head, refusing to believe what his eyes told him. Not an uncommon reaction, she remembered, in the relatives of accident victims. "What?" he gave a nervous laugh. "The doctor? Stealin' stuff?" He shook his head in mock disapproval. Juliet could hear the horror underlying his tones—in a minute or two, it would break through into his conscious mind, and he'd fall apart. Elias's voice cracked. "Whoa, brother! You shoulda come to me. Elias would have taught you how to do it *right*, man!"

A wave of pain from her own injury wrenched a whimper

from between Juliet's clenched teeth. Elias glanced at her. "They got *you*, too?"

Ben coughed again, weakly, and Juliet dabbed thin reddish foam off his mouth. Elias backed away, his dark eyes frightened—the horror was very close to the surface now. "Hey, Julie. I think I ought to call an ambulance . . ."

Ben's eyes opened. "No . . . ambulance . . . Made our prognosis, right . . . Doctor?" Juliet grasped the limp fingers.

"But, man—" Elias paced alongside the car, gesturing. "I just don't *get* it, man! What you wanta try pullin' a heist without your little brother?" The unceasing beat of the rock music gave a ghastly mock party effect to the scene.

Ben smiled faintly. "We did it . . . though." His eyes shifted to Juliet's, and, realizing he couldn't feel her holding his hand, she caressed the side of his face. "The truck . . ." He coughed. "Truck . . . got away?"

She nodded emphatically. "Yes, Ben. It's safe."

"But *look* at you, man!" Elias's voice broke. "You a *wreck*, man!"

"Is . . . Papa . . . home?" Ben's voice was very weak. Juliet was about to tell Elias to turn down the radio, then heard the sound in Ben's throat . . . she held him, awkwardly, through the final spasms as Elias paced up and down, talking, talking—never looking at them.

"Ben, you listen here. Do I try doctoring? Course not. An' the next time you got to boost some stuff, you gonna come to me, you got that, Bro? Elias will show you how to do it right. You dig? Like liftin' these eggs this mornin' . . . shoot. Never broke a one, that's how you gotta do it. Smooth, you see. Shoot. I sound like Papa, don't I?"

Juliet lifted her tearstained face, then, very carefully, lowered Ben's head so it rested against the seat again. Automatically she closed the staring dark eyes. "Elias," she said quietly, but Ben's brother was pacing even faster, in rhythm to the music, never lifting his eyes from the ground.

"*Anyway*—you gonna come to me, and then we'll take 'em *all* on together . . . you an' me . . . the Taylor brothers . . . Man, we'll whomp them upside the head, those jokers."

"Elias . . ." Juliet closed her eyes against the darkness that was hovering at the fringes of her vision.

Elias shook his head angrily, never looking at her. "*Man*— I'll teach you how to do it *right*. You won't get messed up again—"

He paced, every stride like a piston striking, his voice rising into one hoarse prolonged cry: "We'll show 'em, won't we, Ben? And they'll say 'Woooo! What blew through here?' An' we say, the Taylor brothers! *Yeah!* The doctor and . . . the other one . . . the other one . . . whatshisname . . ."

Juliet put out a hand toward him. "Elias—"

"*No!*" Whirling, Elias smashed the radio across the garage. Suddenly all was silent. "The 'other one' . . . can die . . . but not the doctor. Doctor can't die . . . not Ben . . . make it be the other . . . but not . . . not Ben . . ." He was sobbing now, the painful, chest-tearing sobs of one who never weeps aloud. "No . . . no. Dammit, Ben!"

He embraced his brother's body frantically, rocking back and forth. Juliet reached through the haze of her own tears to take his hand. His returning grasp at her fingers was the grip of a man who has lost everything else to cling to . . .

ABRAHAM AND RUBY WERE WALKING SLOWLY TOWARD THE SHOP-ping center when they saw the children grouped by the Visitor propaganda posters. One of the boys held a large can of red spray paint, and was busily drawing a moustache and beard on the aggressively handsome features of the Visitor—Abraham thought distractedly that the posters looked as though Brian, Daniel's friend, had posed for them. The gang giggled, and one of them said, "Do it again, Kenny! Those creeps look better that way!"

Without thinking what he was doing, Abraham reached out and grasped the boy's wrist. "No!" The group moved back, half-fearfully, half-aggressively, in the face of adult authority.

Abraham summoned words. "If you are going to defy them, then do it right. You need a symbol . . . we all need one. We used to use this one." Carefully he sprayed a large red "V" over the poster. "Only we did it with our fingers . . . a long time ago. For Victory—you understand?"

Hesitantly they nodded. Abraham handed the can back to Kenny. "Go tell your friends."

Nodding to Ruby, Abraham turned away. Hearing the hiss of the spray paint behind him, he turned, saw another dripping "V" spread across a smiling Visitor. Smiling for the first time in a long while, Abraham and Ruby walked on.

# 13

MIKE DONOVAN DROVE THE SMALL YELLOW SPORTS MODEL quickly, efficiently, swinging off the freeway into a lesser highway, then, after several miles, onto a two-lane street that led into San Pedro, where Sean lived. He drove automatically, mechanically, his mind busy trying to figure his next move. He'd get the key from Sean, try to talk Margie into loaning him a few bucks—*fat chance*, he thought cynically—then try again with Tony at the Italian restaurant . . .

He slowed the car down, really *looking* at the street for the first time, then stopped with a jerk, staring. Smashed windows marred the storefronts of the ice cream parlor and hairdresser's shop . . . A pickup truck and a sedan were overturned, partially blocking the street . . . The row of houses on the right had suffered damage that looked like burns—even the grass underfoot extending onward to the park where Sean played was singed and blackened.

Grabbing the alien stun rifle from the back of the car, Donovan scanned the area, his heart beating so loud it was hard to hear anything else—he forced himself to take deep, slow breaths—then listened . . .

Silence. Utter and total. It was an ugly sound, Donovan

discovered. He forced himself to listen until he was sure there was nobody in the immediate area but himself. The alien rifle propped beside him, he drove slowly toward Margie's house. He parked, got out, rifle held ready (he'd practiced using it out in the fields—it was a snap to aim and fire), then began to walk toward the house. "Sean? Marjorie! Sean? Hello, anybody!"

Silence . . . silence. Donovan was trembling. He wanted to smash something—scream "Why?"—but only stood . . . silence—

A tiny scrape of leather on concrete, then a muffled sob.

Donovan dropped and spun, crouching, his finger nearly tightening on the firing button—then heard a voice. "*No! Don't shoot me, Mr. Donovan!*"

Mike stood up to see Josh Brooks, Sean's thirteen-year-old friend, peering around the side of the house. The boy walked toward him, and Donovan could see that his clothes were rumpled and dirty, his face tearstained. His eyes were glassy with shock—Mike had seen eyes like that on children in Laos, Nam, and Beirut . . .

He made his voice gentle as the boy, like a frightened deer, walked toward him. "Josh . . . I'm glad to see you. Where is everybody?"

"I dunno." His voice, which had already been changing, was high-pitched with fear, cracking on his words. "They're gone . . . all gone . . ."

As he approached, Mike put an arm around his shoulders, hugging him reassuringly. Josh clung to him, his thin body trembling. Donovan held him for a few minutes. "How long ago?" he asked finally.

"Three days."

"You've been all alone in this town for three days?"

Josh nodded, trembling.

"Well, you're not alone anymore, Josh. I've got you, and I'll take care of you." He gave him another reassuring hug, trying to keep from rushing the terrified youngster. "What happened here, son?"

Josh looked down at the ground, then his legs seemed to give out, and he sat down on the curb. Donovan sat beside him, still keeping his arm around him. "Lots of people were getting tired of what the Visitors were doing. So Sunday a bunch of ranch hands in the area—you know the kind of guys—they drove into town and threw a homemade bomb right underneath a squad vehicle. Blew it up. The local supervisor guy was inside."

Josh trembled at the memory. "They blew it up and killed him."

Donovan glanced at the charred ground inquiringly. Josh nodded confirmation. "Then a lot of folks started shouting, stuff about this was America, and we weren't gonna put up with these goddamn Visitors anymore—" He blushed, looked up. "My Mom doesn't let me say things like that, but I'm just telling you what *they* said, you understand . . ."

"Sure," said Mike reassuringly. "Go on, Josh."

"Then everyone was clapping and cheering. Suddenly the lights went out. All at once. Then everyone got scared, and ran." He shuddered again. "Then there were lights in the sky, so bright you couldn't see where you were going. Roaring toward us. They were troop transports, I recognized 'em when they landed. People screamed and ran. Some shot guns at the Visitors—but the shots didn't seem to hurt 'em much. I lost my Mom and Dad. Then your wife . . ." He hesitated. "Sean's mom, she grabbed me and Sean and pulled us into her house. She slammed the door, but they were everywhere—the lights came through the windows—"

He nearly gagged. "I backed up, toward the kitchen—then somebody grabbed at me from behind, and I turned. I could see a shock trooper in the lights, but his helmet shield was up and I could see his eyes—" He covered his own eyes at the memory. "It was awful! Those awful eyes! They were like—"

"Easy, Josh. I know what they look like. You're all right now. Then what happened?"

"I twisted loose and ran. Just then the front door broke down and they came in and took 'em."

Donovan jerked as though he'd been hit, then, pulling Josh up beside him, walked across the street and into the house. As the boy had said, the front door was a battered wreck. The inside of the house had obviously been the scene of a violent struggle. Donovan walked over to the shattered remains of a vase and picked Sean's Dodger cap out of the middle of it, remembering with a tightness in his throat how his son was forever hanging his cap on Marjorie's best vase—much to her displeasure. Josh's voice came from the doorway, choked with sobs. "He fought real hard and kicked at them to leave his mom alone. He fought and fought—told 'em his dad would come and get 'em."

Mike folded the small cap and thrust it into his pocket, not looking up. "He was really brave, Mr. Donovan. But me . . ." He choked again. "I just . . . I . . . I'm a . . . I hid. In the back of the closet. I was scared, Mr. Donovan. I'm sorry. I should of helped . . . I'm a . . . chick—"

"No, you're not!" Donovan shook his head fiercely. "Don't beat yourself up about this, Josh! There was nothing you could have done. Those guys are tough bastards. I'm not looking forward to tangling with 'em again. Finish telling me what happened."

"They took everybody to the square near the park. I could hear shouts and crying. Then the lights were gone, and so was everybody. Everybody but me."

Josh stopped, drained, and wiped at his nose with the back of his sleeve.

Donovan sighed and said, " '. . . I only have escaped alone to tell thee . . .' "

There was a long pause while Mike tried to think what to do. Josh looked up finally. "Mr. Donovan . . . will . . . will I ever see my Dad and Mom again?"

Mike's throat tightened again, then he looked squarely at the boy. "You bet. If I have anything to say about it." He thought suddenly of his original purpose for the visit. "Josh, the last time I came here, I brought Sean something—do you know where he kept it?".

Josh nodded and went over to the mantel. A picture of Donovan and Sean, glass now cracked, lay on its side atop it. Josh reached behind it, then pulled the golden key out of the small crack between the mantel and the wall. "Here it is. What is it, sir?"

"A key," Donovan said, hefting it and staring at it thoughtfully.

"To get into where?"

"The belly of the leviathan . . ." He stood thinking for another long moment, then nodded. "C'mon, Josh. You look like you could use a square meal."

The boy nodded. "Thanks, Mr. Donovan."

The two walked back out into the lonely streets and the overwhelming silence.

THE CORK SLID FROM THE CHAMPAGNE BOTTLE WITH A SATISFYING pop. Daniel Bernstein smiled. The young man continued to grin as he poured the foaming wine into Lynn's, Stanley's, and Abraham's glasses, then into his own. "Pretty classy, eh? Champagne for breakfast?"

Stanley didn't pick up his wineglass. "Where'd you get it, Daniel?"

"From a local merchant. One who knows the value of having

friends, especially Visitor Friends." He held up his glass. "And now a toast—to my engagement!"

"What?" Lynn said blankly. "To whom?"

Daniel grinned crookedly. "To Robin Maxwell."

The adults glanced at each other furtively as he drank. Finally Lynn ventured, "But she's gone away, Danny."

Daniel smiled winningly. "Oh . . . not *that* far away, hm-mmm?"

They glanced at each other again. "How does Robin feel about this, Daniel?" Stanley asked.

His son's fatuous grin widened. "She doesn't know about it. But I want her . . . so I'll get her. Just the way I wanted this champagne . . . and I got it." He sipped his wine. "Or else I'll turn her whole damn family in."

He set his empty glass down, smiling brightly at his family. Slowly his grandfather raised his glass, his dark eyes holding Daniel's eyes, so like his own . . . then the old man threw the wine directly into his grandson's face. Daniel choked and sputtered furiously, momentarily blinded. Abraham got up and left the room, heading for the pool house.

A moment later Daniel shoved Abraham out of the way, slamming through the door. "Oh, God!" Lynn cried as the rest of the Bernstein family followed.

They rounded the corner to the pool house to see Daniel, his hand clamped brutally around Robin's wrist, dragging her out of the pool house. His face was twisted into that of a stranger. "Come *on*, you dumb little bitch! I'll teach you what Brian couldn't do on a bet!"

"Let me go! *Danny!* You're crazy!" She struggled harder, hearing the frightened wails of Katie behind her, her father's startled questions. "Stop it! Daniel! I'm not going anywhere with you, you freak!"

He continued to pull her along as her father and mother

stormed out of the pool house. There was blood in Robert's eyes. As much to save his son as Robin, Stanley grabbed Daniel, spinning him around, then pushed him into the swimming pool. "Cool off, you idiot!" he shouted.

Daniel came up out of the water, eyes deadly, his Visitor sidearm in his hand. *"Daniel! No!"* Lynn shrieked, interposing herself between her husband and her son.

He hesitated, then the muzzle of the gun dropped. Furiously Daniel sloshed out of the pool, heading inside. They all stood frozen, until Kathleen Maxwell's voice broke their paralysis. "We've got to get out of here, Bob. He'll call his friends."

"He wouldn't—" protested Stanley, then Lynn put a hand on his arm.

"You saw his face. Yes, I think you'd better get out of here. We'll help—what can we do?"

SANCHO GOMEZ FROWNED AS HE MANEUVERED HIS ANCIENT BLUE pickup around the corner. Looking both ways, he pulled out slowly, in marked contrast to his usual cheerfully slapdash style of driving. His eye fell on a package of silver-wrapped teardrop shapes on the seat next to him, and he cursed softly. Finding a parking spot, he pulled over, then sauntered casually toward the back of the truck, carrying the Hershey's Kisses. He opened the tailgate and made a show of checking the ropes holding his lawn mower and some shrubbery to be transplanted, while whispering, "You all right?"

Robert Maxwell and his family lay squashed together beneath the false bottom of Gomez's truck, gasping greedily at the fresh air. "Fine," whispered Maxwell, and was immediately contradicted by Katie's whimpering. "How are we doing?"

"Okay so far—but the roadblock is close now."

Katie whimpered again, and Kathleen shushed her. Robin grimaced as she squirmed to give her little sister more room. "We're never gonna make it if she doesn't stop crying, Mom!"

"Yeah, I almos' forgot." Sancho handed down the Hershey's Kisses. "These ought to help."

"You've thought of everything!" Robert Maxwell sounded surprised.

Sancho grinned, looking off across the roof of the truck at the distant clouds. "Well, I've had some experience at this . . ."

For a second he looked down, winked, then walked back and climbed into the driver's seat. As he put the pickup in gear, Eleanor Dupres came out of her house on the opposite side of the street, her car keys in her hand. She looked thoughtfully at the truck as Sancho tipped his hat to her. He began to sweat when he heard the little girl whimper, then a muffled wail as he pulled away from the curb. He glanced quickly in the rearview mirror at Mrs. Dupres to find her staring after him speculatively.

A few minutes later the roadblock loomed dead ahead. Sancho grimaced slightly as he took a large onion from the dash and bit into it, chewing vigorously, then forced himself to take another bite.

He put the truck in gear, and, still chewing, headed for the two cops manning the roadblock. But his eyes kept traveling back to the silent shock trooper standing guard.

One of the officers approached the cab as Sancho pulled up, waving at the other man. "Check out the back, Randy." The other man nodded, walking to the back of the truck.

Sancho smiled brightly at the policeman and leaned toward him. "Hello, Officer! How are you?" The man recoiled visibly from Gomez's killer breath.

"You're headed where?"

"El Tepeyac, just outside of town. Best food north of Ensenada." Sancho glanced in the rearview mirror, seeing the officer called Randy inspecting the back of the vehicle. The gardener's sensitive ears picked up a fretful whimper from the rear of the truck—he saw Randy tense, knew he'd also heard it. *Keep the kid quiet, Maxwell, or we've all had it,* Sancho thought fervently.

"El Tepeyac? Never heard of it," the cop was saying, examining Sancho's driver's license. He turned back to his partner. "So what's the story back there, Randy?"

The man shook his head, and Sancho closed his eyes momentarily in relief. "No story, Bob. It's okay."

"All right." Officer Bob stepped back, relieved to be out of range of Sancho's breath, waving the truck through. "Move it out, then, Pedro."

"*Sancho, señor.*" He put the truck in gear, glancing in the rearview mirror as he did so, found Randy watching him. Sancho smiled, nodding pleasantly. "Thank you, *señor.*"

JULIET PARRISH LOOKED OUT ACROSS THE ENORMOUS CULVERT TO the ramshackle building that had once contained offices and machinery for part of the L.A. wastewater processing system. Elias took her arm. "Now you be careful, Julie. Kinda steep here."

Awkwardly Juliet made her way down the slope, bracing herself on her cane. Brad followed them. It had been a week since Ben's death—his funeral had been the day before yesterday. Caleb was now, along with Elias, a confirmed member of their steadily growing underground. Juliet hissed with pain as a rock turned under her foot, jarring her hip. She wasn't sure if the nerve damage there would prove permanent—the burning jolt of electricity from the alien weapon had certainly left a hideous, disfiguring scar on her right hip.

When she'd unwrapped the bandages this morning, Ruby Engels helping her, Juliet had winced, and tears had filled the older woman's eyes as they surveyed the still-livid weals. Juliet had smiled wanly. "Good thing bikinis were never my style . . ."

Remembering that scene now, Juliet grimaced. She wasn't thrilled about the prospect of permanent disfigurement, but at the moment, her lack of mobility was more worrisome. How could she lead this group if she couldn't get around? And nobody else appeared willing to assume that responsibility. (If anyone did, she'd gladly renounce it.)

With a final skid that made her bite her lip, they were down, walking across the massive concrete flooring, looking into the dark mouth of the runoff tunnel. It was a good twenty feet high at this point. Elias indicated it. "The tunnel runs down underneath the city. Connects up to some nifty places. It ain't the Beverly Hills Hotel inside, you dig? Spiders an' rats is probably the nicest critters we're gonna have to persuade to relocate. But there's a lotta space down underneath . . . even an old train station at the end of one of the tunnels. Bums sleep in there, sometimes."

"We'll need every hand we can get," Juliet said, looking around. "Think they'll help us?"

"I'll talk to 'em." He looked back at the building. "Course the electricity don't work."

"I'll take care of that," Brad said.

Elias looked back at Juliet. "Then it's okay? Course, bein' near the hills like this, we're all gonna have to drive to get here—"

"It's *perfect*, Elias," Juliet said warmly. "Completely hidden from overhead surveillance—which is why we've got to relocate from the mountain camp. And I have hopes of converting the tunnel into living quarters, so we won't have to travel— we'll be able to live here full time. We've got a lot to do!"

"Dynamite." Elias looked relieved. "Now while you get the stuff moved in, I'm gonna counsel with the Angels. This here's part of their turf."

"The street gang?" Juliet thought rapidly. She didn't know

how they'd respond to the idea of a woman as leader, but they'd make good scouts.

"Sure. They hate the Visitors as much as we do—they've never taken kindly to bein' leaned on."

"You really think you can talk them into helping us?"

Elias shifted rapidly into his jive act. "You kiddin', mama? You is talkin' to de Henry Kissinger of East L.A. I'll catch you-all *later*."

He strutted off, then turned back as Juliet spoke. "Elias . . ."

As he looked, she smiled, nodding wordless thanks. He flashed her a "V" sign, and left, whistling "We Are Family."

DANIEL BERNSTEIN UNLOCKED HIS FRONT DOOR, THEN HEARD THE telephone ringing. He sprinted across the room and caught it on the fifth ring. "Hello?" As he spoke, he reached for a glass from the bar to his right, pouring a stiff shot of Scotch. "Yes, this is his son, Daniel. No, my dad hasn't been here. They *what*? Took him? When? But they probably just wanted to give him a ride home . . . They *said* 'arrested'?" He hesitated for a second, then hung up without saying good-bye.

Punching buttons with quick stabs, he made another call. "Hello . . . may I speak with Mrs. Bernstein, please?" He hesitated. "She what? Lunch? But that was *four hours* ago! What time did she *go* to lunch? No, she's not at home! *I'm* at home, alone . . ." The reality hit him then, and he hung up the phone, looking around at the silent television set, the locked doors . . .

Maybe it was time for Grandpa's walk, that must be it . . . He wandered from room to room, sipping uneasily at the Scotch. Two hours later, he realized, drunkenly, that they weren't coming bck.

SANCHO GOMEZ SMILED TENTATIVELY AT THE SAME TWO POLICE officers as he pulled up before the roadblock on his way back into the city. Neither smiled back. The officer called Bob and a Visitor guard walked to the rear of the truck, jerked the tailgate open. "That report from Mrs. Dupres was right—he *was* smuggling someone in here—but it's empty now," he called. "You sure missed it this time, Randy!"

The policeman next to Sancho raised his gun sadly. "Get out of the truck . . . slowly."

Sancho looked around to see four shock troopers with stun rifles centered on him. Shrugging, he got out of the pickup.

MIKE DONOVAN AND JOSH BROOKS PAUSED ACROSS THE STREET from Vitello's. The Italian restaurant's sign illuminated a van parked in front of it. "Right on time," Donovan said, taking Josh's arm. They crossed the street, scrambled into the van. Tony and Fran Leonetti nodded, then the vehicle began to move. Tony threaded through the dark streets for several minutes before stopping.

"We ought to be safe here . . . at least for a couple of minutes," he said. "How you doin', Mike?"

Donovan quickly introduced his companion and recounted the main events of the past weeks since his foray into the Visitor ship, concluding with what he'd found in the deserted town of San Pedro. Tony and Fran both shook their heads, looking sympathetically over at Josh. "Josh needs to stay with Fran for a while," Donovan said. "Are you still at home?"

"Not much," she answered. "Most of the time I'm helping out with the underground." She turned to Josh. "You like spaghetti?"

The boy nodded. "Sure."

She smiled back at him. "My name's not Leonetti for nothing. We'll get along fine."

"Where's this underground camp?" Donovan asked.

"Several around the city, Mike," Tony said. "One is in the mountains, a decent drive away, but recently they've found another location . . . an abandoned wastewater plant on the verge of the foothills."

Donovan grinned. "The mountains? Like in El Salvador?"

Tony chuckled. "Yeah. I also hear that there's another place downtown somewhere, but I don't know which building."

"We ought to find out," Donovan mused. "But the first thing I want to do is see what this unlocks." He held up the alien key. "They must have some Achilles heel . . . some chink—"

Tony wagged a warning finger. "Watch it there, pal . . ."

Mike laughed. "Some *flaw* in their armor. *Something* we can use against them. And we need to find out where they're taking the people who've disappeared."

"Okay, you've convinced me." Tony restarted the van. "So let's get going."

"You guys be careful, okay?" Fran said, looking from one to the other. Her hand came out to clasp Tony's as he drove. "I couldn't do without either of you."

"Where are you going, Mr. Donovan?" Josh wanted to know.

Mike jerked his thumb straight up. Josh's eyes widened, then clouded with worry. As the van threaded its way through the streets, the boy leaned back against the seat, looking out the window, up at the enormous ship hovering over the city.

DANIEL BERNSTEIN SAT AT THE HEAD OF THE DINING-ROOM TABLE, a bottle in front of him. The burgundy was two-thirds gone. The remains of a TV dinner littered the kitchen, but out of force of habit, Daniel had cleared the table. Now he sat, pouring another glass of wine, trying not to let his gaze shift from one empty chair to another. A knock on the hall door made him look up hopefully, but his face fell when he saw Brian. Daniel looked down at his glass, not asking the Visitor Friends' leader to sit down.

Brian sighed. "Daniel, I apologize. I know you must be very disappointed with me. I promised your parents amnesty, but . . . my superiors overruled me and ordered your family taken in for questioning. But they'll be back home soon, I promise."

Daniel looked up. "They will?"

"You have my word." Brian's tone was very reassuring.

"Did you manage to capture the scientist I told you about?"

"No . . . I'm afraid by the time we got here, they'd disappeared. We'll get them, though, don't worry. Who are they, anyway?"

"Just a scientist and his family . . ." Daniel took a sip of wine. "You sure my folks will be all right? How about my grandfather? He's kind of old . . ."

Brian looked uncomfortable for a second, then his smooth tones resumed. "He isn't well, Daniel."

"But he was fine this morning!"

"Well, you know how old people are. Excitement isn't good for them. But our doctors are taking care of him . . . They're very, very good. They hope to get him feeling better right away. How about you? Are you feeling better now?"

"I guess so . . ." Daniel mumbled, his eyes on the table.

Brian dropped into a seat beside him, and put a comforting hand on the younger man's shoulder. "Well, I've some other news that ought to help. You're getting a promotion."

Daniel looked up. "Huh?"

"To my second-in-command."

"What?!" A light began to dance in Daniel's dark eyes.

"Congratulations!" The Visitor reached over and grabbed Daniel's hand, shaking it vigorously, then patted him on the back.

"Well. I . . ." Daniel stammered, grinning.

"That's not all. When I informed Diana of your loyalty, she

gave me this for you." Brian took out a Lucite case, handed it to Daniel. He opened it to see a man's gold ring, set with a large diamond.

"Brian! Wow!" He tried it on. It fit perfectly.

"Glad you like it. And, again, I'm proud to have you in my unit." He held out his hand, and this time Daniel took it enthusiastically, pumping it up and down, smiling gratefully at his friend.

# 14

DARK WAVES SLOSHED, GRABBING AT MIKE DONOVAN'S SNEAKERS as he and Tony Leonetti crept along the base of the Richland refinery seawall. To their left, a high stone wall butted up from the rocks, with a narrow service ladder leading upward from a ledge midway up. Donovan paused, his stun rifle slung over his shoulder, looking up. "We're gonna have to get up there," he whispered, his mouth nearly touching his friend's ear. "Can you boost me?"

Leonetti grimaced. Donovan was nearly six inches taller and forty pounds heavier than Tony was—but his reach and strength were also greater. Tony nodded. "Yeah—but be quick about it!"

Donovan nodded, handing Tony his gun. Leonetti slung it over his shoulder, cupped his hands, then braced his back. "One. Two. Three . . . Alley-oop!" As Tony hoisted, every muscle protesting, Donovan sprang upward. Finally his groping fingers caught on the ledge, and grunting, he drew himself up, his feet scraping softly as he found a toehold on the wall.

Once up, he rested for a long second, then cautiously climbed a few rungs up the ladder. He scuttled down more quickly than he'd gone up. "Sentry posted," he hissed down into the darkness where his partner waited. "They're not taking any chances on any more unauthorized joyrides like I took . . . Toss the gun up."

A moment later his groping fingers caught the sling of the alien weapon, then he leaned over, extending one hand. "Jump high, Tony!" With the other hand he gripped the ladder behind him. A grunt of exertion—then a muffled curse and a splash. "You okay?"

"Yeah."

"You're gonna have to jump higher than that, pal."

"Damn you, Mike!" But this time Tony's grasp met his. Donovan braced himself, pulling slowly, and in a minute Leonetti was crouched beside him.

The Asian fingered the alien gun. "You know how to use this thing?"

"It's pretty easy. This thing controls the intensity—how strong a jolt it shoots . . . the higher the notch, the stronger the intensity. You prime it here, and this is the firing button."

"Did it come with extra batteries?"

Donovan chuckled. "I figure they're rechargeable. If I just could figure how to hook it into an outlet, I'd have it made."

Tony's hushed whisper held amusement. "Clever guys, these Japanese. Think of everything . . ."

"Look out!" Donovan ducked as a searchlight beam swung out over the water.

"Shit! That was close!"

"Irregular cycle," Donovan hissed, looking up at the tower built near the refinery. "Or else it's hand-operated."

"How are we gonna get by him?" Tony jerked his head at the sentry. From this angle they could barely see the top of his helmet every so often as he paced his beat.

"How about the direct approach?"

"You mean like that time in Cambodia?"

"Yeah."

"And I get to be the pigeon again, I suppose." Tony sounded disgusted.

Donovan hefted the gun. "I'm the one with the firepower."

"Okay." Tony sighed. "You're also the one that'll have to explain it to my widow."

He scuttled up the ladder, rubber soles making almost no sound, then swung over the wall. Donovan swarmed up behind him. As he got to the top, he saw the back of the sentry ahead of him, rifle pointed at Tony, who stood, hands over his head, talking rapidly. "Uh, hi. My name's Tony, you see, and, uh, my shrimp boat had a flat on the way from Korea, and I've been walkin' across this water for so long that—" Donovan swung the butt of his rifle, hard, and the sentry went down and lay still.

Tony scooped up the Visitor's weapon. "Took you *forever*, Donovan. You're losing the old touch."

"C'mon."

A few minutes later, within the refinery grounds, they heard a cry from the seawall and knew that the sentry had been discovered.

"We should have heaved him over the wall," Donovan said, annoyed that he hadn't thought of it at the time. "Would have bought us a few more minutes while they looked for him." He squirmed between two huge pipes, ducking to avoid a third in the maze that surrounded them as they worked their way toward the parking lot.

"Hindsight is always twenty-twenty," Tony grunted, dropping to hands and knees to follow him, "but somehow I'd hate to think we've sunk to the level of cold-blooded murder. Even if they are a bunch of lizards under those pretty faces."

Several minutes of squirming through the piping brought them within sight of a Visitor shuttle, cargo bay doors open.

But this time there were no workers connecting hoses to transport chemicals. The tanks inside were gone, and before the doors, hands atop their heads, stood *people*.

Donovan and Leonetti crouched, watching, as the Visitor shock troopers roughly pushed and shoved the prisoners into the shuttle. Men. Women. Little children, some of whom sobbed brokenly, others who stood glassy-eyed with shock. One little girl clutched a ragged teddy bear. There were bruises on her face. There was a mother with an infant. A young woman swollen and awkward with the last stages of pregnancy. A boy Sean's age wearing a baseball cap . . .

"Jesus, Mike!" Tony turned horrified dark eyes to his friend. "What the hell is going on?"

Donovan shook his head. "I don't know. But we've got to find out." He looked around, forcing himself to study the people they were taking. They seemed a cross section. He noticed one man, wearing a battered cowboy hat and work shirt, with dark eyes and Hispanic features. Blood oozed from a cut over his eye, but he stood defiantly, unbowed.

"Okay, Tony. Same drill." Donovan readied himself as the cargo bay doors began to close, and the pilots stepped inside.

"Right. This time, I ain't gonna trip . . ."

They gathered themselves, moving forward—but suddenly, a burst of alien gunfire surrounded them. Looking up, they saw shock troopers on the catwalks above them, shooting. Donovan fired back, but another burst nearly caught both of them. They ducked back, away from the shuttle, realizing they were caught in crossfire. Donovan took aim at the power cables overhead running to the spotlights in the parking lot. "The cables, Tony! Shoot the cables!"

"I can't make the damn thing work!"

Donovan reached over to Tony's weapon. A burst of blue electricity filled the air with the smell of ozone barely two feet from his head. Mike flipped a switch. "The safety! Now try!"

Tony raised his weapon, aimed, and a burst of blue fire ruptured one of the cables. The lights flickered, and several went out. A swinging cable fell, showering a golden spray of sparks, to strike one of the shock troopers. The creature gave the peculiar ululating cry Donovan had heard earlier as it died.

Donovan shoved his partner. "Up to the catwalk! We can move faster there! Go! I'll cover you!"

Tony sprang for the stairs and pounded up them. At the top, he turned the corner onto the catwalk, only to find another Visitor facing him. Almost without thinking, Leonetti swung his weapon, striking the guard in the face. The creature staggered back, catching hold of the railing on the way over, and Tony raised his gun to hit it again—just as it turned its face.

Its true face—Tony's blow had knocked its mask off. Leonetti shrank back for a second from those reptilian features, and the creature hissed and spat at him. A cloud of venom surrounded the Asian's face. He staggered back, hands to his eyes, which felt as if they'd been seared with hot needles. "Mike! My eyes!"

A bolt from Donovan's gun pulsed in front of Tony, then the Asian heard the thud of a heavy body. He clawed at his eyes as he heard his friend run toward him. There were sounds of a struggle, then another alien death cry—then the pulse of a rifle, followed by a human gasp. Something fell at Tony's feet.

"Mike?" Tony dropped to his hands and knees, feeling the suede of Donovan's jacket beneath his groping fingers. "Mike—oh, God, are you okay?" He crouched over his partner, trying to feel—

A step behind him. Tony began to turn, just as something hard connected with the back of his head. He pitched forward over his friend's body, and lay still.

# 15

DAYLIGHT WAS ONLY A DISTANT GLOW BEHIND ROBERT MAXWELL as he hefted the box of bottled chemical reagents, then ducked under a sagging beam. Cautious in the dimness, he picked his way along the old sewer tunnel. The soil beneath his feet was dry, but his nose wrinkled at some of the scents the dust brought to life as he walked. Robin, picking her way behind him, sniffed audibly. "Stinks down here, Daddy."

"What did you expect, Binna? It's an abandoned sewer network."

"Why couldn't we get to this building on top of the ground?" Robin whined. "It's been a week already. I'm sure they're not looking for us anymore!"

"Don't bet on it," Maxwell said. "The reports in the mountain camp were that Sancho got picked up on his way back into the city . . . poor guy. If there were only something I could do to help him . . ." He ducked to avoid a cobweb, seeing a distant glow ahead. "We're coming to the end, Binna."

"Terrific." Robin was completely unimpressed. Maxwell frowned, fighting to keep his temper. Their week in the mountain camp had been hellish, thanks to his eldest daughter's endless whining and complaining. Several times Maxwell had to turn away to keep from shaking her physically. *Why are teenagers so damn selfish?* he wondered. *Is it just my daughter, or are all of them like this? God knows, Polly's got more spunk than Robin's ever shown, and she's only twelve . . .*

He immediately felt ashamed of his thoughts. Polly had always been his favorite of his three daughters, and Maxwell felt guilty every time he acknowledged this fact to himself. It was partly this guilt that had led him to bring Robin with him this morning—along with the realization that if he didn't distract her, she might try something harebrained. Robin had never been very good at visualizing the consequences of her actions—a fault that drove Maxwell particularly crazy because it was also one of *his* faults.

The two Maxwells emerged from the tunnel, picking their way across the rock-strewn culvert, then approached the headquarters' main door. A sentry looked them over pleasantly, but her hand rested on the butt of the police .38 she wore at her hip. "Robert Maxwell and my daughter, Robin. From the mountain camp."

"Hi, Doctor Maxwell. They told me you were coming. Password, please?"

Robert grinned. "I wish I knew who comes up with these things. 'Jabba the Hutt eats Visitors . . .' "

She laughed. "Yeah, I'd like to know too. Must be Robin's generation. They had to explain the reference to me."

Robin stared stonily ahead. The guard glanced at her, raised an inquiring eyebrow in Maxwell's direction, who shrugged helplessly. "Well, now that I'm here, I'd like to talk to whoever's in charge. See what I can do to help."

"Ever do any carpentry?"

"I got pretty good at banging my thumb," Maxwell said.

"See Juliet Parrish, she's upstairs. Short, blonde. Walks with a cane."

"Okay, see you." Beckoning to Robin, Maxwell headed for the stairs.

At the top of the stairs, he saw a woman walking away from him, leaning on a cane. "Juliet Parrish?" Maxwell called hesitantly. She turned at the sound of his voice. "Ms. Parrish?" he repeated, putting down the carton of chemicals he was carrying. "Robert Maxwell, anthropologist. My daughter, Robin." The young woman turned to smile at Robin. Maxwell was surprised at her youth; she seemed about the same age as his grad assistants, twenty-three or -four. No makeup, blonde hair caught back off her shoulders, a button-down shirt and brown sweater. Only her blue eyes, shadowed with weariness, betrayed an age beyond years.

"Glad to have you with us, Mr. Maxwell, Robin," she said with a smile.

"Robert, please. Mr. Maxwell is my father," Maxwell said, looking around. "They said you were organizing things up here."

She laughed. "They did, huh? Shows you they're easily fooled. But I'm trying. C'mon, let me show you around."

They followed her through the crumbling, dusty interior of the old wastewater plant. Maxwell saw the red "V" symbol sprayed on several of the broken-plastered walls. The sounds of hammering and sawing reached Robert's ears, and they came upon several people mending holes in the walls and floors. Juliet spoke above the noise. "We're trying to get this place ready so we can bring down all of our people and equipment from the mountain camp. We're trying to make it livable—" She ducked a shower of plaster from overhead, where a lightbulb hung nakedly through a hole in the ceiling. "Or at least safe."

Robert sighed. "I don't think any place is safe anymore."

"You're right," she agreed.

A woman with tousled brown hair stuck her head out of

one of the rooms. "Hey, Julie! Where's the water cutoff valve?"

Juliet made a hand-spreading gesture, sounding a bit frazzled. "I don't know, Louise. Try in there . . ." She pointed across the hall and turned back to the Maxwells. "The toilets, by the way, are out through that hall . . . They're *very* picturesque." She grinned wryly, brushing a strand of hair out of her eyes with a grimy hand.

Robin rolled her eyes. "I'll bet."

They passed a room holding a microcomputer and a bank of radio equipment. Juliet gestured at it as they passed. "There's our poor man's BBC. The kitchen's over there. We try to keep snacks, as well as mealtime stuff. Be careful, Robin—" The girl had wandered close to the elevator shaft. "The holes—"

"Yeah," said Robin, "I see the holes." Her voice also said she'd noticed the dirt, the cobwebs, and the roaches. Juliet looked over at Robert.

"One can ascertain that she's *not* thrilled to be here."

He nodded. "Yeah. It's not the Galleria, is it? I brought her here because I thought she'd *really* go crazy up at the mountain camp."

"Poor thing." Juliet looked at Robin's back as the girl hesitantly peered into the kitchen. "There aren't many others her age around here."

Robert had poked his head into the laboratory. "I see you're getting things under control here . . . There's quite a bit of stuff left up at the mountain camp, you know. I was impressed. An electron microscope! How'd you manage *that*?"

Juliet smiled and shrugged. "We've . . . paid for everything we've gotten. One way or another." She looked at Maxwell. "We can't leave the more sophisticated, hard-to-replace gear up there much longer. We've got to get it down here. Every day I worry that they'll fly over the camp and suddenly tumble that it's no longer a summer resort for rich brats." She smiled at him. "Which reminds me, this is where those chemicals belong. Mind bringing them in?"

"Of course not," said Maxwell. "I'll get them immediately."

The box of chemicals in his arms, Maxwell followed Juliet into the laboratory. "You can put them over there, please." She pointed to a scarred old laboratory table next to a sink. Two other people bustled around the room. One, a young black man, looked up at Juliet. "Julie—where'd you say you wanted this Bunsen burner set up?"

"Over there, Elias." She pointed to the corner of the table. "Did you manage to find some bottled gas?"

"No problem." He jerked his chin at a bottle in the corner. The other young man, white, with glasses and curly brown hair, looked up.

"Hey, boss. Where'd you say you wanted the sterilizer?"

"Over there, under the cabinets." She turned back to Maxwell. "Robert Maxwell, I'd like you to meet Elias and Brad. Doctor Maxwell is an anthropologist."

They nodded pleasantly. Maxwell looked around the lab, seeing with a wry, pleased grin that it was by far the cleanest room he'd seen in the complex. Juliet Parrish, it seemed, had her priorities straight.

Louise, her hair festooned with a cobweb, entered the room. "Julie, I *can't* find that water cutoff valve!"

Juliet nodded at Maxwell with a "What can you do?" expression. "I'll get it, Louise."

Outside the lab, Juliet saw Robin Maxwell standing in the corner, looking up at the sun shafting in from one of the boarded-up windows. Something about the girl's expression reminded Juliet of Algernon's wistful expression just before feeding time. She bit her lip. She'd deliberately avoided thinking about the college, or Doctor Metz, or Ruth . . . or Ben . . . or Denny. Juliet tried to swallow the tightness in her throat as she looked for a wrench before heading into the storeroom where she'd seen some piping. Sure enough, both the hot water pipe and its cutoff valve were there.

Juliet began tightening the cutoff valve with the wrench. Suddenly the pipe over her head began to spray rusty water as the pressure caused an ancient seal to blow. Juliet gasped, choking on the dirty water, feeling it spray her hair and clothing—she'd need to take another bath when she was done, and their current water supplies were so limited! Frustrated, she fitted the wrench back onto the lug, tightening it with quick, furious jerks, but the water made it slippery—the wrench loosened and slipped off, banging her knuckles so hard Juliet saw stars.

Her breath coming in angry sobs, Juliet tried again—only to have the consarned thing peel back the skin from the already sore knuckles. Juliet yelped and threw the wrench down, cradling her bruised hand. "Julie, honey . . . are you okay?"

It was Ruby Engels. The older woman peered in the doorway, then, seeing Juliet dissolve in angry tears, she came in, closing the door behind her. "I'm okay, Ruby," Juliet said, gesturing at the spewing water pipe and shaking her head.

"Sure you're okay, Julie," Ruby said, coming over to put her arms around her. "But you shouldn't be struggling with the plumbing with your hip still injured! I'll get somebody to help."

Juliet hugged her, breaking down completely at the sound of a sympathetic voice. "Oh, Ruby! I can't handle this! Most of the time when something has to be done there *isn't* anyone else willing or able to do it! Look at me!" She pushed her dripping hair back from her face. "I'll have to take another bath . . ." She wrung the hem of her wet sweater ineffectually. "I'm supposed to be a *scientist*, Ruby! A doctor—maybe someday a biochemical researcher! Not a plumber! Or—or some kind of rebel guerrilla leader!" She sniffled, swiping at her nose with her soaked sleeve. "You all look at me like I know what to do, but—"

"Yeah." Ruby hugged her again, patting her back. "I know. You're just as scared and lost-feeling as everyone else."

Juliet hiccuped slightly as her sobs abated. "More."

Ruby stroked her wet hair gently. "'These are the times that try men's souls . . .' and women's too. I'll tell you why we all look to you. You're a natural for the job, and we see it, even if you don't. A natural leader."

"I don't feel like it," Juliet said, raising her head.

"You don't have to. All you have to do is trust your instincts, and your fine mind. Trust yourself as much as everybody else trusts you."

Juliet took a deep, hesitant breath. "And if I can't manage to feel that kind of trust in myself?"

Ruby shrugged, assuming her "Yiddish momma" manner. "So then you fake it. We won't know the difference."

Juliet began to laugh, her first genuine laugh since Ben's death. Ruby grinned back at her.

Later that evening, Juliet heard Elias's triumphant voice call her name. "Julie! Hey, Julie! Special delivery! Specimen time!"

She hobbled out of the tiny room she was using as an office/bedroom, leaning on her cane. Elias was coming down the hall, accompanied by his friends, the Angels. The street gang members were carrying something long, bulky, and red—after a second, Juliet realized their burden was a Visitor trooper with a trash can over his head. Brad and Robert Maxwell joined them.

The booted legs kicked as they put the alien on his feet, then, with a "Ta-da!" from Elias, jerked the trash can off.

"Be careful of his gun!" Juliet cried, and Brad hastily grabbed the alien sidearm as it skidded to the floor. The Visitor staggered, raising a hand to his thick brown hair, turning to inspect the varied range of weapons leveled or pointed at him. Juliet gasped sharply in recognition. It was Mike Donovan, the cameraman!

"Goddamn it, you bozos!" Stunned, he pulled his fingers away from the spot where the garbage can had landed, then, seeing the red smear on his hand, his mouth twisted sardonically. "Anybody got a Band-Aid?"

"Doesn't sound like one of them," commented Robert Maxwell, baseball bat still poised.

"He's not," Juliet said. "But he may be a sympathizer. Where did you find him, Elias?"

"In an alley, couple of blocks from here. He was wanderin' around, lookin' lonely, so me and the Angels here decided he'd make a perfect specimen for your lab. You hardly ever see them out, 'cept in pairs."

Juliet's words had apparently penetrated Donovan's mind, and he whirled on her so rapidly he staggered again. *"Sympathizer?* Where do you come off with a load of shit like that?"

Juliet addressed the group rather than him directly. "He knows Kristine Walsh. We'll have to be careful of him. It could be a setup." She turned back to the stunned Donovan, who rallied after a moment.

"I don't have to stand here and take this! Who's in charge here, anyway?"

Brad shrugged, the muzzle of his rifle never leaving Donovan's midsection. "Guess you could say she is." He jerked his chin at Juliet, who, dressed in a faded red sweatshirt, her hair still bedraggled from her battle with the plumbing, looked even younger than usual.

"Who? *Her?*" Donovan barked a short, incredulous laugh. "That *kid?*"

Maxwell grinned and winked at Juliet. "One smart kid, I'd say." She returned his grin with a wan smile, before turning back to the indignant Donovan.

"Would you like that bandage now, Mr. Donovan? Or would you prefer to go on bleeding?"

Brushing coffee grounds from the stained shoulders of the Visitor uniform, Donovan followed her into the lab. She motioned to a stool as she washed her hands, then, when he sat down, she limped over with some disinfectant. He eyed her warily. "You walk with a cane?"

"Yes," she said, parting his hair with quick, competent fingers, and inspecting the wound.

"You get hurt too?"

"Yes . . ." She moistened a cotton ball with disinfectant. "How'd you get the uniform?"

"They had a sale." She dabbed at the wound. "Owww! You did that on purpose!"

"Of course I didn't," Juliet said coolly, dabbing again. "Hold still."

"You a doctor?"

"More or less," she answered, dabbing again, holding him with a hand clenched in his hair as he jerked, breath hissing through his teeth.

"How comforting—ouch! Don't you have any Novocain?"

"Yes, but I have to save it. If you'd hold still—" Juliet said, inspecting the lump, then dabbing at it again. "How'd you get the uniform?"

"On the Mother Ship. My partner and I—ouch, dammit!— Tony and I were going up for a little reconnaissance, and they knocked us over with those stun guns. When I came to, two of the Visitors helped me escape. One was a guy I'd met before, named Martin—the other was a woman named Barbara. They gave me the uniform, told me when a shuttle was coming down. I climbed aboard, and then, when I got down here, I stole a truck and crashed out through the fence. Things got kind of sticky for a while, but I managed to ditch the rig outside of town. I was wandering around, looking for a headquarters I'd heard of downtown . . ."

"In that uniform? That was very foolish, Mr. Donovan. Elias and the Angels might have killed you if they'd been in a different mood." She dabbed at his cut again, thoughtfully. "Your escape sounds like maybe it was a setup, to me."

"I don't think so—damn! When are you gonna be done?"

"Why don't you think so?"

"Because . . . they sounded so damn sincere, talking about some kind of organized Fifth Column within the Visitors . . . said there weren't nearly enough of 'em, but that not all of 'em agreed with their leader's plans for us—ow!"

He twisted away. "That's enough! Dammit, you're torturing me as bad as Diana is torturing our people up on that Mother Ship!"

"Is she?" Juliet wasn't particularly surprised.

"Yeah. Apparently the bitch gets some of her kicks that way." He felt his head gingerly.

"Sneaking aboard that Mother Ship was no easy job," Juliet observed. "What made you try it?"

"I'm highly motivated." He glared at her.

"Why did you do it?" Her questions were gentle, but inexorable.

With a muttered curse he swung on her. "Because, kid, my son Sean is aboard that Mother Ship, along with my ex-wife and my partner, and God knows what's happening to them! Or to the rest of San Pedro—they just scooped up the whole goddamn *town* and transported 'em all to the L.A. Mother Ship!"

"I suppose I should believe you?" Juliet said quietly, staring at him. "After all, *you* sound so damn sincere . . ."

"That's it!" With a short, bitten-off laugh, Mike Donovan threw his hands up. "I'm leaving!"

He turned to do just that, but even as he stepped out of the lab door, Brad cocked his rifle ostentatiously, and the air was filled with the snick of switchblades and the hiss of chains. Mike Donovan hesitated, crouching low, his hands poised to slash. Juliet stepped up behind him. "I wouldn't, Mr. Donovan. We're also short on bandages."

She paused for a long moment, then, as Mike slowly straightened, continued, "You have to understand our point of view, Mr. Donovan. You were among the first to go aboard their ship; you worked in close proximity with them for quite some time; several nights ago you met with Kristine Walsh—"

Donovan turned, his surprise plain. She nodded. "And now you show up here, escaped from someplace no one ever escaped from before . . . wearing that—"

"*Goddamn it!* I know what I'm wearing! How'd you know about Kristine?"

" 'Cause I was there. Outside. Watching."

"Listen, kid, you want to talk about *setups*—"

She nodded. "Yes, I saw it."

"Then why the hell didn't you let out a yell and warn me?"

"I wasn't sure who was setting who up—or which side you're really on."

Mike looked at her, his green eyes very serious. "I'm on the right side, kid. Believe me."

There was a long pause, then finally Juliet nodded. "Well. Why don't you tell us what you know?"

The group gathered in the conference area, and Donovan faced them, looking out across the expanse of still-suspicious faces. "Did any of you see the interrupted broadcast the night the Visitors declared martial law?"

A general murmur of assent followed.

"Well, indirectly, I suppose I'm responsible for that move on their part . . . though I'm pretty sure they would've done it eventually. That evening I got aboard the Mother Ship. I filmed Diana and Steven, one of her lieutenants, eating animals as large as guinea pigs *whole*. They're not humanoid at all. They're reptiles of some sort, wearing very clever masks to hide their alien features. Up till tonight, I thought they were all just as ugly on the inside . . . as evil . . . as they appeared to my eyes on the outside. But tonight, two of them, Martin and Barbara, risked their lives to get me off the Mother Ship and back here—so I guess looks really aren't everything. That's it, in a nutshell."

An excited babble—mixed equally of belief and skepticism—swelled after Donovan finished speaking. Elias waved an excited hand. "Reptiles? You *sure,* man? What did they look like?"

Donovan grimaced. "I'm no artist, guys."

"But Roger is!" A young black woman pushed a dark-haired man forward. "Go on, Rog!"

Taking a piece of charcoal from someone, Roger, in response to Donovan's description, began to sketch on the concrete wall. Mike watched in admiration—and with a shudder of recognition—as the reptilian features he'd glimpsed twice now (the second time had been just prior to his capture at Richland) took shape as a result of his words. As Roger drew, Donovan continued to give a detailed summary of the Visitors' behavior.

"How's that?" Roger asked, stepping back.

"Yeah." Donovan gave him a respectful nod. "I'd have to get my tape to check every detail, but that's pretty close."

"Where is that tape, Mr. Donovan?" Juliet asked. "We could use it in our studies. We really need to recruit a herpetologist. Does anybody know one?"

"Herpetologist!" Elias rolled his eyes in mock horror. "Julie, don't tell me you is *diseased,* mama!"

Amid general laughter, Robert Maxwell admitted that he'd

minored in paleontology, so had some background in animal biology. "But, *reptiles* flying around in spaceships?" Brad asked. "That's crazy! Lizards are stupid—I used to have a chameleon for a pet, and they make a cat look like a genius by comparison."

"Cats are smart!" flared Louise, who had adopted a stray tabby within days of their move into the ancient building.

"It's really not crazy, Brad," explained Maxwell. "It could have happened here on Earth."

"What?" Donovan said.

"Up till about sixty-five million years ago—the end of the Cretaceous period—reptiles ruled this planet. They had been evolving and changing for *millions* of years . . . far longer than man has been around. Who knows what they might have evolved into? But then, the geologic evidence shows, a meteor—a really *big* one—impacted with the Earth, probably landing somewhere in the ocean. Its impact messed up the environment—probably screwed up the food chain, by first raising temperatures, then by creating so much dust the whole planet was dark for a couple of years. Nobody knows definitively whether this raised temperatures—via the greenhouse effect—or lowered them—by blocking out the sun's rays. But either way, the impact probably contributed to wiping out most of the reptile population—allowing the mammals—us—to gain the ascendancy."

"Wai-i-it a minute, Doc!" Elias shook his head. "How the hell you know all this if it happened so long ago?"

"Iridium," said Juliet.

"Right, iridium. It's a common substance in asteroids, comparatively rare here on Earth. Sediment layers around the Earth show marked increases in iridium in the soil layer sixty-five million years ago. The asteroid impact has been pretty well accepted as an actual occurrence—what they're still arguing about is how it affected the ecology of that time . . ."

Elias looked impressed in spite of himself. "So you're sayin' that maybe this meteor heated up the place, and those reptiles couldn't handle it?"

"Reptiles here on Earth are cold-blooded, Elias," Juliet said. "Their internal metabolism can't adjust to handle wide temperature variations as well as the metabolism of mammals."

"Hey!" Elias snapped his fingers. "So all we got to do is heat up all our outdoor barbecues at once and—boom! Kentucky-fried horny toad!"

Everyone laughed. Maxwell shook his head, grinning. "It's not that simple, I'm afraid. Wish it were. Extreme heat *would* probably drive them away—only problem is, with their technology, we'd have to get the whole planet so hot *we'd* probably fry too. Besides, to generate that much heat quickly would take something on the order of a nuclear holocaust."

"Forget that, then," Brad said. "Killing off the human race just to get rid of the Visitors is definitely cutting off your noses, so to speak."

"What about cold?" asked Louise. "Reptiles here on Earth can't handle cold."

"Those suckers sure can," said Caleb Taylor. "The one who rescued me took over two hundred degrees below zero."

"Those fake skins may act as insulation," Donovan volunteered. "Besides, I'm sweating wearing this uniform. This fabric is super-insulated. Maybe that accounts for how he did it." He thought for a moment. "They keep their Mother Ship so dimly lighted . . . maybe bright lights would blind them?"

Juliet nodded. "That may be a very practical suggestion— the most practical offered so far. But even though it may be a partial strategy, we're going to need more effective and longer-lasting means than that."

Everyone murmured agreement. Juliet rested her chin on her hand, thinking. "The eating Mr. Donovan described seems consistent with the biochemistry of reptiles as we know them. I wonder if there's a way to get at their main food source . . . poison it, somehow. If we could identify where they keep it."

"Yeah," said Robert Maxwell. "But we'd have to develop a poison that wouldn't kill the host animal. Reptiles prefer live—or freshly killed—animals."

"What about that poison spray I described?" Donovan asked. "I thought snakes had to bite you—these guys don't have fangs to inject venom."

"It's fairly common for reptiles here on Earth to spray their venom," Maxwell answered. "Besides, it's probably a sort of vestigial trait they've retained from earlier times."

"It's pretty deadly," Mike said, thinking of how Tony had been blinded. "Can you make an antidote?"

Juliet shrugged. "Possible. Procedures for creating an anti-venin are pretty standard—but we'd need a quantity of venom."

"Good," said Robert sardonically. "Let's add that to the old shopping list. We've *got* to get one of those guys for Julie to examine!"

"Yeah . . ." Juliet sighed. "If wishes were horses . . ." She exchanged a quick glance with Ruby, then straightened in sudden decision. "You know what we ought to do? Define our overall plan of resistance."

"Good idea," Robert said.

"How about this," she began, ticking points off on her fingers. "First of all, to undermine all Visitor activity in every way we can. That means by direct methods as well as more passive resistance . . . work slowdowns at the factories, stuff like that. For the more direct means, well, they can't have an unlimited supply of vehicles. Those things sit on street corners unattended . . . sometimes for hours. We ought to be able to bollix 'em somehow." A general murmur of agreement filled the room.

"Then, secondly, I think we've got to find out what their hidden goals are," Juliet continued.

"Hidden?" asked Brad.

"Sure," Donovan said. "They've lied to us about everything so far. They're dumping that supposedly life-saving chemical out into the atmosphere—at least, here in L.A. they are."

"And they've brainwashed so many people with that conversion process of theirs," Juliet said. "We need to find out more about it. And more about who they may have gotten to in that way."

Donovan waved his hand for attention. "When I was captive up there, Diana told them to take me to what she called the 'Final Area'—whatever that is. To forestall that, the Visitor who helped me out, Martin, asked her why she didn't convert me. He made it sound like a challenge. First Diana said that converting me would take too long . . ." He looked slightly sheepish. "There seems to be a popular misconception that I'm stubborn and rather pigheaded."

"Oh, I can't *imagine* that!" said Juliet, with a twinkle. Laughter echoed around the room.

"Yeah . . . Well, anyway, after Martin kinda threw down the glove to her, Diana changed her mind, and told him to lock me up—which was how he was able to break me out of there later. So the success of their conversion process is dependent on the individual involved. Martin told me that if Diana just needs information, she'll go for it in much more ordinary ways . . . like torture. They were strapping one poor little SOB into a chair, and preparing to use something like a miniature blowtorch on him . . ."

Murmurs of unsurprised outrage filled the room. Donovan shrugged. "I guess the message is, don't fall into their hands if you can possibly help it. They're not playing for small change. We also ought to consider whether we can get in touch with other Visitors themselves who are like Martin—opposed to their leader's scheme—whatever it may be—here on this planet."

"Yeah," agreed Robert Maxwell. "And third in our plan of attack should be to analyze them physically. Which brings us back to the fact that we need a specimen."

"We've also got to spread the word about their reptilian nature," Juliet said. "Most people are repulsed by snakes and lizards anyway—unfair as that may be to the creatures here on Earth, it will probably work in our favor. For that, we're going to need Mr. Donovan's tape."

"Agreed," said Mike.

Ruby Engels spoke up for the first time. "We should also circulate the word about them abducting whole towns of people, and torturing them. Most people still think that if they're not scientists, they have nothing to fear!"

"Ycah," said Elias, pain flitting briefly across his dark features, "that sort of thinking is easy to fall back on. We got to let folks know the truth!"

"And, lastly," Juliet said, "and most importantly, we have to establish contact with other groups in other cities . . . around the world."

"Right," said Donovan. "They're sure as hell out there. We're gonna have to bypass ordinary means of communication— we know they've got AT&T in their pockets."

"Right. And once we figure out a way to talk to each other, we've got to organize coordinated plans to get rid of them. That's our only chance at winning."

Everyone nodded, and murmurs of agreement filled the room.

"Now . . ." Juliet said. "Let's make a list of targets locally. We'll make our first overt move tomorrow."

# 16

"WHAT SORT OF THING DID YOU HAVE IN MIND FOR TOMORROW, Julie?" Caleb Taylor asked.

Juliet sighed. "We need weapons. Much as I hate the idea of violence, Mr. Donovan's story about San Pedro pretty well confirms that if we're going to stand against them, we've got to be armed. Our information confirms they've set up an armory here in the city to equip all their roadblocks and the Visitor Friends units. How about it?"

Taut faces nodded silent agreement. Robert Maxwell felt something squeeze his insides at the idea of going up against the shock troopers he'd seen—he'd never had any military experience. Too young for Korea and too old for Vietnam . . . He straightened, deciding that he'd send Robin back to the mountain camp and her mother, tonight, to wait until the attack was over.

Maxwell looked around the assembled group. His daughter wasn't there . . . No great surprise, but he realized suddenly he hadn't seen her since before Donovan had arrived—several hours, now. Leaving the group to plan the logistics of the raid, he searched the headquarters quickly. No Robin.

Venturing outside, he looked around. There was a half-moon, masked occasionally by scudding clouds, but Maxwell could see well enough to tell she wasn't in the culvert. He wandered around the side of the building. "Robin?"

His soft call frightened some tiny creature in the underbrush, but otherwise brought no response. "Binna? It's Dad." In the distance, a police siren shrieked.

Maxwell's heart was hammering by now, the blood thudding so emphatically in his ears that it was hard to listen. He checked his watch—eight thirty. After curfew. If Robin was outside, on the streets that lay just over the hillside and down the road, then she would be fair game for the nightly Visitor patrols. Maxwell hurried through the gap in the battered chain-link fence, his steps coming rapidly.

Once on the streets, he ducked his head into his collar, shuffling along like a man who has had one drink too many and has only just realized the time. He kept his head low, but beneath his brows his eyes were busy, roving every intersection, every alley. His fear was so tangible that he fancied it followed him like a cloud—like that little guy with the unpronounceable name in the *Li'l Abner* comics. Every time he glimpsed a red uniform he was afraid there would be a familiar figure in a white blouse and gray jeans with it.

Nearly an hour passed and there was still no Robin.

Maxwell thought of turning back. His prepared excuse of having had one drink too many was now very thin, it was so late. Maybe Julie could send Elias and the Angels out after her . . . Robert bit his lip. Those young punks in the gang had looked pretty tough . . . *What am I going to do?* Maxwell wondered.

He decided he'd turn back after one more corner.

Robert Maxwell rounded the corner, only to find himself facing a squad vehicle. He stopped, half-turned, then heard a hard, reverberating voice: "Stand right there! You're breaking curfew—let me see your identification!"

*Oh, damn. Damndamn DAMN!* Maxwell halted, though his anguished mind wanted only to run.

"Against the wall."

Robert, moving like an old, old man, walked over to the cement-block side of the building. "Sorry," he said, slurring his words. "Got to drinkin' with a . . . lady friend. You know how it gets . . . forgot the time, I'm sorry . . . m'wife's gonna be *pissed* at me . . ."

He heard footsteps behind him, but realized that the first trooper had not left his original post—so there were two of them. Harsh fingers grabbed his hands, placing them on the gritty surface, then, moving with unpleasant, impersonal familiarity, grabbed his legs at the thigh, first right, then left, so he stood spread-eagled in the position television police dramas had made so familiar. Now he really understood why they did it this way—it was impossible for him to move easily, since all his weight rested on his hands and his toes. It would take him two moves, instead of just one, to free himself and run.

The hands ran over his body, digging hard into pockets, beneath his arms, at his sides, finishing with his thighs. "He's unarmed," said a second Visitor voice. The trooper removed Robert's wallet. "You can turn around now."

Maxwell turned around, so frightened that he was afraid he'd disgrace himself—his stomach heaved and he had a sudden, terrible need to urinate. He took deep breaths, forcing himself to study the man who was going through his billfold.

A black man—or, he amended to himself in the face of Donovan's revelation, this one wore the mask of a black man in his late thirties. Maxwell found himself experiencing a strange double-vision effect, picturing the reptilian features underlying the ones he could see with his eyes. He thought of long, flicking tongues and venom within that grim-jawed mouth, and felt his stomach flip-flop again.

The trooper looked up from his prisoner's driver's license. "Another Maxwell. Now isn't that interesting?"

Robert looked up at him, his eyes widening. *"Another* Maxwell? What do you mean?" But, sickened, he knew already.

"Just that we picked up a young lady late this afternoon with the same address as yours. Her name was Robin. Your daughter?" The Visitor's deep voice was almost sympathetic beneath its alien overtone.

"Yes," said Robert numbly. There didn't seem to be any point in denying it. *Oh, God, Binna! Where are you? What's happening to you? Are you all right?*

"I've got to report this to headquarters," the Visitor said, turning his head to address the guard. "Bring him over beside the hatch."

Maxwell, under the guard's direction, reassumed his spread-eagled position against the side of the squad vehicle, while the black leader went inside. Maxwell turned to the guard. "Please . . . tell me where my daughter is."

The Visitor just smiled. Robert swung the other way at the sound of booted feet on the ramp. "My daughter? You have her? Where is she?"

The Visitor's deep voice still held that touch of sympathy. "She's our prisoner."

Maxwell made a quick lunge toward the interior of the craft. The leader stopped him with a hard hand on his arm. "Not in there. She's been taken to the Mother Ship."

"Is she all right?"

The Visitor looked at him levelly, unblinking. "I'm told that will depend on you, Mr. Maxwell."

Robert looked down, biting his lip. *Oh, God, don't let this happen to me . . . please, no . . .* "What do you mean?" he asked.

"We need some information," the leader said. "We think perhaps you can help us."

Maxwell looked directly at him. "I don't know anything that could help you . . . believe me."

The Visitor went on dispassionately, as though Robert hadn't spoken. "Information about a camp in the mountains."

"No—" Robert tried to keep his voice steady; to his horror it broke. "I never heard anything about a camp . . ."

"We know it exists," the squad leader said, inexorably, gently, "but we need to know its location."

*God help me! Help Binna, please!* thought Maxwell, keeping his eyes steady on the Visitor's ebony features. "I can't help you. I don't know anything about a mountain camp. Really!" He put every bit of sincerity he could muster into his voice.

"Hmmmm." The dark eyes in the dark face were sad. "That's too bad. I'm very sorry . . . for your daughter, Robin." He turned to climb back up the ramp.

One step . . . two . . . "No, wait!" Maxwell yelped, thinking fast. "Wait! You don't understand!" Tears blurred his vision, but he could see the Visitor turn back to look at him. "My wife—my other daughters . . . they're all up there. I can't choose between them—I can't! No matter how much I want to tell you!"

"In the mountain camp?" The deep, sympathetic note was back.

Robert nodded, closing his eyes, trying to think. The night breeze made trickles of coldness as the tears broke free and ran down his face. "Yes . . . in the camp. I can't . . . you can't expect me to . . . God, please . . ."

"Come over here, Mr. Maxwell." The Visitor's hand was on Robert's arm, pulling him a few paces away from the sentry. His voice was low, conspiratorial. "I understand your anguish. Your daughter's position has placed you in a terrible dilemma . . ."

Robert nodded wordlessly.

The leader hesitated for a long moment, then glanced quickly over his shoulder at the sentry, who was looking the other way, paying no attention. "I understand, because, you see, I have children too . . ."

Maxwell looked at him. From some insane corner of his mind that still remained a scientist he wanted to ask if the Visitor young were live births or eggs. He waited.

"Suppose," the leader said, still in that quiet, gentle tone, "that I could guarantee that the mountain camp would not be taken until a certain time, so that you could get your wife and daughters out beforehand. What would you say to that?"

"You'd do that?" Maxwell said, wanting to believe. "But what about Robin?"

"After the camp is no longer a problem, then I could slip her aboard my vehicle and bring her back. Turn her loose, with your message as to how to contact you. She's only a young girl. Nobody will look for her."

"No. Believe me, she doesn't know anything! She's only a kid!"

"I could see that when we found her today. Frankly, I hated to even pick her up, but unfortunately, the others saw her too. So I had to. But she hasn't been harmed, and she won't be— if you help me."

"I—"

"If you warn the others before we arrive, Diana will question Robin. Do you understand what I'm trying to say?"

Maxwell closed his eyes, thinking of Donovan's words. Thinking of Robin's smooth, pretty skin . . . thinking of small blowtorches. "Yes. Yes, I understand. I won't warn them—" *There are only a few still up there,* he thought. *Just a couple left . . . and fewer still tomorrow, because of the attack on the* armory. *Maybe only one or two . . .* "But they're my friends. Can your people take the camp without—without—"

"Yes," said the squad leader forcefully, his hands gripping Robert's shoulders. "It can be done quite easily, with no harm to anybody. And we won't get there until . . . what? Four o'clock tomorrow afternoon? Does that give you enough time?"

Maxwell nodded. He was so exhausted he felt as though he could lie down and sleep right here. The Visitor shook him a little. "All right. Here's the map. Point to the location."

Numbly, Maxwell did so. "Tell Robin to come to the elementary school playground. I'll meet her there tomorrow evening."

"All right. Four o'clock. You have my word . . . as a father." He extended his hand.

Maxwell looked at the hand for a long moment, then slowly put his own into the other's cool, firm grasp. They shook, then the Visitor said, more loudly, "All right then, but don't let me catch you violating curfew again. Do your drinking at home from now on!"

He gave Maxwell a rough shove back toward the street. "Hurry up—and remember what I said!"

"I'll remember," said Robert fervently. "Thanks, Officer!"

He turned, his feet taking him automatically back toward the underground headquarters. He couldn't get back to the mountain camp tonight—but tomorrow. Tomorrow.

Clinging to his numbed exhaustion as a shield against thought, he kept walking, faster . . . faster. Within a street or two, reaction set in and he ran, mindlessly, scurrying through the empty streets like a frightened animal.

DIANA GLARED AT MARTIN. "ESCAPED? HOW?"

Martin took a deep breath. "I'm not sure. I left him in a holding cell, and later sent Barbara to bring him to me so I could begin preliminary injections. When I realized she was late, I went to the cell to see what had happened. Barbara was unconscious, victim of a short-range stun. Her gun and uniform were gone."

"*Shit!*" Diana said explosively. Martin wondered fleetingly where she'd learned the obscenity. She stalked back and forth along the wall of her private office/lab, sending the lab animals into a flurry of hysterical motion each time she approached. Martin waited, tensely, for her fury to abate.

"All right." Calm once more, she turned back to him. "We have to assume the worst—that he's escaped aboard one of the shuttles. Alert all units to report any unauthorized crewmembers. We're going to have to institute some kind of security clearance procedure for all incoming personnel. I'll have to consider what would be most efficient."

"At once, Diana," Martin said, turning away. He was two steps from the door when her voice stopped him. "And, Martin?"

He was almost afraid to turn—afraid that, even with his contacts covering his eyes, she'd discern his fear—but he forced himself to look back at her, showing merely a junior's deference to a superior officer. "Yes, Diana?"

"Send Brian to me."

"At once, Diana."

He left the room fighting the urge to run.

When Brian arrived, Diana nodded pleasantly to him. "Ah, Brian. Thank you for coming so promptly. I need your help."

Brian was puzzled, but tried to remain calm. He'd done his job perfectly so far—he had nothing to worry about. At least he hoped so. "Of course, Diana. Whatever I can."

Her long red lounging robe shimmered around her as she turned to eye him speculatively. "It's come to my attention that you have developed a relationship of sorts with this young lady." She pressed a button, and a screen on the wall awakened to show a girl crouched in one of the holding cells, makeup and tears streaking her rounded young face.

"Robin Maxwell!" Brian exclaimed. "But I thought she and her family had escaped!"

"Not this one." Diana looked at the girl's image reflectively for a long moment. Robin sat quietly, only raising her hand now and then to wipe at the tears which continued to well and drip down her cheeks. "So, you *do* know her?"

"Well . . . Yes, I know her," stammered Brian, wondering if Diana had somehow been told about the times he'd taken a little time off and gone to the video arcade with the girl—but he'd only done it a few times, and mostly to case the place for potential Visitor Friends recruits.

"Is she attractive to you?" Diana's dark blue eyes were very intent.

Brian shrugged. The thought had never occurred to him. He looked directly at his leader, deciding honesty might be the best move in this case. "Not like you are."

She smiled, pleased. "Ah. I see now how you've managed to rise through the ranks so quickly."

"I'm quite serious," Brian said, moving closer to her, his eyes holding hers.

"That's very interesting," Diana conceded. "Because I've had my eye on you for quite some time."

Brian smiled at her. "Of course I'm at your service." His eyes traveled down the length of the red robe, his mind filled with images of Diana in her true form—no wonder even the Leader had found her irresistible. "In any way you require service . . ."

She smiled, glancing sideways at him. "Perhaps presently. At the moment, I want your help with an experiment. A medical experiment. Involving you and . . ." her gaze flicked to the image, ". . . her."

Brian was a little taken aback. "Are you suggesting what

you seem to be? For what purpose? I'm not sure it's even possible."

She smiled, showing her false human teeth. "Oh, I'm sure you can manage. My reports indicate you're very . . . flexible. And the girl has been very sheltered, with little basis for comparison." She nodded. "Will you help me?"

"Will it be . . . painful?" Brian glanced at the girl again.

"We'll have to spend a little time in the science lab first. While I work, I'll brief you on your role. I can't promise complete freedom from discomfort, but most of the action will take place on an intercellular level. And the actual experiment *could* even prove . . . pleasurable."

Brian remained doubtful, but tried not to let it show. "If it's important to you, Diana, then of course I'm willing."

She smiled. "You won't regret your loyalty to me, Brian."

Together they left the room, heading for the lab on the other side of the giant ship.

ROBIN MAXWELL CROUCHED ON THE STRANGE, SHELFLIKE BUNK, sniffling, wishing she had a tissue. It had been hours since she'd been brought aboard the Mother Ship. She was beginning to feel hungry and thirsty.

When she'd first been brought aboard, she'd been handed over to a Visitor woman who had taken her to a strange, laboratory-looking place, then told the girl to remove her clothing. When Robin had indignantly refused, she'd drawn her sidearm and, still smiling politely, had suggested she think again. Robin had taken off her clothes.

Then the woman had made her lie on some kind of couch and passed an alien instrument slowly over her entire body, then a different one over her midsection. It hadn't hurt, but Robin had felt humiliated. The woman wouldn't answer her questions—had only finished whatever it was she was doing, returned the girl's clothing, then, when she was again dressed, gave her a sandwich and a carton of milk—afterward taking her to a remarkably normal-looking bathroom. Since then, she'd been locked here, in this horrible cell.

The tears started again. Robin shivered as she slumped backward and her spine touched the cold metal of the bulkhead. She buried her face in her arms, wondering if she'd ever see her father and mother again. She was only a kid. What could they possibly want with her?

A sound came from the door—a soft hiss. Crouching, she trembled, then, moved by the thought that she'd rather face whatever was coming standing up, she climbed to her feet, hugging herself protectively.

The door slid open, and Robin's eyes widened ecstatically. "Brian! Brian, Brian!" She rushed toward him, filled with relief at the sight of his familiar, handsome features. "Oh, thank God!"

Even as she reached him he stepped forward, and—wonder of wonders—put his arms around her, tenderly, protectively. "Robin . . . just take it easy. You're okay. You're safe now. I won't let anyone hurt you."

She sobbed, half in relief, half in joy. "Oh, Brian! I missed you! I thought I'd never see you again!"

"I'm here now. I'll protect you. I'll get you out of here." He gathered her even closer, and she felt the cool hardness of his muscled body. Tentatively, Robin slipped her arms around him in return, her mind whirling chaotically. Her knees felt rubbery, and she leaned against him. He supported her weight without effort, and his hand came up to caress her thick, tumbled hair. "Robin . . . I missed you."

"Brian . . ." She touched his cheek hesitantly, hoping her eyes weren't red and that her makeup hadn't run—she still couldn't believe he was here, holding her. It was like a wonderful dream, the kind that she woke from at night, her heart beating so hard it seemed it would break out of her body, and then she sobbed to realize it *was* just a dream—that *he*—the wonderful, godlike *he* who lived only in dreams—was gone.

*It's* real *this time,* she told herself fiercely. *He's here. He's holding you in his arms. I think—I think he even wants to kiss you . . .*

He did. His mouth touched Robin's, brushing quickly, exploringly, then returning to press harder. She closed her eyes, feeling faint, her hands clutching at him frenziedly. *Brian, I love you,* she thought, feeling his hand touch her breast, at first hesitantly, then returning to cup it firmly. He slid his hand beneath her sweater.

"No . . ." she said dreamily, as his mouth traveled down her cheek, settling on the tiny pulse in her throat. His hand was pulling at her sweater. "No . . . yes . . . Brian . . ."

Her eyes closed and she swayed dizzily. She was scarcely aware when he lowered her to the bunk. She had one more sharp, insistent return to clarity when she realized her jeans were open, but by then his weight was holding her down. He was heavy; she couldn't get up.

*No,* she wanted to say. *Stop, this is too real . . .*

But it was also too late.

# 17

JULIET PARRISH WOKE JUST BEFORE THE WINDUP ALARM CLOCK
rang at six o'clock. She rolled over and shut it off quickly, before it could jangle; she'd always hated being jarred awake by
alarms. She lay back in her narrow, lumpy cot for a moment,
thinking that as soon as she moved, swung her legs out,
reached for her jeans, she'd be committed to this day and
what it could hold. *Please, God, don't let anybody die. Don't
let anybody get hurt. Please.*

She closed her eyes, feeling sleep nibble at the edges of her
body, wanting to suck her back down into its warm depths.
With a quick jerk that stabbed her hip, Juliet sat up, reaching
for her clothes.

Clad in old jeans and a red sweater, she coiled up her
shoulder-length hair, pinning it into a bun. Then, picking up
her cane, she limped out into the hall. The first person she
saw was Robert Maxwell—from the haunted look in his
brown eyes and the darkness beneath them, Juliet gathered
that he'd slept even less than she had. "You okay, Robert?"
she asked.

"Yeah," he mumbled, not meeting her eyes.

"Is anything wrong?"

He shook his head. "No . . . no. Just nerves, I guess."

"Tell me about it."

Elias came out of the room they'd outfitted as a men's dorm, his usual jauntiness noticeably subdued. "Hi, Julie," he said.

"Sleep okay, Elias?" she asked.

"Oh, sure," he said bleakly. "Like a baby—one with the colic."

By now the main hall was filled with people. Juliet turned, addressing them. "Everybody try to eat something, okay? I know you're nervous, but it's going to be a long day. Can't have anyone passing out from hunger in the middle of this."

Turning, she limped into the laboratory. She was washing her face in a pan of cold water when she heard a step. Mike Donovan lounged in the doorway. "Morning, Doc," he said.

"Good morning, Mr. Donovan," Juliet said primly—she wasn't sure why she treated him with such arms'-length formality, but there was something about his cocky grin that irritated her.

"Caleb's scrambled up a pan of eggs," Mike said, nodding in the direction of the big meeting room. "Aren't you gonna take your own advice?"

Juliet smiled wanly. "I'm afraid it's a case of 'do as I say, not as I do . . .' Quite frankly, I don't think my stomach would cooperate with anything more than a cup of orange juice."

"That bad, eh?" He watched her dry her face with a ragged old towel. Juliet, conscious of his scrutiny, made an effort to keep her hands steady as she emptied the pan into the sink, but, to her dismay, water slopped onto the floor. Donovan continued as if he hadn't noticed. "I gotta hand it to you, Doc—you've really pulled this bunch together. Juiced 'em up. They're ready to go out and fight tigers this morning."

She looked over at him as he continued. "But I'll tell you

something: keep a little of that juice for yourself. Don't give it all away, 'cause you're gonna need it. You've cut yourself a big piece of pie with this raid, Doc."

Juliet smiled wryly at him. "So, it's 'Doc' now, Mr. Donovan? What happened to 'kid'?"

He ducked his head for a moment, then met her eyes again, his own slightly sheepish. "Yeah . . . well . . . you're older than I thought."

"Thanks," said Juliet, grinning. "I think."

"You know what I mean." He gestured.

"Hey, Julie." Elias stuck his head in the door. "I got juice and a doughnut out here for you. A *chocolate* iced one."

"Thanks, Elias." Taking her cane, she went out into the hall. There she sipped her juice and managed to nibble at the pastry, studying her people. There were more of them than yesterday—many members of the new resistance group still lived at home, especially those employed in non-science-related fields. The rebels talked loudly, laughed uproariously, their movements quick and abrupt . . . all except for a few, like Robert Maxwell, who sat silently, still, pulled deep within themselves:

*Better give them something to do, quick,* Juliet thought. *They're really wired.* "Everybody?" she called out, and at the sound of her voice, they all turned to watch her. "Okay, one last time. Everyone clear on his or her assignment?"

A general murmur of agreement accompanied the nodding heads. "Diversionary actions begin at one o'clock. Right, Caleb, Ruby, the rest of you?"

Caleb, dressed for work at the Richland plant, his friend Bill Graham beside him, nodded. "They'll know we're alive and well at the plant, all right."

"And downtown," Ruby said. "Especially at the police stations."

"Good," Juliet said. "Our main assault at the armory will begin just before two, when they should be at the most disorganized."

"*Two?*" Robert Maxwell said, paling. "I—"

"Yes," said Juliet. "You missed the end of the meeting last night. You're coming with us to the armory, all right?"

"Uh . . . yeah, okay," Maxwell said.

A pulse jumped beneath his eye. Juliet frowned. "By the way, I haven't seen Robin. Did you send her back to the mountain camp, so she'd be safe?"

Maxwell nodded without speaking, not looking up. Studying his pallor, Juliet was tempted to tell him to go back to the camp himself—it was obvious the man was terrified. But they needed every hand they could get.

While she was considering, Maxwell looked up, saw her concerned gaze, and smiled weakly. "I'm okay, really. Just a little nervous . . ."

"All right, Robert," Juliet said doubtfully. "Now, those of you who will be in on the raid on the armory. We've got to keep in mind our primary objective—"

"To grab as many high-powered weapons as we can get our little patty paws on, without gettin' ourselves wasted," Elias supplied.

"Right." Juliet nodded emphatically. "It's critical for all our future operations that we be able to defend ourselves. For that we'll need arms. Then we'll be able to protect all our equipment when we bring it down from the mountains."

Mike Donovan stirred restlessly. "Listen, gang, while you guys are stirring up a ruckus down here, I think I'm gonna try to infiltrate the Mother Ship again. I want to—"

"Find your family?" Juliet interrupted, remembering Donovan's single-minded outburst of the previous evening.

"Yeah, that too. I won't deny it. But I also have an idea on how to get into a place where I'll be able to find out just what their real plans are. With the uniform, I should be able to get in and get back out."

Ruby turned to look at him. Her expression said plainly that she thought he was crazy. "That sounds really suicidal to me."

"Yeah." Donovan shrugged. "Maybe I was a kamikaze pilot in a previous incarnation. That's what my partner, Tony, always says. Don't forget, he's still up there. I won't sleep nights until I find out what's happened to him—to all of 'em."

"In that case, you'd better tell us where you hid that tape," Juliet said. "As a precautionary measure."

He grinned crookedly. "And I thought you loved me for my mind. It's in a locker at the bus terminal." He dug in his pants pocket, handed Juliet a key. "A kid I know named Josh has been paying the rental each day."

"Good enough," Juliet said, her eyes on his, her fingers gripping the key. "Take care, Mr. Donovan. We'd hate to lose you."

"I'd hate to lose me, too."

"Good luck," Juliet said, still looking at him, then added abruptly, turning away, "To all of us."

Caleb's deep tones cut through the other murmurs. "Hey, Julie . . . how 'bout a prayer? One for the road, so to speak."

The young woman nodded. "Go on, Caleb."

"Me?" He glanced around, then composed himself for a second. "Well, Lord. We sure do need your help on this one. Please help every one of us to do our best, 'cause a lot of folks are counting on us. Give us wisdom and strength and courage, if that be your will. Thanks, Lord. Amen."

Juliet was surprised to hear Donovan's voice mixed with the others as they echoed Caleb's "amen." She faced them, taking a deep breath. "Let's do it."

HARMONY MOORE HASTENED TOWARD THE COMMISSARY, CARRYing a tray of refilled salt, pepper, and sugar containers. It was a nice day, she thought, looking around her at the blue sky, the gently scudding clouds. Her eyes were so accustomed to the huge Visitor ship hanging over the city that she didn't even notice it consciously anymore.

As she walked along, her eyes turned upward, wondering if it would rain by evening, her foot jerked as her shoe stuck to something on the concrete. "Huh?" Harmy stopped, put the tray down, and lifted her foot. Tendrils of bright pink chewing gum clutched her shoe lovingly. Harmy made an exasperated sound.

As she attempted to scrape the mess off her shoe, she braced her hand against one of the massive pipes thrusting outward from a huge refinery tank. Her fingers brushed something yielding at the same moment as she heard the ticking sound. Harmy looked up at her hand. Attached to one of the pipes was a wad of grayish-white goop, with a small black box attached. There was a clock face on the box. A red pointer showed one o'clock, while the time read twelve forty-five.

*What the heck is that?* Harmy wondered, staring at it. *It almost looks like . . . like . . .*

Swallowing, forgetting the tray, she backed away, jerking her foot free of the gum with a sudden panicky yank. She wondered what the range of the thing was . . . if there were others planted to go off. She ran the little distance to the parking lot, and her truck, her mind racing. *The resistance! This must be something they're doing. What should I do?*

Harmony had watched Kristine Walsh's reports on the television, listened to the radio—and wondered what the real truth was. Her father had died in Korea, her brother in Vietnam—she'd been a pacifist since high school. She didn't like seeing armed shock troopers on the streets of her city. But setting bombs where they might hurt or injure people, destroy property, was something else.

Harmy bit her lip as she sat on the tailgate of her truck, the minutes ticking by in her head, on her watch. There was nobody else in sight. Maybe she ought to call the cops. But from the rumors she'd heard, that could result in reprisals from the Visitor troops. She'd even heard a rumor that they'd apprehended a whole town that tried to rally against them. One of Harmy's best friends, an X-ray technician, had disappeared over a month ago. She missed Betty horribly—they'd been so close.

Harmy checked her watch again. Twelve fifty-eight and thirty-three seconds.

She looked back up. A figure in a red uniform was walking around the tank, a clipboard in his hand.

"*Willy!*" Harmy shrieked. Without thinking, she jumped up and ran toward him. "*No! Get away!*" Racing over to him, she grabbed his arm and dragged him toward the parking lot.

The blast knocked both of them off their feet. Wild-eyed, they stared at each other. Then they heard the other blasts. The alarms shrieked. Harmy climbed to her feet and offered a hand to William. "Harmy?" he shouted as he stood up. "What's coming on?"

"*Going on,*" she corrected automatically. "I think it's the resistance people."

"You saved my life," William said, still clutching her hand. "I am thankful to you always."

In the midst of the chaos of running feet and shrieking sirens, she smiled at him. "You saved Caleb. It was the least I could do."

MIKE DONOVAN HESITATED FOR A SECOND BEFORE THE YELLOW door, feeling in his pocket for the gold and crystal key he'd given to Sean so long ago. It slipped into his hand, cool and smooth. Glancing quickly down the shadowy corridor of the Mother Ship to make sure he was unobserved, he pushed the key into the slot. With a tiny hydraulic hum, the door slid aside. Donovan pulled the key out and stepped through.

*So far, so good*, he thought. He hesitated for a second, blinking to accustom his eyes to the even dimmer light within. A dark corridor stretched ahead. Behind him, the door slid shut, making him jump.

He hadn't had any trouble getting aboard the Mother Ship—it had simply been a matter of keeping his dark glasses on and lingering near a shuttle until it was ready for departure, then scramming aboard at the last moment. Under his pulled-down Visitor cap, the dark glasses masking his features even further, he'd been just another anonymous figure in uniform.

Just as the shuttle had landed, an announcement had echoed through the docking bay that the Richland plant was under attack. In the resulting confusion of troops and departing squad vehicles, he'd slipped away into the bowels of the alien ship.

Donovan moved forward, trying to keep the heavy uniform boots from echoing on the metal-gridded floor of the corridor. He passed no one. Finally his way opened out into a huge central room, so large that even the echoes of his footsteps were lost and muffled. The cavernous room was filled, floor to ceiling, with huge tanks—but not the heavy-duty refinery tanks that he'd seen at Richland. These tanks—he tapped one to be sure—were thin-walled and bore no pressure gauges or instruments to indicate the condition of their contents.

A valve led out of one of the tanks. Donovan twisted it. A stream of clear liquid trickled out. Bending over, Mike eyed it, then, frowning, put out a finger. The cold liquid felt familiar on his skin. Donovan sniffed it, then cautiously tasted.

"Jesus, it's *water*. In all these tanks?" Turning the valve wider, Donovan took a few swallows; he was thirsty. Then he roamed through the huge room, trying valves at random. After the first ten or so confirmed that each tank had the same contents, Donovan stood, trying to count them. He lost track after five hundred, but there were more than that, many more. How many millions of gallons did they represent? And were there similar holds with the same cargo on the other ships?

Mike rubbed the back of his neck as he stood in the dim coolness of the hold, puzzling. There was something going on that he didn't understand here, and that he *ought* to. Comprehension niggled at the fringes of his mind, tantalizing him, but staying just out of his reach.

When he stepped out of the corridor, he went looking for another of the yellow doors. He found it, inserted his key, and stepped in. As he moved along the corridor, he heard footsteps approaching. Quickly, he flattened himself into a darkened alcove, seeing a technician pass. Donovan heard the yellow door hiss, then peered out cautiously. He jerked back quickly at the sound of more footsteps, then cocked one eye around the edge of the alcove. *Martin!*

As the Visitor officer walked by, Donovan reached out and grabbed him. He felt the false, cool flesh of the alien's nose and mouth beneath his stifling hand, saw the contact-covered eyes widen as they recognized him. Cautiously, Donovan removed his hand.

"Donovan!"

"Yeah." Mike regarded him grimly. "I want to know what's going on. I just got back from the hold where the tanks are. The *water* tanks. I asked you before about the real reason for your little visit to our small planet here, and you said there wasn't enough time if I was going to escape. But right now I've got all the time in the world, and I want you to level with me."

Martin looked at the floor for a long moment, then sighed. "All right. Yes, the tanks are full of water, there's no chemical."

"Then you *are* dumping the chemical out into the atmosphere?"

"Yes."

"*Why?*" Mike shook the Visitor's shoulders a little in frustration. Then his eyes widened as it hit him. "Ohmygod—I've been an idiot. The *water*. You're stealing the water. The chemical is just a smoke screen. All the water that gets pumped into the plants to supposedly process the chemical is actually taken up here. But why?"

"Pure liquid H-2-O is the rarest and most valuable commodity you can imagine. It's one of the first resources any industrial society destroys and pollutes. You've already started here, so you should know. Unlike most planets, ours included, your world has a lot more water than it has land area. We need water desperately—for sustenance, industry . . . everything."

"But we would have shared it—"

"Some of us proposed the idea of telling you the truth, asking you to do just that. But our Leader wants it *all*. Now that Earth is regarded as more or less secured, other ships from our home are already on their way. The whole plan will take a generation—our life spans approximate yours—but in the end, we'll have it all, if the Leader has his way."

"Earth will be a desert," Mike said hollowly. "Humanity . . . all of us . . . will die without water."

Martin sighed. "There won't be any people left when we leave."

Mike looked at him.

The Visitor officer nodded. "There's something else I have to show you."

With a terrible sense of foreboding, Mike Donovan followed Martin along the corridor. Like the other one, it opened out into a huge room, but this one contained smaller, cylindrical chambers, each about three feet by seven. The hair prickling on the back of his neck, Donovan looked around. "What the hell are these for?"

Martin gestured wearily. "See for yourself."

Stiffly, Mike walked the short distance to the nearest cylinder. It was filled with some kind of gelatinous, gray-colored substance that flowed and eddied within the container. As Donovan peered into it, the thick gray gel swirled and thinned, and, abruptly, a face drifted into view. It was an older man, with a thick moustache. His eyes stared, vacant; his mouth hung open. He was naked.

Martin's voice came from behind Mike. "They're your people. The ones who disappeared."

Mike whirled to face him, his mouth so dry he had trouble speaking. One name burned in his mind—*Sean*. He choked on the question. "Dead?"

"No. Not dead." Donovan closed his eyes in momentary relief, then forced himself to listen. "Metabolism slowed extraordinarily, perfectly preserved—they can be revived in a matter of minutes. Diana developed the technique."

Mike looked out at the thousands upon thousands of cocoons, then, turning, directly at Martin: "My son is here. Someplace."

"He was taken?"

"Along with the rest of San Pedro. I have to find him."

Martin rubbed wearily at his forehead with a very human gesture of frustration. "Mike, there's no way, short of looking him up in the central computer—and I have only limited access to it. We don't even know for sure he's on *this* ship. He could be on the San Francisco ship. Or the Seattle one. I'm sorry."

Donovan gestured at the cocoons. "There's a way of finding him—there's *got* to be. But Martin, *why*? Why are they being taken—stored—like this? Because they're troublemakers, or scientists who'd like to do tests on you, reveal your true faces?" Martin gave him a quick glance, then looked away. Mike grinned ironically. "You know I've seen 'em. It's weird to stand here talking to you as though you're human like I am, and know you're not. Really weird."

"Yes, I know about your fight with Jerome. He said you're—what's the term? A mean customer?"

"I do my best," Donovan said absently. "But if that's so, why not kill 'em? Why keep them here?"

"The Leader wants them living. Some of them will be conscripted into fighting his battles. I think the term is 'cannon fodder.'"

"How did somebody like that get into power anyway?"

Martin looked grim. "Charisma. Circumstances. Promises. Financial backing. A doctrine that appealed to the unthinking—assurances that he, as their leader, would bring them to greatness. Not enough of us spoke out to question him—or even took him seriously—until it was too late. It's happened here on your planet, hasn't it?"

"Yeah. It has." Mike remembered something abruptly. "I've been meaning to ask about Barbara. She ordered me to shoot her—told me they'd never believe I overpowered her and stole the uniform, otherwise. Is she okay?"

"She's recovering."

"Good. I want to thank her someday." He looked back at the cocoons. "So many. There must be thousands of 'em."

"Yes."

Mike looked at him. "*Some* of them, you said, would be used for troops in your leader's army. What about the rest?"

Martin looked off across the chamber, refusing to meet the human's eyes. "In addition to water, there's another basic shortage on our planet."

Donovan felt the blood drain out of his face, leaving his features stiff. His lips moved silently. "Food?" But even though he hadn't spoken aloud, Martin, who was watching him again, nodded.

"Yes."

Shaking violently, Donovan put a hand to his face. "Oh, God. Should'a known. I think . . . gonna be—" He swallowed gulpingly, trying to control his nausea, rubbing furiously at his mouth as though Martin's revelation had left a bad taste on his lips—a foulness that could be wiped away.

"Take it easy, Mike," Martin said. "We don't have time for that."

"I know." Still trembling, Donovan forced himself to take deep, slow breaths. "God. I should have guessed. You could . . . do that? To a kid like Sean?" He looked over at another container where a young woman's face floated. "To her?"

Martin shook his head. "Don't. I feel terrible about it. Making both of us sick isn't going to help. I'm not going to say that I'm a vegetarian—that's not our way. But intelligent species? No. When this expedition was first mounted, we were told the inhabitants of this world were . . . like cattle. Not intelligent. Then, when we came here, there were those who protested when they saw the truth. They were . . . disposed of."

"Yeah? Iguana burgers?"

"What?"

"Never mind. Bad taste." Mike spat into a dark corner. "We'd better get out of here."

As they walked back toward the door onto the main corridor, he whispered, "Just promise me something, Martin."

"What?"

"If you can, find out where my son is. Sean Donovan. And his mother too. Her name is Marjorie."

Martin nodded bleakly. "If I can. It won't be easy. I have to be very cautious."

As they reached the door, Donovan put a hand on the Visitor officer's arm. "Now for Tony. I want you to take me to him."

The alien hesitated for a long moment. "I know which

holding cell he was in, but Diana said she was going to question him personally. I didn't hear anything else."

"Let's go there, then."

Martin was obviously frightened. "That's a well-trafficked area, with a lot of security. If I'm seen with you, I'll never be able to explain it away."

"You're not taking nearly the chance I am. Let's go."

The Visitor hesitated as though he would argue further, then stopped when his eyes met Mike's. "All right," he said reluctantly.

They walked quickly, purposefully, Donovan with his cap pulled down and his dark glasses on. It made seeing difficult—the ship itself was already dim for human vision. But he had little choice.

Finally they reached the detention area. Martin checked door numbers, then inserted his key. "I must warn you, Mike, this will be unpleasant."

Donovan nodded. "Okay."

They stepped inside. The room was cool and still and smelled of blood and excrement. In its center was a draped gurney. Martin stepped over to the drape, picked up the edge, and looked beneath it. As Mike stepped over to join him he turned and nodded wordlessly.

Mike's breath caught in his chest. "Tony," he said softly, knowing his friend could not hear. Gently he pushed Martin aside and picked up the sheet.

Tony Leonetti's face was composed, serene. Someone had closed his eyes. There were no bruises on the features. Looking for the cause of death, Mike raised the sheet higher, scanning the body. The cause of death was obvious. Someone had cut Tony open, someone with consummate surgical skill and technique—but they'd neglected to sew him back up. The gurney on which he lay was slightly hollowed, and he was inches deep in blood.

Donovan choked, then gently touched his friend's face. "Tony . . . God, I'm sorry, buddy. I'm so sorry . . ." He lowered the shroud back over the still, pale features. "Diana?" he said, keeping his voice steady with an effort.

"Yes." Martin sounded nearly as anguished as Donovan felt. "She's authorized some . . . medical experiments. She occasionally demonstrates surgical techniques for her staff . . ."

"I want to kill her," Mike said, his voice hard and brittle.

Martin's voice was weary. "You'd have to stand in line."

A groan from the corner made both of them start and turn. A figure in a blue work shirt lay curled in the dark, on the cold floor. Donovan hastened to turn the injured man over, gently. He'd obviously been beaten by someone who was obsessed with doing a thorough job—his features were bruised so badly that it was difficult to get any idea of his age or normal appearance. His left eye was swollen so badly it made a hideous reddish-blue bulge on the side of his head.

Battered, cracked lips moved, and Donovan made out a hoarse whisper. "Who . . . who are you?"

"A friend."

"You're . . . not . . . one of them?"

"No."

The man tried to smile, weakly. Mike realized from his dark hair, the intonations of his speech, that he was Mexican. "They tried to make me talk . . . I told them nothing." He grinned, the expression hideous. "Do you have . . . any water? I used . . . the last of mine . . . to spit at Diana."

"Here," said Martin, holding a cup to the man's lips. He swallowed with an effort, but managed to drink the whole cup, seeming the better for it. Martin came back with some medical supplies. While Donovan cleaned and medicated the man's face, Martin bound his ribs to support them, and gave the man several injections.

At Donovan's inquiring look, he explained, "To prevent

infection. Antibiotics, mostly, but the second one should get him on his feet. I assume you're going to want to take him back with you?"

Donovan hadn't actually thought about it until Martin spoke, but at the Visitor officer's words, he nodded. "Yeah. Think we can smuggle him into a squad vehicle?"

"I'll scout ahead, see what I can turn up. There's someone else you ought to take with you. They picked up a young girl yesterday, and I understand she's being used as a hostage to make her father betray one of the underground bases. Diana seemed particularly interested in her, so you'd better get her out of here. She's only a kid."

"Okay, I'm game. I'll take care of him while you go check on the kid. I'll meet you in the docking bay in . . . ten minutes?"

Martin checked his chronometer. "Make it fifteen. See you, Mike."

When he'd gone, Donovan got his patient another cup of water. "Think you can stand now?" he asked, when the man had finished it. "We're gonna try and get off this crate. You up for that?"

"Believe it, *amigo*," the man said.

"Good. My name's Mike Donovan, by the way." They shook.

"Sancho Gomez."

"Nice to meet you, Sancho. Too bad it couldn't have been under better circumstances."

When his chrono indicated that it was time to move, Donovan took Sancho's arm, unstrapped his Visitor sidearm, then put his hand on its butt. "Just a little prisoner transfer to another cellblock," he said, "that's all we are. Try and look scared of me, Sancho."

"*Comprende.*"

They reached a hiding place just inside the docking bay

without incident. A few minutes later, Martin entered, holding the arm of a terrified-looking teenage girl, her face dirty, tearstained, smeared with eye makeup.

Glancing quickly around, Martin motioned to the girl to climb into one of the small squad vehicles. Even as he turned back, Donovan and Sancho were beside him. They climbed into the Visitor craft. Martin nodded, preparing to climb in also. "Let's go."

"You're coming too?" Mike was surprised.

"I have to. It's silly to think that nobody saw me with you or Robin. It'll be dangerous for me here now."

"You ought to stay here, Martin." Donovan leaned out of the craft, his green eyes very intent.

"What? Why?"

"We need somebody up here on our side. You'll be invaluable to the underground."

"But, Mike—" Martin looked frankly scared. "I've got to fly this thing for you."

"Shit on that. I can fly it. You stay here, Martin."

"You can't fly this thing!"

"Wanna bet? I'm a good pilot, and I spent every trip we made together watching everything you did. I can fly it, I know I can."

"But listen—"

"Dammit, Martin, admit it!" Mike leaned close to the Visitor, his eyes holding the alien's. "You're scared, right?"

"I—" Martin's shoulders sagged and he glanced behind him. "It's going to be very dangerous for me."

"You'll make it." Mike clasped his shoulder. "Nobody even gave Sancho and me a glance. Nobody will connect this little caper with you. Just duck outa sight, so I can get out of here."

Martin still hesitated. Donovan shook his shoulder roughly. "Dammit, Martin! Dangerous for you? It's dangerous for all of us! I've lost a son, and my partner. And what about Barbara? She was willing to risk me shooting her to help! What does Sancho look like, a day at Disneyland? Hell, we're all damn scared, Martin, but each of us has got to help in the best way we can." He hesitated for a long moment, seeing Martin's quick glance at Sancho. "How about it, man, you game?"

Martin nodded suddenly. "All right." He pointed to the controls. "You'll have a tendency to overcompensate, Mike. It's very sensitive."

"Which one controls direction?" Martin showed him. "Good. Speed?" He watched and nodded.

"And that one over there is your altitude gauge. It's fully fueled. Good luck, Mike."

"I hope so." Mike hesitantly started the craft. It whined into immediate life. "You ought to sell these babies in New England," he mumbled. "Make a fortune." As Martin turned to leave, Donovan caught his arm.

"Hey . . . Martin. Thanks. I'm proud to have you as a friend. Our side is lucky you're around."

Martin nodded. "I'm glad to have *you* as a friend. Now, if you don't get this thing out of here, we won't live to be old friends—which would be the best of all. So, 'scram' is the word, I believe."

"Right." Martin hurried away as Donovan closed the hatch. "Strap in, everyone." Just as the newsman began to ease the lever forward, there came a shout. "Damn! We've been spotted! Hang on!

He goosed the squad vehicle, which leaped forward with a rush, heading for the landing bay doors. They began to close as the fugitives neared them, and Donovan had to make a quick swerve. The craft bounced slightly as they struck the opposite door—then they were away.

They soared out into the open blueness of the upper atmosphere. As Donovan eased the lever forward, trying to get the feel of the craft, they were abruptly aimed at the roiling blue-green of the Pacific. The girl sitting next to Donovan gasped shrilly as the vehicle dived, "Pull it up!"

"I'm *trying*!" Donovan snapped, pulling back on the lever, fighting panic as the ocean grew in the windscreen. The nose of the craft came up . . . up . . .

With nearly equal suddenness, the three humans found themselves upside down as the Visitor craft looped violently. The girl screamed. "Shut up, you idiot!" Donovan shouted, fighting the controls. Finally, by using only the lightest of touches, he was able to right the craft and fly in a fairly straight path. He banked into a long, gradual turn that would lead him out to sea. Martin was right—the thing nearly flew itself. But he wanted to practice awhile before attempting a landing.

"Where are you going, *amigo*?" asked Sancho, who was sitting in the rear of the craft.

"Out to sea, so I can try this baby out without being hassled by any other air traffic," Mike said. "I want to practice before I have to even *think* about any fancy moves or trying a landing. Out here I'll have a little peace and quiet."

"Uh, I hate to tell you this, *Señor* Donovan, but I'm afraid we're being hassled."

"Huh?"

"There are two other craft like this one chasing us, and—"

Sancho was interrupted by something striking the squad vehicle, making it shudder.

"What was that?" yelped the girl.

". . . and shooting at us," finished Sancho. "I think we're in trouble."

# 18

RUBY ENGELS DRAGGED HER ANCIENT SHOPPING CART BEHIND HER as she walked slowly up the familiar sidewalk. She checked her watch for the twentieth time—twelve forty. Only a few minutes to go. She took a deep, shivering breath, hoping that God would give her the strength to do what had to be done. In spite of her bravado of that morning, Ruby was scared. All her life she'd been a law-abiding person, and it was hard to change at her age.

As she walked along, she saw two familiar figures just ahead—people she'd never expected to see again. Quickening her pace, she smiled and waved. "Stanley! Lynn! You're back!"

Stanley and Lynn Bernstein were standing in their backyard, out near the pool house. They both looked up at Ruby's hail. "Ruby!"

Leaving her cart at the corner of the driveway, Ruby hastened toward them. "I'm so glad to see you! I thought maybe you wouldn't be coming back!"

Stanley's arm was bandaged from the elbow down—he held it stiffly, as though the slightest jar would bring agony. Lynn appeared uninjured, but her blue eyes looked changed—as though they'd beheld the worst she could have imagined, and was only now beginning to realize it hadn't destroyed her. She reached out to embrace the older woman, her arms shaking. "Ruby, it's so good to be back!"

"Where's Abraham?"

The Bernsteins looked at each other. "We never saw him," Stanley said dully. "When we got home, we saw Daniel." He said the name as if it hurt him. "He hadn't seen him either. He promised to ask his leader, Brian, where Father is, but—" He swallowed. "I'm afraid it's better not to know."

Lynn put her face in her hands, shaking. "Daniel said he . . . was sorry . . . that we'd been—"

"Take it easy, Lynn," Stanley said, putting his good arm around his wife.

"I understand," said Ruby clearly. "Please, Stanley, take care of yourself. Lynn, I'll see you later. Try to get some rest." She patted the younger woman on her bowed shoulder, then walked quickly away.

She refused to think. Her legs moved mechanically, one-two, one-two, as she reclaimed her shopping cart and followed the path she and her friend had walked so many times. At the first corner, one of *their* vehicles was parked, hatch open, next to two police cars.

Ruby stopped. Halfway down the side block, several shock troopers, accompanied by two policemen, were searching some tough-looking youths in front of Visitor posters festooned with the "V" symbol. Cans of red spray paint bore mute witness to the kids' crime. Quickly, Ruby took one of the Molotov cocktails out of its concealment in her shopping cart, then pulled her Zippo lighter out of her pocket. Holding the gasoline-filled bottle concealed beneath her huge purse, she lit the rag fuse as she passed the open hatch. Nobody was watching—the troopers were concentrating on the kids.

With a quick, sure gesture, Ruby tossed the cocktail into

the open shuttle. "This one's for Abraham," she muttered, giving a defiant glance at the Visitors' backs. Then she trotted on, the cart bumping.

The first, small explosion was joined a second later by a much bigger one. Ruby cast a quick, satisfied glance back to see the shuttle in flames; one of the police cars had also caught. The Visitors and cops were staring at the flames; the kids were only flying, distant figures. She smiled tautly, before she noticed that one of the policemen was watching her over his shoulder.

Ruby's back stiffened—then she saw his grin, quickly stifled, and the "V" sign he made behind his back for her benefit.

Ruby Engels walked on down the street, her eyes scanning for another target.

# 19

AS THE DELIVERY TRUCK LURCHED AROUND A CORNER, ELIAS'S hands slipped on the steering wheel. "Sorry 'bout that," he said, wiping first his right, then his left palm on the thigh of his jeans. "Hands are sweaty." The sound of another explosion echoed in the distance. "You scared too?" He checked the rearview mirror; the garbage truck was still back there.

Juliet, sitting beside him, looked tensely through the window at the hulk of a burning police car. "Yeah. I just hope nobody gets hurt. I would hate to lose one of us."

Robert Maxwell, sitting beside Juliet on the swaying seat of the fast-moving truck, was thinking fast. He stole a quick look at his watch, which showed one forty-seven. *Two hours to go. I'll have to break free during the attack and steal some transportation so I can get Kathy and the girls out.* He thought of the people in the mountain camp, imagined Juliet's face if she knew how he was betraying them, then resolutely pushed such thoughts out of his mind. *Robin. Think of Robin, up there in that damn hulking ship . . .*

The truck turned another corner. Directly ahead of them was a huge concrete and brick building, enclosed within a twelve-foot chain-link fence. Two shock troopers stood guard at the gate. Inside the fence they could see army vehicles parked.

"There. There's the loading dock, Elias." Juliet pointed.

"I see it. Hang on!" The truck accelerated toward the gate. With a huge lurch it struck the chain-link and burst through.

"Look out for the two on the roof!" Juliet shouted. They slewed around, bouncing off a parked troop carrier, then backed up to the loading dock.

The garbage truck trundled in through the wreckage of the gate and its back door began to open as the pulsing whine of Visitor weapons filled the parking lot. Armed resistance fighters jumped out and began firing at the Visitors. Several fighters produced large framed mirrors, using them to flash the bright sunlight in the faces of the roof guards.

Juliet jumped out of the delivery truck and ran around to the back, her hip stabbing with pain—she barely felt it. "Open it up! Let's get it loaded! Fast!"

The rear door of the truck opened and more resistance fighters tumbled out onto the loading dock. They raced inside the armory with Juliet, the sounds of the battle outside following them. Elias came up beside Juliet as she grabbed several guns. "Whoo! Lookit all this hardware!"

"No time to pick and choose," she snapped. "Load 'em on." Quickly they formed a chain, passing weapons from hand to hand into the truck. Elias and Brad raced around, handing machine guns, a bazooka and ammunition, then a rocket launcher and rockets to the chain. Juliet looked up at a shout to see one fighter dragged in by another, then Robert, who half-carried a moaning woman. "Oh, no!" She hastened over to the wounded. "We've got to get them into the truck!"

Robert's eyes were wild, his mouth anguished. "I've got to get out of here, warn the mountain camp! They're going to be raided this afternoon!"

"*What?!*"

"Robin is a prisoner—I was only trying to protect her! But there are too many lives at stake—I can't keep quiet and let them be taken!"

Without waiting for a response, he turned and dashed out of the armory, located a parked jeep, scanned to see if the keys were in the ignition, then climbed in. Juliet hesitated, but there was nothing she could do. Robert started the jeep, gunned the motor, and, crouching low over the wheel, roared away.

"Elias!" Juliet called. "Help me get these people into the truck!"

As they carried the wounded man and woman out, she shouted to the other rebels: "The truck's getting full—pass the word. Get ready to haul it out of here! We've got to head straight for the mountain camp—they're going to be raided!"

The next few minutes passed in a blur, a hideous one. Several more wounded were slung hurriedly into the truck, and Juliet saw that at least one of them wouldn't make it as far as the mountain camp. Elias and Brad oversaw the retreat, while Juliet remained in the rear of the delivery truck with the wounded.

When she peered out to see how the courtyard fighting was going, Juliet saw many red-clad bodies. All of the alien vehicles were in flames. Even as she watched, the fire spread toward the munitions storage. "Elias!" she shrieked. "Get us *out* of here!"

Brad leaped into the rear of the truck just as the engine rumbled to life. "Did everyone else make it into the trash truck?" Juliet asked.

"Yeah." Brad looked around at the jumbled stacks of weapons. "We did okay, looks like."

"If you can call five wounded, one probably critically, okay then you're right. Come over here." When he reached her side, she continued, "Okay, hold this rag here, until the bleeding stops. How much first aid did they give you as a cop?"

"I've delivered a baby," he said. "But mostly it was just basic wait-for-the-ambulance stuff."

"That's better than most people. At least you don't upchuck at the sight of blood."

"What were you yelling about the mountain camp?"

"Robert got away just after telling me that the Visitors captured his daughter, Robin, and forced him to give the location of the mountain camp. They're going to raid it. We've got to get our equipment out of there!"

"Oh, shit! That sonofabitch!"

"Brad, are you crazy? What do you expect the poor guy to do, just throw away his own daughter's life? I just hope that somehow we can manage to get her back. Maybe this 'Martin' Donovan spoke of can help."

"Damn. Somebody better."

By the time the truck left the city behind, they had done all they could for the wounded. Juliet sat on the swaying floor, her back against a pile of army rifles, Lenore's head in her lap. Her hand held the young black woman's, partly for comfort, partly to check her thready, erratic pulse. Brad looked over at them. "She gonna make it?"

Juliet looked at him soberly and shook her head from side to side. She didn't want to speak aloud because it was barely possible that Lenore could still hear, even though she seemed to be unconscious. Hearing, she knew, was one of the last senses to go.

"We must be nearly there by now," Brad said, checking his watch. Juliet nodded, looking down at Lenore. The pulse beneath her fingers fluttered, throbbed, fluttered as the woman twitched and gasped. Then it stopped.

"She's gone," Juliet said. She noticed that her hip ached terribly and that she was crying. Neither fact seemed very important.

Brad looked closely at her face in the dimness of the wan

overhead light, then scuttled across the floor. "Hey, Julie. Hey . . ." Awkwardly he put his arm around her. Juliet leaned against him for a long time.

The truck banked into a sharp turn. Lenore slid bonelessly out of Juliet's lap. "That's the turn onto the mountain road," Juliet said. They could feel the alteration in the truck's engine now as it strained to take the incline. "Just a little way to go now. What time is it, Brad?"

She could see the tiny glow of his watch. "Two-fifty."

"You mean it only took a half-hour in the armory?"

"Less," Brad said. "It's weird, isn't it? We used to notice that in Nam. We'd be in a raid, or pinned down somewhere under fire, and time would get real short—or sometimes real long."

Juliet stiffened. "I hear shots!"

A moment later, the pulse of Visitor weapons was plainly audible, as well as screams. "They're attacking the camp!" Juliet jumped up and pounded on the wall separating the truck from the cab. "Hurry *up*, Elias!"

"He can't hear you, Julie!" Brad said. They braced themselves against the rear door, waiting, holding guns ready to toss out to the fighters.

The truck's brakes squealed, then it jolted to a halt. Immediately Brad pulled the rear door open. "Here! Guns!" Pulses from the Visitor weapons resounded, and as Juliet watched, a squad vehicle swooped down to strafe the center of the camp. Blue fire blazed from its weapons, exploding on impact with the ground, the tents, the people. Juliet handed out arms, hardly daring to watch. She felt light-headed with horror.

Brad and Elias dragged the bazooka out of the truck and hastily set it up. Juliet grabbed the nearest gun and clumsily crawled out of the truck, grabbing the arm of a man she recognized as Terry. "There are wounded in the truck with the guns! Get some people and get them both out! If they shoot the gas tank, they're dead and we're unarmed!"

"Right!" he shouted, turning away. Juliet stayed still for a moment, then heard one of the craft coming in again.

"Get him, Brad!" Elias yelled, and the ex-cop fired the bazooka at the craft sweeping at them head-on. A brilliant burst of light impacted against the Visitor craft, which spun away, out of control, arcing beyond the trees. A second later they heard the explosion, saw the ball of greasy orange flame reach greedily for the sky.

Juliet gave a wordless yell of encouragement at the two, who hurriedly reloaded the bazooka. One of the other craft— they moved so fast it was hard to tell how many there were— bore down on the camp. It fired a burst just as a brown-haired woman dashed from a burning tent. She crumpled with a shriek of pain. A boy of about thirteen raced out behind her. He wasn't strong enough to lift her. "Help!" he shouted, but none of the panicking figures seemed to hear. Juliet grabbed a weapon and started across the campground toward him. "I can't lift her!" he yelled.

Juliet's hip stabbed as she moved, and it seemed to take an eternity for her to reach the boy. She took the woman's arm in her right hand and, together with the boy, began to drag her toward the cinderblock building housing the scientific equipment. Ahead of her, she saw another group setting up the rocket launcher.

*Hurry . . . hurryhurry . . . Faster!* Juliet's mind screamed. Dimly, from the stabbing pains in her hip, she realized she was running. But her movements felt thick, gluey, as though she were trapped in an eternal nightmare. Out of the corner of her eye, she saw the largest of the Visitor craft diving directly at them. Dropping the woman's arm, she turned, the weapon she'd grabbed in her hand.

It was a .45 automatic. She recognized it from Brad's lessons. Her mind screamed that it was crazy—a handgun against an aircraft—but, possessed by the unreality that was surrounding her, Juliet took the stance Brad had shown her, the gun braced carefully in both hands, aiming. It was the first time she'd ever fired at anything but a straw target.

The gun bucked in her hand as she squeezed off several rounds. Would the bullets even penetrate the skin of the craft? It swooped by, its weapons firing, and she recognized one of the occupants.

*Diana.* That dark, beautiful countenance had been on too many magazine covers for her to be mistaken. Juliet's finger squeezed the trigger again, and this time she *saw* the spark of impact on the alien craft.

The squad vehicle sailed by, unharmed. Elias and Brad fired the bazooka at it, but missed. Juliet turned to grab the fallen woman's arm again. "Come on!" she screamed at the boy.

She heard the craft zooming in again for another strafing pass, and knew, with a terrible certainty, that this time the pilot had their range—he wouldn't miss. She waved frantically at the boy. "Get out of here! I'll get her!"

He stubbornly shook his head. They began dragging the fallen woman again. Juliet fixed her eyes on the building facing them, refusing to look elsewhere. She couldn't stop her ears, though, and she could hear the pulsing whine of the Visitor weapon coming closer . . . closer . . .

Suddenly she heard the whoosh of another squad vehicle, then the pulse of its weapons. "Look!" the boy yelled, pointing.

Diana's craft spun crazily, plainly hit, while the new vehicle swooped toward them—heading for the fighter that had been strafing the other side of the camp. Diana's craft recovered, then flew slowly, awkwardly, back in the direction of the city and the Mother Ship, escorted by the other alien ship. As Juliet and the others watched, the newcomer tailed them almost out of sight, firing steadily, then, turning, came back to the camp.

It landed clumsily, throwing up clouds of dust. The hatch opened, and a face they all recognized emerged. "Hi, there."

"Mike!" the boy beside Juliet shouted, jumping up and down ecstatically. "How'd you get the ship?"

"Trading stamps," answered Donovan. Juliet felt a hand on her arm, pushing her gently aside, then realized Louise and Bill were picking up the woman, who was still unconscious, but groaning now.

Limping, Juliet started toward the alien craft, conscious again of that odd arms-length impulse. "Mr. Donovan," she said coolly, "it's good to see you. You have a knack for knowing when to drop in." Other fighters were collecting around them.

"Yeah," Donovan said. "You're lucky Sancho managed to figure out where the firing button was in that baby." Elias and Brad were lifting a nearly unconscious man out of the craft. His battered face managed a grin as Donovan gave him a "V" sign. Robin Maxwell climbed out of the passenger seat, looking considerably more chastened than the last time Juliet had seen her.

"Ms. Parrish, have you seen my Dad and Mom?"

"No," Juliet said. "Has anyone seen Robert Maxwell?"

"I saw him," one of the men said. "He drove in here just before you folks did. He was heading for the dorm."

ROBERT MAXWELL STUMBLED PAST THE FLAMING CHAOS OF THE dorm, calling his wife's name. The building sent out waves of heat that did nothing to still his trembling. If Kathy had been in there . . .

Refusing to continue the thought, he walked on. "Kathy?" Dimly, he was aware that the Visitor craft were gone—he didn't even wonder where, or why. "Polly? Kathy! God, answer me, please!"

In front of him was a small shed that held canned goods

and other supplies. Maxwell rubbed blearily at his eyes, trying to focus. There was a splotch of blue draped on a picnic table under the overhang of the shed. *Blue,* Robert thought fuzzily. *My favorite color.* He remembered Kathleen complaining once, because every birthday he gave her a sweater, always a blue one . . .

His vision sharpened as he rubbed, enough so he could see that the pretty expanse of blue was marred by red—

"Kathy!" The scream clawed his throat. "No!" He ran toward his wife.

She lay sprawled across the picnic table, legs dangling. Dark blood pooled on the table, oozed down her thighs from the gaping maw that had been her stomach. Her face was streaked with crimson, but her green eyes opened as he lifted her. "Kathy? Where are the girls? Are they okay?"

Her head moved with the tiniest of shakes, back and forth.

He put his face against her forehead, feeling the spattered silk of her hair. "Oh, God, Kathy! This wasn't supposed to happen." Sobbing, Maxwell cradled her head against him, rocking back and forth. "No . . . no . . ."

Time slowed, stopped, narrowed to this one moment, the urge to shelter his wife, hold her against the inevitable. It didn't take long. He knew immediately when it was finally over; her body was heavy in his arms . . . so heavy.

When he finally released her, staring into her empty, fixed, and huge pupils was like looking down into an eternity of darkness. He reached out and closed her eyes quickly, unable to stand looking at that loneliness. Carefully he lowered her body to the table, then took off his jacket, placing it gently over her face. Something bumped his side, and he looked down to see the pistol in its holster. It seemed an eternity since he'd buckled it on in preparation for the raid this morning.

*My fault,* he thought, looking at his wife's covered form,

then at the desolate camp. *All mine. Kathy's dead. My little girls . . . the people who trusted me . . .* He thought of Robin, helpless in that damned ship, and cursed himself with a bitterness that seared his entire being. *I cannot live like this,* he thought. *I just can't.*

The gun slid into his hand, cool, heavy, and comforting. Absently he clicked the safety off, staring into the little round darkness at the end of the muzzle, the darkness that promised relief from this guilt, this pain, then his finger found the trigger.

"Daddy! *Daddy!*"

Maxwell turned, the gun slipping from his hand, to see Polly running awkwardly toward him, carrying Katie. Both girls were sobbing, but obviously unhurt. "Katie! Polly! Oh, God!" He raced toward them, caught them in his arms. They cried together, clutching each other, and then, miracle of miracles, Robin was somehow there too.

MIKE DONOVAN STARED INCREDULOUSLY AT JULIET PARRISH. "What do you *mean,* 'It sounds like we'd better focus our attention on destroying as many of the Mother Ships as we can . . .'? Are you *crazy,* Doc? Haven't you been listening to what I just told you? They've got thousands . . . *thousands* . . . of our people on board! People they've kidnapped! Destroy the Mother Ships, and they go with 'em!"

"Yes, I understand," Juliet said, not looking at him. She was watching the camp evacuation that was under way. "Elias! Get those trucks out! The ammunition ones go *first!* And, Mr. Donovan, we'll try, of course, to find a way to get them off the ships, but—"

"*Try?*" He reached out and grabbed her arm, swung her to face him. She saw he was wearing a baseball cap that was ridiculously small for him, perched on top of his thick shock of brown hair.

Juliet nodded, her eyes holding his. "Yes, *try*. Mr. Donovan, you have to understand that we may have to sacrifice those thousands."

"*Sacrifice?*" He was so angry his voice broke on the word.

"To save *millions*—even billions—that are still here on Earth. I don't like it either, not a bit—but we may not have a choice!" She gestured to someone behind Mike, shouting, "*Now* the lab equipment. And get started on the wounded!"

Mike stood in the center of the compound, watching her limp away, conscious of a strong feeling of déjà vu that he couldn't quite identify. His gaze wandered past her to a group of stretchers waiting to be loaded into a truck, and, seeing a familiar brown head among the wounded, he sprinted over.

"Fran! What happened?"

Fran Leonetti looked pale, her arm and side swathed in bandages, but she turned her head as Donovan ran up. Josh stood by her side. "Hi, Mike," she said. "I got hit during the attack, but Juliet Parrish and Josh toted me off the battlefield before anything more permanent happened. Where's Tony?"

Mike felt a pang of guilt, realizing he'd completely forgotten Tony Leonetti's death during the rush to reach the camp. Looking down at Fran, he knew suddenly that he'd hesitated a moment too long. Her brown eyes were slightly fogged, probably by painkillers, but they didn't leave his face. "Bad news?" she asked in a small voice. "Mike? Tell me."

Donovan swallowed, then picked up her unbandaged hand and held it gently. "I'm sorry, Fran. They'd beefed up their security patrols, and they nailed us. Knocked me out. When I woke up, a couple of 'em helped me get off the ship, but said they couldn't get to Tony. When I could, I sneaked back aboard to find him, but it was . . . too late."

"Dead," she stated, not wanting to believe it. "You're telling me Tony's dead?"

"Yeah. God, I'm sorry, Fran. I can't ever say how much."
The grief that he'd repressed threatened to overwhelm him
now. He swallowed heavily, trying to keep his breathing
steady. If he gave way an inch, he had a feeling he'd be unable
to stop—and Fran needed him. He held her hand in both of
his, wishing he could put his arms around her, but the bandages forestalled him.

"It hurts . . ." Fran sounded as much surprised as grief-
stricken. "God, Mike, it's making a real pain inside me. Now
I know why they talk about heartache . . . broken hearts . . .
Oh, it hurts!" Tears were running down her face, but she
didn't seem to realize it. "He was only twenty-eight . . . three
years younger than I am. Things were going so well. Did you
know we were talking about starting a family? I didn't want
to be pregnant in the summer, so we were gonna wait a couple
of months . . ."

"Fran," came another voice. "We're going to lift you now."

Looking up, Donovan saw Elias and Brad. "Is there room
for me to ride with her? I had to give her some really bad
news about her husband . . . I want to stay with her."

"What about the lizard go-cart over there?" Brad asked,
jerking his chin at the Visitor squad vehicle. "Juliet said we
should move it down and hide it in the woods near headquarters. You're the only one can fly that thing."

"Yeah," Donovan said. "I guess you're right. Fran?" He
brushed her hair back from her wet face. "I'm going to have
to go. But I'll see you down at the other camp, okay?"

"Okay," she whispered.

Josh looked up. "I'll ride with you, Fran, if they don't mind.
I'm awfully sorry to hear about your husband . . ."

"Yeah, I think we can scrunch you in," Elias said.

Mike got up and walked toward the squad vehicle through
the carnage of the wrecked camp. *We won this one*, he

thought, *they didn't get the lab equipment, and we've got weapons. But it's only starting, and already the price has been so high . . .*

STANLEY AND LYNN BERNSTEIN LOOKED UP FROM THEIR DINNER AT the knock on their back door. Favoring his bandaged arm, Stanley went over to peek out the window, then opened the door hastily. "Robert!"

Robert Maxwell stepped in soundlessly, then pointed to a picture of Daniel on the counter with a questioning look. "He's gone for now," said Stanley. "He's out with Brian."

"Why have you come here, Robert?" Lynn twisted her napkin worriedly, her expression verging on hostility.

"Please. I have to talk to you."

She shook her head wildly, a feral, frightened light in her eyes. "You have to leave! Our son might come home any moment! Don't forget, he's the one who—"

"I remember," Robert said. "But the resistance needs your help."

"What?" Lynn said blankly, then turned to her husband in bewilderment.

"We want this to be known as a 'safe' house—a place where some of us can hide if we're in the neighborhood and get into trouble."

"Are you out of your mind?" Lynn was on her feet now. "Robert, I don't like what's happening either, but we've been arrested once already. Look at him." She indicated her husband. "He's the one who has really suffered. They tortured him! He didn't know anything that could have helped them— but they did it anyway! The only reason they let us go was that our son—*my son*—is an informer. They wanted to stay on *his* good side. We meant nothing to them!"

"That's part of our reasoning. They know that you know

nothing, so they won't try here again. It's like lightning—they won't strike the same place twice."

"The only reason they let us go was so we could tell others what happened—how they could be tortured if they don't co-operate fully. If they took us again, we'd be killed!"

Robert looked at her for a long, long moment. When he spoke, his voice broke hoarsely. "Lynn, three days ago they killed Kathleen. My little girls have no mother anymore. If I die, my kids will have nobody. But I've decided that even so, it won't be so bad to have to die myself if that means others . . . thousands, maybe millions of others . . . can be saved. Some fights are worth even terrible personal loss and risk, and *this is one of them!*" He looked back at her, his dark eyes very se-rious. "Please, Lynn . . . reconsider."

Lynn slumped back into her seat, her eyes filling as she took in his news. "Kathleen? Oh, Robert, I'm so sorry. Truly sorry. But—" she looked over at her husband protectively, "we can't. We simply *can't.*"

Stanley Bernstein moved for the first time since Maxwell had entered, heading for a chest that stood in the dining room. He was back in a second, carrying a piece of paper, which he handed to his wife.

"What's this?"

"Father left it for us. It's dated the morning they took us . . . he must've figured they would. Read it, Lynn. Aloud, so Robert can hear."

Automatically, Lynn began to read:

*My dear family. It's painful knowing I won't share the days ahead with you. I pray that I am the only one who will be taken today. It hurts to know that I'll not see your faces anymore. Already I am missing you . . . Stanley, my son . . . Lynn, who is as dear to me as the daughter I never had, and Daniel, for whom I worry the most. But*

*I am too old to run away this time. What I must do is to
stay instead, to show I have faith in what is right.*

*You may think that an old man wouldn't be afraid to
die, but this old man is very frightened. I keep hoping
that I'll find a little of my wife's dignity and strength, but
so far I am as frightened as a child who fears the dark.
Yet I am determined.*

*We must fight this darkness that is threatening to
engulf us. Each of us must be a ray of hope. We must
each do our part, and join with all the others until each
ray joins together to become a blinding light, triumphant
over the dark. Until that task is accomplished, life here
on Earth will have no purpose, no meaning. We cannot
live as helpless victims.*

*More than anything we must always remember which
side we're on . . . and be willing to fight for it.*

*Your mother and I will march beside you . . . holding
hands again. We'll sing your song of victory—you'll feel
us in your hearts. Our spirits will be—*

Choked by sobs, Lynn stopped, but Stanley quoted the last
line from memory. "Our spirits will be with you always . . .
and our love."

He looked at his wife. "Don't you see, Lynn? We *have* to
help . . . or else we won't have learned a thing."

# EPILOGUE

LITTLE KATIE MAXWELL WOULD ALWAYS REMEMBER THE DAYS IM-
mediately following the attack on the mountain camp as being a time of tears. A great many of them had flowed from her
own young eyes. The four-year-old felt certain that her
momma would somehow magically reappear. Several times
Katie seemed to hear the warm, safe, familiar voice or
glimpse a promising shadow, but disappointment always followed. And Katie felt a deep ache expanding inside her little
chest and behind her eyes.

Then came the strange and sad night when her father
Robert held her tightly as they watched the long box being
lowered into the earth. Katie was told that it contained her
mother. Katie was very worried that her momma wouldn't be
able to breathe down in there.

Robin and Polly leaned heavily against their dad on either
side. The family stood among the other solemn freedom fighters who had gathered to pay final tribute to Kathleen and
their other fallen comrades. The cemetery was nestled in the
foothills of the San Bernardino Mountains near the small,
quiet town of Monrovia, east of Los Angeles. Katie heard
people saying that the burial was taking place at night to

avoid notice by the Visitors. Katie heard Robin choke back a sob and saw that tears were streaming down her oldest sister's anguished face.

Katie saw that twelve-year-old Polly was more stoic and resolute, as was ever her nature. Polly's jaw was set and her young body was stiff with anger as she stared at the coffin sinking down out of view into the dark ground. Katie had heard Polly say she would avenge their mother's death. That determination burned in Polly's fierce eyes and she angrily wiped away the single tear that had escaped.

Katie saw that her father also had tears tracing down his cheek. When a soft rain began to fall, Katie gazed up into it as she pressed her cheek against Robert's, saying, "Look, Daddy, even the sky is crying."

THE ABANDONED WASTEWATER RECYCLING PLANT HAD ITSELF BEEN recycled into a new headquarters by Juliet and her resistance compatriots. And in the last week the old facility had become decidedly more crowded. Many new people had joined the primary resistance group and gone underground. Living in the neglected plant they were quite literally underground. The concrete facility had been constructed for utilitarian purposes and had all the charm of a boiler room. Part of it, in fact, was precisely that.

Many family groups had created some small amount of privacy for themselves by hanging an old blanket or sheet on a stretched rope or wire to form a semblance of walls. Whatever meager belongings they had managed to bring with them gave each space a slightly personalized feeling, a touch of memory of their former homes and lives.

Because the Maxwells had been among the earliest arrivals they had settled into a small cubicle with three real walls. The best feature of their location, however, was the tiny half-bathroom which was right beside it. The gray paint was peeling badly off the door. Katie picked at it with a fingernail as she and Polly stood waiting impatiently outside of it. "I really have to pee, Robin," Katie insisted loudly toward the closed door.

She and Polly heard the sound of a toilet flushing within, then the door opened slowly and Robin appeared. She was wiping the corner of her mouth. She smelled faintly of bile and Polly saw that she looked pale.

"Sorry about that." Robin forced a wan smile, "Go on, Katie. And then brush your teeth."

The towhead looked up at her big sister. "You sound like Momma."

Robin tousled Katie's ringlets. "Guess I'll have to, huh?"

The three girls felt a wave of sadness roll over them. That was how it often came. They'd occasionally have more cheerful moments, even a laugh or two, then the loss of their mother would return like the tide carrying that bone-deep ache back into their chests.

They shared a sad look, then Katie went inside. Robin leaned against the concrete wall, feeling its coolness. Polly studied her sister, whom she could see was clearly unwell. Being a very astute twelve-year-old, Polly's suspicions had been growing. "Barfing again, huh?"

"I'm fine." Robin sniffed, forcing her eyes to open wider as she tried to put on a look of adult nonchalance.

But Polly wasn't buying her act. "Yeah, right." Robin heard the sarcastic edge in Polly's voice. Polly realized it, too, and softened her approach slightly, saying, "Look, I just think you ought to have Julie take a look at you."

"I'm okay," Robin said, hoping that she sounded more convincing than she felt. "It's nothing. Really."

"Come on, Robin. You've been sick all week." Then Polly hesitated, weighing whether or not to let the other shoe drop. She finally decided to. She watched carefully for Robin's reaction as she said, "Particularly in the morning, huh?" She let the innuendo hang, but Robin didn't address it, so Polly pressed further, but confidentially, sister-to-sister. "And I see you hiding it from Dad."

Robin still shrugged it off, gesturing toward the huddled masses spread across the expansive, musty area. "It's all these new people crowding in, you know? I've just got a bug."

"Or a *guy*, huh?"

Robin's eyes glanced up reflexively before she could stop herself. She quickly looked away from Polly and forced a small chuckle. "Oh yeah, I wish."

Polly watched her a moment with genuine concern. Her voice grew softer still as she said, "Robin, listen, you can talk to me, okay? Did Daniel get you alone and like force you or . . . ?"

"Daniel?" Robin said with a smirk of dismissive incredulity. "Get real." Robin walked past Polly into the small cubicle where they had fashioned a makeshift bunk bed to take maximum advantage of the limited space. Polly watched her closely, catching Robin's reflection in the fragment of mirror they had hung on one wall.

Robin remained silent. But as the twelve-year-old deciphered the mixed emotions crossing her sister's face, Polly knew that her suspicions were on the right track. "Okay, not Daniel, then. But . . ." Polly suddenly felt a chill stiffen the hairs on the back of her neck as it dawned on her *whom* Robin might be involved with. "Holy shit, Robin—tell me it wasn't *Brian!*"

Robin remained calm as she turned down the frayed sheet on the bottom bunk and adjusted the stuffed rabbit that Katie always slept with. "No, Polly, it wasn't Brian. It wasn't anybody."

Polly was barely breathing, she stared at her sister's back. "It *was* him, wasn't it?" Robin's silence continued. Polly took a hesitant step closer, her voice very tense and fearful. "Jesus,

Robin! Haven't you seen the sketches of what they look like *underneath*?"

"I don't believe that crap," Robin said, her face assuming a sour, patronizing expression to imply that only an idiot *could* believe the rumors of the Visitors being reptilian. She continued fussing with the threadbare bedclothes, looking natural and calm.

Polly's mouth had gone dry. She stared at Robin's back as she whispered, "I heard Donovan has a tape."

"But have you seen it?—No."

"Not yet, but—"

"Listen, Polly." Robin finally turned toward her younger sister, explaining patiently, "People believe all kinds of ridiculous stuff."

"But if it's true, you can't just—"

Robin's eyes riveted onto Polly's. "It wasn't him, okay? It wasn't anybody."

The tomboy stared back. She wanted to believe her sister, but her sharp instincts still waved red flags. She decided on a gentler tack. "Okay. Good. I'm glad to hear it. Then there's no reason why you shouldn't talk to Julie or—"

Robin's ire flared. She drew a breath to shout at Polly, but held it, quelled it, determined to defuse the issue. She said, in a softer, more congenial voice, "Yeah, you're probably right. I will." Then she touched Polly's arm, adding, "Thanks."

Robin smiled and walked off through the shadows of the dilapidated facility, leaving the younger girl confounded and concerned. But what most troubled Polly was that Robin had touched her arm. Polly couldn't even remember the last time that had happened.

Large dusty pipes ran parallel to the concrete floor and low ceiling in one of the many service tunnels of the treatment plant. Robin moved through the narrow, darkened tunnel, squeezing past a new family clutching their belongings and headed in the opposite direction. She was desperate for a breath of fresh air. She climbed a set of rusting metal stairs to the next level, where there was a small window she often visited.

The industrial metal frame creaked as she pushed it open slightly and gratefully drank in the evening air. Looking out and upward she could see the curve of the gigantic Mother Ship glowing in the moonlight against the night sky. She gazed at it for a long moment, recalling her experiences aboard it. Then she realized something. She looked down and saw that her hand had instinctively come to rest atop her abdomen.

A private expression of wonder formed on Robin's young face. Then she sensed that the area around her was growing darker. She looked back out the window and saw that a cloud was gliding over the moon and obscuring it. The subtle change in light was also affecting the Mother Ship, lending it a darker aspect that Robin found somehow discomforting.

ONE NIGHT SIX MONTHS LATER ELIAS WAS LOOKING OUT OF A DIF-ferent window. He was standing inside an extremely clean and well-maintained electronics laboratory, peering out across the Plains of San Agustin, which spread to the horizon about fifty miles west of Socorro, New Mexico. The nearly full moon cast a wash of soft light over the two dozen massive radio antenna dishes forming a symmetrical Y, which stood like giant sentinels aimed upward at the starry night sky.

Elias was in the control room of the National Radio Astronomy Observatory, but he was having a little trouble with its informal name. " 'The *Very Large Array?*' "

"That's right." Juliet smiled up from where she was working at one of the consoles under the subdued control-room light. Some delicate woodwind music by Mozart was playing quietly.

"Shoot," Elias puffed, "they couldn't have picked a cooler name? Like *Dish City*? Or *Big-Ass Antennas*?"

A seven-year-old girl appeared from the small kitchen area carrying a paper plate with cookies and said, "I call it *Space-Com Central*."

"Yeah!" Elias grinned broadly at her. "Now that's what I'm talkin' about. Why don't they listen to you, Margarita?"

The little girl smiled assuredly. "They will someday."

Elias was impressed by the kid's spunky confidence. "I think you got that right, girl." He tousled her rich auburn hair, which was pulled back in a tight, utilitarian ponytail. A few ringlet wisps had escaped to soften the edges around her bright face. Her eyebrows were the same rusty hue as her hair, and a sprinkling of freckles saddled her nose. Elias got a kick out of her tomboyish quality, but her features also suggested there might have been some exquisite royalty in her Scottish-Canadian heritage.

She held out the plate to him. "Want some chocolate chippers? Made 'em myself."

"You bet." Elias snagged a couple.

Juliet also reached out, saying, "I never met a cookie I didn't like. Thanks, Margarita." Then she took a bite and her expression showed she was very impressed. "Mmmm. Deadly!"

Margarita's hazel eyes sparkled with pleasure at the good review. She set the plate near to where her father, Kenneth Perry, was working beside Juliet. Doctor Perry was an astrophysicist who looked to be in his late thirties. His hair was thinning, but the ruddy color of it and of his full, closely trimmed beard securely identified him as Margarita's father.

During their drive out to the remote facility, Juliet had told Elias how Margarita had been fascinated by her father's job as an astronomer since early childhood. Margarita loved climbing around the frameworks that surrounded each of the massive antennae. She thought it was the world's biggest jungle gym. And she greatly enjoyed coming into the control lab with her dad.

Elias gestured past the high-tech equipment toward the antennae outside as he asked the girl, "So are those big dishes outside there as good as your cookies?"

"Oooh, yeah," Margarita said with an emphatic nod as she took a cookie for herself. She sat on a lab stool, which she rotated back and forth as she delivered her litany, "The VLA is one of the world's premier astronomical radio observatories."

" 'Premier'? Yow." Elias raised his eyebrows at her use of the word.

Kenneth chuckled as he adjusted some control. "She knows the stats better than I do."

"That for real?" Elias looked to the girl, encouraging her.

Margarita picked up her cue and drew a big breath. "The VLA has twenty-seven radio antennas in a Y-shaped configuration. Each antenna is twenty-five meters—that's eighty-two feet—in diameter."

"Eighty-two feet," Elias faked, "yeah, that's about what I figured."

"The data from the antennas is combined electronically," Margarita continued, "to give the resolution of an antenna thirty-six kilometers—that's twenty-two miles—across."

"Whoa," Elias blinked, "twenty-two *miles*? Get outta here!" He wasn't sure which impressed him more, the description of the facility or the girl herself. "Are you serious?"

"Yep," Margarita chirped, happy that he was so interested.

"So does that make these like *the* most powerful antennas in the world?"

"Yep," Margarita said offhandedly as she twirled herself in a complete circle on the stool while munching her cookie.

Juliet smiled at her, then at Elias. "So if we're going to get a signal out, this is our best hope."

Doctor Perry moved behind a console to repatch a connection. "Robert told me he was using sideband frequencies like I am to skirt the Visitors' surveillance monitoring."

"Yeah." Elias nodded and licked some chocolate off his finger. "He finally made some contact with other resistance groups."

"But just sporadically so far, Kenny." Juliet sighed.

"Still," Perry said as he plugged in another cable, "that's good news."

"Got that right," Elias agreed. "Just knowing there's some other fighters out there helps pump up our troops."

The astronomer moved back around to the front of the console. "Well, maybe there're even more fighters *way* out there." He sat down at the controls and typed in some adjustments, then said, "Okay, Julie. Whenever you're ready."

They looked at each other. All of them knew that this was a weighty moment in their lives and perhaps critical to the future of planet Earth. Juliet drew a breath. "Let's start sending."

Perry nodded. "Who wants to do the honors?"

"Can I do it, Daddy?"

Kenneth Perry looked at his bright-eyed daughter, then glanced at Juliet, who smiled ironically, saying, "Absolutely, Margarita. It's really *your* future we're dealing with here."

The girl jumped off her stool and came to stand between her father and Juliet. The child's hazel eyes scanned the complicated information on the console's main flat screen. Elias noted that Margarita actually seemed to comprehend a good deal of it. But she double-checked with her dad. "Looks like I just hit the 'enter' key, huh?"

"That's right, kiddo." Her father put his arm around her shoulders.

"O-kaaay."

But then Margarita paused. Juliet noted that the youngster somehow instinctively recognized the ceremonial aspects of what she was about to do. She raised her young hand above the keyboard, then spoke carefully and slowly, "Here's one small step for a girl . . ." She pressed the enter key.

A staticky computer buzz began issuing from the large speakers mounted on the ceiling above the console and blended with the Mozart. Elias scrunched his face curiously. "Wait a minute, that *buzzing* is our call for help?"

Kenneth Perry nodded. "In binary mathematical code."

"Lots of little ones and zeros," Margarita clarified help-fully.

But Elias was still confused. "Just numbers?"

"Mathematics is the universal language," Juliet explained. "If the Visitors do have an enemy advanced enough to do battle with them, they'll be intelligent enough to translate this distress call."

"If they ever even receive it," Perry added.

Elias frowned. "How long's it gonna take to reach 'em?"

"Depends how far away they are," Margarita said as she took another cookie.

"A few years probably," Juliet said. "At least."

"God . . ." Elias scrunched his face quizzically again. "*Years?*"

"Yeah." Perry leaned back in his chair. "The signal can only travel at the speed of light—"

"A hundred eighty-six thousand miles per second," Margarita said while toying with a chocolate chip.

Her father continued, "So if they're, say, ten light-years away, then it'll take—"

"I get it." Elias nodded. "Ten years for it to reach 'em."

"Right," Juliet said. "And even if they could travel at or near the speed of light, which is very unlikely, it would take at least—"

"Another ten years for them to show up here." Elias felt the wind diminishing from his sails. "Wow. Twenty years from now."

"Or probably longer," Perry cautioned.

Elias's eyes had taken on a thousand-yard stare as he pondered, "Wonder what Earth'll look like by then?"

Juliet was also considering it. "Hopefully we'll be around to find out." Then she drew a breath. "Meantime, Kenny and Margarita will keep sending bursts of transmission. In different directions. Night and day, huh?" She put a hand on the young girl's shoulder.

"You betcha, Julie," Margarita said, smiling back with keen resolve in her eyes.

"Well," Elias heaved a long sigh, "I sure hope they got their ghetto blasters tuned in on us."

"And if they do . . ." Juliet said as she met his dark brown eyes, "let's hope they'll be on our side."

Elias gazed at her, weighing that very serious consideration. He looked over at the main console monitor, which was streaming with ones and zeros as the computer buzz continued.

A few minutes later Juliet and Elias stepped out of the control room. She drew a long breath, and a slight grimace crossed her face. The chill night air always caused the injury to her hip to ache more than usual. She leaned on her cane and looked up at one of the giant dishes that loomed behind them, knowing that it was invisibly streaming their call for help out toward the distant stars. She also knew that it was, at best and in every sense of the phrase, a long shot. "The reality we have to face, Elias, is that help may *never* come. We may end up having to rely completely on ourselves."

But Elias was feeling empowered. "Well, we ain't done bad so far. The first battle's been won."

"That's right," Juliet said, then articulated the reality, "but the *war* is just beginning." He looked into her sky-blue eyes and was contemplating the daunting future they were facing as Juliet asked, "You up for it?"

A cocky grin broke across the young man's face. "Girl, who you talking to?" He pulled a can of aerosol paint out of his oversized jacket. Then, with gusto, he stepped up to the concrete wall beside the control room door and onto it he sprayed a big, bright, red **V**.

YSABEL ENCALADA MOVED WITH URGENCY THROUGH ONE OF THE shadowy, pipe-lined service tunnels of the wastewater facility. She'd heard that Juliet had returned, and Ysabel was searching quickly among the other resistance members to find her. Ysabel was fifty-one. She had lived in the United States for the last seventeen years, but she had been born in Lima, Peru. Her thick black hair was a legacy from her Aztec ancestors. She kept it cut short in a very no-nonsense style that matched her personality. She was extremely feisty and had spoken out against several Visitor policies. When three of her fellow workers at Microsoft had disappeared after voicing similar complaints, Ysabel realized the danger and slipped away into the Underground so she could continue her fight against Visitor tyranny. She had hooked up with Juliet's primary resistance cell several months earlier. Her skills in computer science and communication technology had served her and the resistance very well.

Her compatriots were also cheered by her colorful blouses that echoed her South American tastes and heritage. A half-dozen thin bracelets of polished wood and silver were always clicking together on her wrist.

She emerged into a high-ceilinged chamber that once housed large pumps. It had been transformed into one of the galleys that helped supply food to those encamped inside the water reclamation plant. She spotted Elias and Juliet across the dingy room. They both looked weary from travel. They were surrounded by others who were anxious to know how the transmission had gone. Elias was guzzling a soda while Juliet filled in her compatriots.

Ysabel hurried toward her. "Thank God you're back."

Juliet blew out a puff. "Yeah. A couple of close calls coming up through Lake Elsinore. We need to think about moving further north. San Jose, San Francisco, or—"

"Robin's in labor."

Juliet glanced up sharply. "What? I figured she was only about five or six months along." Juliet was already on the move, falling into step beside the older woman who was pointing the way. "Where is she?"

"We put her in your medical unit."

They hurried into the service tunnel as Juliet peeled off her jacket and said, "Are you sure it's true labor?"

"Her water broke."

"How long ago?"

Ysabel glanced at her watch. "Eight hours and twelve minutes."

Juliet's voice was low as she considered it. "Oh my God . . ."

"And Julie . . . there was a lot of blood in it."

"Well, that's not unusual."

"But this blood looked . . ." Ysabel frowned, searching for words.

Juliet glanced at her. "Looked how?"

The older woman was at a loss. ". . . Strange."

Juliet was about to ask more when a pain-filled cry pulled her attention toward the resistance medical area that they were approaching. Juliet saw that Robin was covered with sweat, strands of hair stringing across her face. She cried out again in pain. Her father, Robert, was at her side, mopping her fevered brow, saying, "Easy, honey . . . easy." When he saw Juliet a wave of relief swept through him. "Oh, thank God. You've got to help her."

Juliet was already hurriedly washing her hands at the big metal industrial sink nearby. She saw that Brad, the sturdy former L.A.P.D. sergeant, had pumped a blood-pressure cuff on Robin's arm. Juliet knew Brad had some EMS training and asked, "What are you getting, Brad?"

"One-ten over fifty-five," Brad said. "And it's been dropping steadily."

"Pulse?"

"On a roller coaster. From twenty up to a hundred and twenty and back. Getting weaker in the last hour."

Juliet shook the water from her hands, then slipped on latex surgical gloves as she glanced at Robin's IV bottle. "What's hanging?"

"Ruby started a saline drip," Robert said. "We didn't want to medicate her until you got back."

Juliet had moved to Robin's side and was checking her eyes, then her gums. "She's getting shocky. Raise her legs." She leaned over the teenager, saying, "Robin. Can you hear me?"

The girl's hazy eyes lolled toward Juliet. She managed to nod vaguely.

"Good girl. That's a girl." Juliet moved to the foot of the bed. She lifted the sheets and said, "I'm going to examine you, okay? To see how far along you are." Robin was too weak to respond. Ysabel was wheeling over a small lamp. "Over my left shoulder, Ysie, thanks." Juliet saw Ruby approaching with some additional sheets. Juliet had attended a few births, but since she was only an intern she was comforted by the presence of Ruby, who was a retired RN. "Better prep an epidural, Rube."

"Right away . . . *Doctor*." Ruby emphasized the word. Her kind eyes met Juliet's, which gave the younger woman a much-needed boost of confidence. Ysabel stepped closer, aiming the lamp between Robin's legs. Juliet began the obstetric exam.

Robert wiped his daughter's brow, then saw her tensing up. He placed a hand gently on Robin's enlarged abdomen. "She's having another contraction."

Juliet nodded. "Yeah, I feel it." Juliet stood up. Her mouth was dry, her mind racing.

Brad saw her concern. "What's wrong?"

"She's not dilated at all. Not one centimeter." Juliet struggled with the problem, then Robin cried out loudly in severe pain.

Ysabel glanced at the girl, then to Juliet. "What should we do, boss?"

Robert was growing distraught. "She can't keep suffering like this."

Juliet knew it and took control, speaking decisively, "Ruby, forget the epidural. Prep a spinal. We'll get it into her, then get gowned and scrubbed. You, too, Brad. Robert, you better also."

Robert stood up, his voice nervous, "What're you going to do?"

"A C-section. I don't see any choice."

As Robert moved to the sink and started to scrub, Juliet drew alongside him, speaking quietly, "Did she ever tell you who the father is?"

He shook his head. "No." He continued scrubbing, unaware that Polly was standing nearby in the shadows. She had heard Juliet's question. The twelve-year-old looked across at Robin, who was in agony, but who was focused sharply on Polly. Robin's gaze had an aspect of warning. It was clear to Polly that Robin wanted her secret kept.

But when Robin's attention was pulled away by the severity of another strong contraction, Polly made her own decision. She stepped closer to her father and Juliet, saying, "It's Brian."

Robert was confused. "What?"

The girl's intense eyes met his. "He's the father."

As Robert stared at Polly the blood drained from his face. He reached to the wall for support.

Juliet was startled by his reaction. She looked sharply at Polly, though she was fearful of asking, "What's wrong? Who's Brian?"

Polly's voice could barely be heard. "He's one of *them*."

Juliet went even paler than Robert had. Then her mind began calculating, and she said, "No . . . I don't think that could be possible. They're different *species*. The chromosomes wouldn't recognize each other . . . fertilization couldn't occur."

Polly's eyes held firmly on Juliet's. "Then what's inside of her?"

Juliet stared back at Polly, then glanced over at Robin on the bed, writhing in birth agony.

ELEANOR DUPRES LIFTED A SMALL CUT-CRYSTAL ATOMIZER. SHE sprayed a mere breath of vermouth over the ice-cold gin she had poured into her fine-stemmed glass. She called the drink a Fallout Martini. This was her third cocktail within the hour, but she blamed that on her son, Mike Donovan, as she often did. He always seemed determined to irritate her to the point that she needed a little extra bolstering.

Her back was to him, but in the beveled glass mirror behind the black marble wet bar she could see him standing obstinately with that self-righteous intensity that she always felt was designed to annoy her. She was determined, however, to maintain her superior dignity. She slowly skewered an olive as though it were the voodoo doll of an adversary. Then she placed it into her martini as she chuckled condescendingly. "Reptilian? Mike, *really*!" She turned to look at him as though he were still in third grade. "That is positively the most outrageous story I have ever heard." She lifted her glass in a mock toast to him and sipped it delicately with her perfectly lined lips.

She saw that Mike was doing his best to remain calm as he said, "Shall I bring the tape and show you?"

Eleanor waved her martini glass as though dismissing courtiers. "Oh, Hollywood creates that sort of nonsense all the time. I could never take it seriously. Besides, you and your left-wing friends have been determined to demonize them from the very beginning."

Donovan watched her walk across the thick Persian carpet in her elegantly appointed lanai. Through the paneled windows behind her he could see the marine layer rolling in, darkening the moon's reflection on the surface of the Pacific. Eleanor sat down carelessly on one of her large, two-thousand-dollar wicker thrones. Mike knew that some workhouse Chinese child had likely been paid two dollars for making it. Eleanor settled regally back, adjusting her pale yellow Chanel dress. Then the manicured fingertips of her free hand idled on the surface of the side table, which was inlaid with real ivory in the shape of little elephants.

Though he still maintained his composure, Mike's voice took on an edge as he said, "Mother, I shot the footage myself."

"I'm sorry, but that doesn't make it any more believable, because I know you have an *agenda*." She spoke the word with a smirk, as though his notions were ill-conceived and absurd. "Besides, the Visitors have always been perfectly lovely to me and—"

"Listen, Mother!" Mike suddenly bellowed as he came furiously uncorked. "Whether you believe it or not, the truth is that my son"—he took a step closer to emphasize—"your *grandson*—and tens of thousands of others are all prisoners! Aboard those big ships of your perfectly lovely friends." He waited for some reaction. She merely sipped her cocktail and glanced around the lanai, noticing a bit of dust on the Degas bronze. Mike stepped into her line of vision. "Good God, don't tell me you're unaware of all the people who have disappeared! Or the war that's going on in the streets or—"

"Of course I'm aware of all that," she said harshly, surprising him with her sudden intense focus. "I'm not a fool, Michael."

"I know that. So why won't you—"

"I'm a *survivor*." Her dark eyes drilled into his. "Otherwise I never would've gotten here from that hick town in Louisiana where I started. Or made it through your father's goddamn drunkenness!"

Mike faced her with equally resolute strength, saying, "That's not nearly the same thing as what's happening in the world!" He tried to speak with a voice of reason. "Do you know how much help you could be to us who are fighting back if you'd just—"

"I'm a *survivor*," Eleanor repeated stridently, staying her course. She cocked a wise eyebrow as she continued, "And if *you* are going to be one, then you'd better change your ways immediately." She anticipated his response and waved him down before he could speak. "I know the Visitors aren't saints, for Christ's sake. But they're in power." Her eyes narrowed as she tried to get her son to understand the essential point. "They *are* Power. Anyone who fights back will be crushed. This world belongs to them now."

Mike nodded. "And to the people who sympathize with them?"

"Exactly. Yes!" Thinking she was perhaps finally getting through to him, Eleanor took on a softer, more pliant tone. "You and I are in incredibly unique positions, Mike. Don't you realize that?" Her face formed a genuinely charming smile that Mike had seen her use to beguile so many people, particularly men, over the years. "Come on now, why not take advantage of the rare gift that Fate has placed in our hands. Why not?"

He was incredulous, holding the concept with both hands in the air between them as he shouted, "Because I can't *survive* at the expense of other people! That's not *right*!"

She stared at him, then breathed a long sad sigh at his bull-headedness. She sipped the last of her cocktail and fiddled with the olive. Donovan gazed at her, his brain a theater of turmoil and dark emotion. He tried to fashion words, but every line of logic, of compassion, of humanity seemed utterly useless. He was hurting deeply.

Finally, very quietly, he spoke. "You know, Mother . . . when I was a kid there was a woman who taught me what was right and what was wrong." Eleanor's eyes flicked up to his. She saw from his face that strong emotions were coursing underneath. He looked very young, almost boyish, almost as though he was fighting back tears. At length he spoke very softly through his pain, "I wonder whatever became of her . . . ?"

Eleanor grew uneasy under his gaze. She looked away. Mike tried to find more words, but they simply didn't exist. Disheartened to the depths of his soul, her son quietly left the room.

Eleanor sat, unmoving, coldly staring straight ahead.

Outside, the thick marine layer had spread up and over the Pacific Palisades. It enshrouded the neo-Mediterranean Dupres estate that rested comfortably atop a three-hundred-foot bluff facing the ocean, which was now invisible in the foggy darkness. Mike could smell the salt air, though, as he moved carefully past the Greek statuary on the pristine lawn toward the wrought-iron security gate. His heart was heavy from his confrontation with his mother. And from knowing that if the Visitors' plan continued unchecked, in twenty years there would no longer be much sea air to smell.

In spite of that weight upon him, Mike was trying to keep sharply attuned to the moment. He was very well aware that his mother might have already called the authorities to report his presence.

He paused just inside the iron gate that was moist from the vaporous fog. The gate's vertical bars and the corresponding parallel shadows they cast onto his face suggested a fate that Mike definitely wanted to avoid. He peered carefully through the bars. Though he saw nothing amiss on the clean, upscale residential street, he paused yet a moment longer to listen. The blanketing fog had deadened the air. A numb silence prevailed. There was only a slight creak of the gate as he opened it.

Mike kept to the shadows, skirting the hazy illumination from the streetlamps. He moved across the damp street to where he had sequestered his vintage Indian motorcycle within some bushy landscaping. He had just climbed onto its leather seat when a pulse burst ricocheted startlingly off the fender. Mike ducked and snapped around to look behind him.

Across and up the street he glimpsed a uniformed member of the Visitor Youth, whom Diana had recently renamed the Teammates. The excited boy ran across a shadowy lawn, took cover behind a parked car, and again fired his pulse pistol at Mike. He was Daniel Bernstein. He shouted to others off somewhere in the misty darkness behind him, "Teammates! Down here! He's down here!"

Mike could see several more young Teammates, followed by two Visitor troopers, apparitions gaining definition through the swirling fog as they came running toward Daniel's position. Mike pulled his own weapon from a sleeve on the Indian and fired back. His pulse bursts splashed electrically off the car, forcing Daniel to duck. Mike swung a leg over his big bike, kick-started it, and peeled out as a fusillade from the troopers' weapons burst on the pavement around him.

The thick air whipped Mike's hair as he piloted the bike with motocross skills and increasing speed. In his side mirror he spotted through the fog the lights of a Visitor fighter craft banking in over the trees. Even in the heavy fog, it would have a clear shot at him in a few seconds. Mike swerved the heavy bike sharply. He jumped the curb and sped off the road into a wooded arroyo. The sycamore, pine, and eucalyptus foliage was knitted into a thick canopy above him, giving him some cover from the pursuing fighter. Mike killed the bike's lights as he sped on with gritty determination. He dodged between the tree trunks and finally disappeared into the foggy darkness.

THANKS TO THE ANESTHESIA ROBIN WAS NO LONGER FEELING THE birthing pains as intensely, but three or four times a minute she suddenly shivered as unexpected icy waves of nervous tension coursed through her. A clear oxygen mask covered her nose and mouth. Brad sat near her head, monitoring her vital signs, which had stabilized slightly. He spoke toward Juliet, "Still a hundred ten over sixty."

"Good." The young intern nodded. "Let's try to keep it there." Juliet and the others had put on scrubs, masks, and surgical caps. They had moved Robin into the makeshift surgical suite that Juliet had arranged several weeks earlier for emergencies. At the time Elias had put up a hand-lettered sign that read *M.A.S.H.*

In an attempt to keep the space as sterile as possible, temporary walls of thick plastic sheeting had been hung to create an area about ten feet square. A portable air-conditioning unit provided clean, filtered air. But Juliet was perspiring anyway as she leaned over Robin. She was well along into the operation, "All right, I'm down to the bag of waters now, there's still quite a bit of fluid left in it . . ."

Robert sat opposite Brad at Robin's head. He wiped his daughter's brow with a cool cloth, saying, "You're doing great, honey." He tried to keep his voice even, tried to contain the growing dread he felt. He looked toward Robin's abdomen, which had been coated with the blue sterilization fluid and draped so that only her pregnant belly was visible.

Juliet had opened an incision about seven inches long just

above the teenager's pubic bone and was now stretching the skin wider. She could see Robin's uterus beneath the incision, and within the sac she could discern the ghostly form of the unborn child. "Hold this clamp, Ysie." The Latina slipped her hand over Juliet's and took possession of the instrument. Juliet nodded. "Good. Wipe, please."

Polly, also in surgical gear, swallowed her own queasiness and reached around to dry Juliet's damp brow.

"Thanks, Polly." Then Juliet looked down into the open incision and took a breath. "Okay . . . Here we go . . ." Juliet willed her novice hands not to tremble as her scalpel cut a fine, straight line through the venous membrane of the sac. Bodily fluid instantly pooled around the new incision. Ruby was ready for it. She leaned in from opposite Juliet and suctioned off the excess liquid.

". . . I'm into the sac . . ." Juliet said quietly. Everyone attending grew even more tense. They were barely breathing. Robin the least of all.

". . . I can see one hand," Juliet said, smiling. "Five fingers . . ." Then Juliet's expression clouded slightly.

Ysabel saw the young woman's reaction. She leaned closer, whispering, "What's wrong?"

Juliet murmured back, barely audible, not wanting Robin to hear, "Look . . . at the fingers . . ."

Ysabel leaned closer. She could see the baby's tiny hand protruding out through the uterine sac. The little fingers were tremulous with life. As Ysabel watched, the fingers spread slightly, revealing paper-thin membranous webbing stretched between them.

Robin, sweating and fearful, felt the sudden hush around her. "What is it?"

"Nothing, honey," Juliet lied smoothly, but Robert caught the disquieted look in the intern's eyes and knew something was wrong. Juliet tried to sound confident. "We're doing okay. You're going to feel some pressure now . . ." Juliet had been studying the uterine cavity. She could see that the baby's back was presenting. To Juliet's eye the spinal cord seemed slightly more convex and prominent than it should have.

Ruby noticed something else. She whispered, "The skin, Julie. It looks . . ."

Ysabel finished her thought. ". . . Weird."

Juliet's hands separated the uterine membrane. She carefully eased the little form out. It was covered with birthing fluids that were not entirely pink or red, as would be expected. Instead, they had an odd, sickly yellow tinge. Juliet was very cautious with the umbilical. "Okay, the baby's out . . . Clamp the cord, Ysie."

Ysabel nervously applied the clamp. There was a gurgle, then a whimper. Juliet glanced at the baby's bottom, announcing, "It's a girl."

There was positive reaction and relieved laughter from Robert and Brad. But not from Ysabel, Ruby, or Juliet, who were the closest. Juliet slowly turned the infant, which was dripping with the strangely colored birthing fluid, so that she could look full at the baby's face in the light. When she did, Juliet stopped breathing.

Its eyes were squinted closed. It had a normal human facial configuration, nose, mouth, and ears, but where the hairline should've been there were layered rows of infinitesimal scales. The baby's cheeks were flushed as would be expected. But lying flat against either cheek and pointed toward the back of the little head were at least a dozen tiny spikes of what appeared to be cartilage, like those of a blowfish. Juliet saw they were pulsating outward ever so slightly.

Juliet, Ruby, and Ysabel stared at it in stunned disbelief as the newborn emitted a strange squeal and opened its sticky eyes. Juliet inhaled a startled breath and her whole body shuddered as she saw that the eyes were red with vertical yellow irises.

Ysabel choked back a gasp as she crossed herself fearfully, gasping, "Jesus, Mary, and Joseph!"

Juliet realized that she was holding in her hands the first of a new species. A bizarre comingling of human and reptilian. A macabre half-breed.

Everyone stood dumbstruck. They had all seen it now. All of them except Robin, who was still lying flat and becoming increasingly fearful. "What's wrong?" When no one responded immediately, her voice caught in her throat, "What's *wrong*?!"

"Nothing, Robin," Juliet said, trying her utmost to sound professional. "I just need to get the cord cut and get you closed up, so that—"

"I want to see my baby!"

Brad saw that Robin's respiration rate was ramping up.

"In just a few minutes," Juliet insisted.

Brad warned Juliet, "BP's jumped to 190 over 110."

Robert tried to calm his daughter, saying, "Just lay still, honey, everything's going to be—"

"I want to see her now!" The teenager was nearing panic; she strained against her father to raise herself up. "I want to see her *now*!"

Brad also reached out to hold her. "Robin, no. Lie back." But the girl's will was too strong. She crunched herself upward, ignoring the stabbing pain it caused her. Juliet tried to turn the child away, but the cord was too short and at that moment the infant also squirmed, twisting around in Juliet's hands so that Robin found herself staring directly at her progeny with its yellow-red eyes glaring at her.

Robin stared as her mouth worked soundlessly.

Another dreadful squeal came from the baby's purple-green lips. And then its ten-inch, forked tongue lashed out.

Robin's eyes went wide as her blood turned to ice and her brain short-circuited. She emitted an unearthly shriek.

MANY LIGHT-YEARS ACROSS THE SILENT DARKNESS OF DEEP SPACE, in the direction of the Horse Head Nebula, there was a yellow main sequence star somewhat larger and hotter than Earth's sun. It was part of a binary system. Its sister star was a red dwarf. Six planets of varying size were in orbit around the pair of them.

The fourth planet was half again larger than the Earth. Small patches of blue, which might have been water, reflected the light of its two suns and suggested a nitrogen-rich atmosphere, but the world's overall surface colors were shades of dusty beige and green. It was traced with thin, irregular lines that looked from space like blood vessels. And they seemed to likewise pulsate with flowing movement.

From a position several thousand miles above the planet, someone was looking down at it. He was within a six-foot-wide viewing port. He looked like a strong and sturdy human male in his mid-forties. He was nude.

His skin appeared to be Caucasian but had an unusual, faint sheen to it. Except for the short hair on his head, which was brushed forward in a style similar to ancient Romans, and a slight dusting around his compact genitals, he was nearly hairless. His nose was also Roman in form. His face had a squareness to it, with a particularly strong jawline. There was an old, thin scar along his right cheek that ran from his ear almost to the tip of his chin. Several other long-healed battle scars were evident on his torso, including a deep, uneven one on the outside of his left thigh about twelve inches in length.

His eyes appeared human, except that the color of his irises was amber. They had a particularly piercing quality befitting the high level of command that he had achieved.

He stood looking out of the bulbous viewing port with his back to what appeared to be a shadowy natural cavern. The walls were as curved and uneven as the inside of a termite mound. They might have been carved or created by insect excretion. The lighting was indirect, phosphorescent, and dim, the atmosphere thick. Three of the commander's aides were sitting sideways on the wall, defying gravity as though the wall was their floor. One of the two males had black skin, and the lone female had skin of a tone that would have been taken for Hispanic on earth. The three were sitting nude at their control stations. Flashes of complex data flickered constantly on illuminated crystalline sections before them.

A female voice spoke to the commander in a language that was not of Earth. "Pardon me, Admiral."

The commander turned to face the woman. She was also nude. Her smooth skin was very black and her features fine. On Earth she might have been taken for an athletic, thirty-year-old Ethiopian, except that her eyes were a vivid pink and her skin had the peculiar sheen common to all the others in the chamber.

The commander acknowledged her nodded salute. "Yes, what is it?"

She held out a small gossamer ribbon and said, "This distress call was picked up by one of our wormhole probes."

The admiral took it from her. He scanned it carefully and glanced up at her with some surprise. She smiled. "I thought you'd find it interesting."

"Yes," the admiral said as he nodded slowly and examined the ribbon again. "Definitely primitive . . . but very interesting."

The dark-skinned woman raised one of her thin eyebrows slightly. "Perhaps an opportunity, sir?"

He pondered it further, chewing the inside of his lip. "Perhaps." He looked up at her again. "How long ago was it transmitted?"

"We're still trying to determine that, sir. It may have been quite a while. Quite a long while."

"Very well. Good work. Keep me closely advised."

"Of course, sir, and thank you." But she had an additional question. "Sir? Would you like to take any immediate action?"

"Yes." His eyes met her gaze pointedly, for an extended moment. Then he said slowly, "I'd like to think."

The woman smiled knowingly. She nodded and gracefully exited.

The admiral looked at the gossamer ribbon again, studying the message it contained. He contemplated the possibilities. And the dangers. Then he turned his head to look back out the port.

He turned *only* his head, until it had rotated a full 180 degrees on his shoulders.

A shuttlecraft that might have been mistaken for a small meteor was passing close enough outside for the pilot to see her admiral within. His naked back was fully facing the port, but his face atop it peered straight out. His eyes were focused far into the void. His expression was deeply thoughtful.

The pilot continued on her mission. She skirted the admiral's ship, which was gargantuan, asymmetrical, and organic. It looked as though it might have been daubed together by impossibly gigantic wasps.

The shuttle accelerated as it flew downward beneath the bottom of the admiral's flagship, and then the full expanse of the fleet revealed itself to the shuttle pilot. There were scores of other gigantic craft stretching into the far distance against the starry blackness. They were all similar in organic construction, but in various shapes and sizes. Dozens of tiny shuttles buzzed around them like flies. To human eyes the scene would have appeared mind-bending: unsettlingly alien and fearfully forbidding.

But from a far greater distance, the eerie ships with their unusual inhabitants, the strange planet, and even its binary stars were mere pinpoints in the vast, unknown, and decidedly unpredictable universe.

# ABOUT THE AUTHORS

**Kenneth Johnson** is the award-winning writer, director, and producer of numerous television shows, TV movies, and feature films. He is the creator of the miniseries *V* and the author of the sequel novel *V: The Second Generation*. Johnson is also responsible for creating such popular Emmy-winning TV series as *The Bionic Woman, The Incredible Hulk*, and *Alien Nation*. He directed the feature films *Short Circuit 2* and *Steel*. He is the recipient of the prestigious Viewers for Quality Television Award, multiple Saturn Awards, and the Sci-Fi Universe Life Achievement Award and has been nominated for Writers Guild and Mystery Writers of America Awards. He lives in Los Angeles with his wife, Susan.

**A. C. Crispin,** the author of the original novelization of *V* and other *V* novels, has published many science fiction novels, including a number of bestselling Star Trek™ and Star Wars® novels. She also created the successful Starbridge series. She lives in Maryland.